The author of almost a hundred books and the creator of Jeeves, Blandings Castle, Psmith, Ukridge, Uncle Fred and Mr Mulliner, P.G. Wodehouse was born in 1881 and educated at Dulwich College. After two years with the Hong Kong and Shanghai Bank he became a full-time writer, contributing to a variety of periodicals including *Punch* and the *Globe*. He married in 1914. As well as his novels and short stories, he wrote lyrics for musical comedies with Guy Bolton and Jerome Kern, and at one time had five musicals running simultaneously on Broadway. His time in Hollywood also provided much source material for fiction.

At the age of 93, in the New Year's Honours List of 1975, he received a long-overdue knighthood, only to die on St Valentine's Day some 45 days later.

Some of the P.G. Wodehouse titles to be published
by Arrow in 2008

P. G. WODEHOUSE
Piccadilly Jim

arrow books

Published by Arrow Books 2008

5 7 9 10 8 6

First published in the United Kingdom in 1918 by Herbert Jenkins Ltd

Arrow Books
The Random House Group Limited
20 Vauxhall Bridge Road, London, SW1V 2SA

www.randomhouse.co.uk

www.wodehouse.co.uk

Addresses for companies within The Random House Group Limited
can be found at: www.randomhouse.co.uk/offices.htm

The Random House Group Limited Reg. No. 954009

A CIP catalogue record for this book
is available from the British Library

ISBN 9780099513889

The Random House Group Limited supports The Forest Stewardship
Council (FSC®), the leading international forest certification
organisation. Our books carrying the FSC label are printed on FSC®
certified paper. FSC is the only forest certification scheme endorsed by
the leading environmental organisations, including Greenpeace. Our
paper procurement policy can be found at
www.randomhouse.co.uk/environment

Typeset by SX Composing DTP, Rayleigh, Essex
Printed and bound by CPI Group (UK) Ltd, Croydon, CR0 4YY

Piccadilly Jim

CHAPTER 1

The residence of Mr Peter Pett, the well-known financier, on Riverside Drive, New York, is one of the leading eyesores of that breezy and expensive boulevard. As you pass by in your limousine, or while enjoying ten cents' worth of fresh air on top of a green omnibus, it jumps out and bites at you. Architects confronted with it reel and throw up their hands defensively, and even the lay observer has a sense of shock. The place resembles in almost equal proportions a cathedral, a suburban villa, a hotel and a Chinese pagoda. Many of its windows are of stained glass, and above the porch stand two terra-cotta lions, considerably more repulsive even than the complacent animals that guard New York's Public Library. It is a house that it is impossible to overlook; and it was probably for this reason that Mrs Pett insisted on her husband's buying it, for she was a woman who liked to be noticed.

Through the rich interior of this mansion Mr Pett, its nominal proprietor, was wandering like a lost spirit. The hour was about ten of a fine Sunday morning, but the Sabbath calm which was upon the house had not communicated itself to him. There was a look of exasperation on his usually patient face, and a muttered oath, picked up no doubt on the godless Stock Exchange, escaped his lips.

'Darn it!'

He was afflicted by a sense of the pathos of his position. It was not as if he demanded much from life. He asked but little here below. At that moment all that he wanted was a quiet spot where he might read his Sunday paper in solitary peace, and he could not find one. Intruders lurked behind every door. The place was congested.

This sort of thing had been growing worse and worse ever since his marriage two years previously. There was a strong literary virus in Mrs Pett's system. She not only wrote voluminously herself – the name Nesta Ford Pett is familiar to all lovers of sensational fiction – but aimed at maintaining a *salon*. Starting, in pursuance of this aim, with a single specimen – her nephew, Willie Partridge, who was working on a new explosive which would eventually revolutionize war – she had gradually added to her collection, until now she gave shelter beneath her terracotta roof to no fewer than six young and unrecognized geniuses. Six brilliant youths, mostly novelists who had not yet started and poets who were about to begin, cluttered up Mr Pett's rooms on this fair June morning, while he, clutching his Sunday paper, wandered about, finding, like the dove in Genesis, no rest. It was at such times that he was almost inclined to envy his wife's first husband, a business friend of his named Elmer Ford, who had perished suddenly of an apoplectic seizure; and the pity which he generally felt for the deceased tended to shift its focus.

Marriage had certainly complicated life for Mr Pett, as it frequently does for the man who waits fifty years before trying it. In addition to the geniuses, Mrs Pett had brought with her to her new home her only son, Ogden, a fourteen-year-old boy of a singularly unlovable type. Years of grown-up society and the absence of anything approaching discipline had given him a precocity on which the earnest efforts of a series of private tutors had expended themselves in vain. They came full of optimism and self-confidence, to retire after a brief interval shattered by the boy's stodgy resistance to education in any form or shape. To Mr Pett, never at his ease with boys, Ogden Ford was a constant irritant. He disliked his stepson's personality, and he more than suspected him of stealing his cigarettes. It was an additional annoyance that he was fully aware of the impossibility of ever catching him at it.

Mr Pett resumed his journey. He had interrupted it for a moment to listen at the door of the morning room, but a remark in a high tenor voice about the essential Christianity of the poet Shelley filtering through the oak, he had moved on.

Silence from behind another door farther down the passage encouraged him to place his fingers on the handle, but a crashing chord from an unseen piano made him remove them swiftly. He roamed on, and a few minutes later the process of elimination had brought him to what was technically his own private library, a large, soothing room full of old books, of which his father had been a great collector.

He stood outside the door, listening tensely. He could hear nothing. He went in, and for an instant experienced that ecstatic thrill which only comes to elderly gentlemen of solitary habit who in a house full of their juniors find themselves alone at last. Then a voice spoke, shattering his dream of solitude.

'Hello, pop!'

Ogden Ford was sprawling in a deep chair in the shadows.

'Come in, pop, come in. Lots of room.'

Mr Pett stood in the doorway, regarding his stepson with a sombre eye. He resented the boy's tone of easy patronage, all the harder to endure with philosophic calm at the present moment from the fact that the latter was lounging in his favourite chair. Even from an æsthetic point of view the sight of the bulging child offended him. Ogden Ford was round and blobby and looked overfed. He had the plethoric habit of one to whom wholesome exercise is a stranger and the sallow complexion of the confirmed candy fiend. Even now, a bare half-hour after breakfast, his jaws were moving with a rhythmical champing motion.

'What are you eating, boy?' demanded Mr Pett, his disappointment turning to irritability.

'Candy.'

'I wish you would not eat candy all day.'

'Mother gave it to me,' said Ogden simply. As he had anticipated, the shot silenced the enemy's battery. Mr Pett grunted, but made no verbal comment. Ogden celebrated his victory by putting another piece of candy in his mouth.

'Got a grouch this morning, haven't you, Pop?'

'I will not be spoken to like that!'

'I thought you had,' said his stepson complacently, 'I can always tell. I don't see why you want to come picking on me, though. I've done nothing.'

Mr Pett was sniffing suspiciously.

'You've been smoking.'

'Me!'

'Smoking cigarettes.'

'No, sir!'

'There are two butts in the ash-tray.'

'I didn't put them there.'

'One of them is warm.'

'It's a warm day.'

'You dropped it there when you heard me come in.'

'No, sir! I've only been here a few minutes. I guess one of the fellows was in here before me. They're always swiping your coffin-nails. You ought to do something about it, Pop. You ought to assert yourself.'

A sense of helplessness came upon Mr Pett. For the thousandth time he felt himself baffled by this calm, goggle-eyed boy who treated him with such supercilious coolness.

'You ought to be out in the open air this lovely morning,' he said feebly.

'All right. Let's go for a walk. I will if you will.'

'I – I have other things to do,' said Mr Pett, recoiling from the prospect.

'Well, this fresh-air stuff is overrated anyway. Where's the sense of having a home if you don't stop in it?'

'When I was your age I would have been out on a morning like this – or – bowling my hoop.'

'And look at you now!'

'What do you mean?'

'Martyr to lumbago.'

'I am not a martyr to lumbago,' said Mr Pett, who was touchy on the subject.

'Have it your own way. All I know is—'

'Never mind!'

'I'm only saying what Mother—'

'Be quiet!'

Ogden made further researches in the candy box.

'Have some, Pop?'

'No.'

'Quite right. Got to be careful at your age.'

'What do you mean?'

'Getting on, you know. Not so young as you used to be. Come in, Pop, if you're coming in. There's a draught from that door.'

Mr Pett retired, fermenting. He wondered how another man would have handled this situation. The ridiculous inconsistency of the human character infuriated him. Why should he be a totally different man on Riverside Drive from the person he was in Pine Street? Why should he be able to hold his own in Pine Street with grown men, whiskered, square-jawed financiers, and yet be unable on Riverside Drive to eject a fourteen-year-old boy from an easy-chair? It seemed to him sometimes that a curious paralysis of the will came over him out of business hours.

Meanwhile, he had still to find a place where he could read his Sunday paper. He stood for a while in thought. Then his brow cleared, and he began to mount the stairs. Reaching the top floor, he walked along the passage and knocked on a door at the end of it. From behind this door, as from behind those below, sounds proceeded, but this time they did not seem to discourage Mr Pett. It was the tapping of a typewriter that he heard, and he listened to it with an air of benevolent approval. He loved to hear the sound of a typewriter; it made home so like the office.

'Come in,' called a girl's voice.

The room in which Mr Pett found himself was small but cosy, and its cosiness – oddly, considering the sex of its owner – had that peculiar quality which belongs as a rule to the dens of men. A large bookcase almost covered one side of it, its reds and blues and browns smiling cheerfully at whoever entered. The walls were hung with prints, judiciously chosen and arranged. Through a window to the left, healthfully open at the bottom, the sun streamed in, bringing with it the pleasantly subdued whirring of automobiles out on the Drive. At a desk at right angles to this window, her vivid red-gold hair rippling in the breeze from the river, sat the girl who had been working at the typewriter. She turned as Mr Pett entered, and smiled over her shoulder.

Ann Chester, Mr Pett's niece, looked her best when she smiled. Although her hair was the most obviously striking feature of her appearance, her mouth was really the most individual thing about her. It was a mouth that suggested adventurous possibilities. In repose it had a look of having just finished saying something humorous, a kind of demure appreciation of itself. When it smiled a row of white teeth flashed out; or, if the lips did not part, a dimple appeared on the right cheek, giving the whole face an air of mischievous geniality. It was an enterprising, swash-buckling sort of mouth, the mouth of one who would lead forlorn hopes with a jest or plot whimsically lawless conspiracies against convention. In its corners and in the firm line of the chin beneath it there lurked, too, more than a hint of imperiousness. A physiognomist would have gathered correctly that Ann Chester liked having her own way and was accustomed to get it.

'Hello, Uncle Peter,' she said. 'What's the matter?'

'Am I interrupting you, Ann?'

'Not a bit. I'm only copying out a story for Aunt Nesta. I promised her I would. Would you like to hear some of it?'

Mr Pett said he would not.

'You're missing a good thing,' said Ann, turning the pages. 'I'm all worked up over it. It's called "At Dead of Night", and it's full of crime and everything. You would never think Aunt Nesta had such a feverish imagination. There are detectives and kidnappers in it and all sorts of luxuries. I suppose it's the effect of reading it, but you look to me as if you were trailing something. You've got a sort of purposeful air.'

Mr Pett's amiable face writhed into what was intended to be a bitter smile.

'I'm only trailing a quiet place to read in. I never saw such a place as this house. It looks big enough outside for a regiment; yet when you're inside, there's a poet or something in every room.'

'What about the library? Isn't that sacred to you?'

'That boy Ogden's there.'

'What a shame.'

'Wallowing in my best chair,' said Mr Pett morosely. 'Smoking cigarettes.'

'Smoking? I thought he had promised Aunt Nesta he wouldn't smoke.'

'Well, he said he wasn't, of course, but I know he had been. I don't know what to do with that boy. It's no good my talking to him. He – he patronizes me!' concluded Mr Pett indignantly. 'Sits there on his shoulder-blades with his feet on the table and talks to me with his mouth full of candy as if I were his grandson.'

'Little brute!'

Ann was sorry for Mr Pett. For many years now, ever since the death of her mother, they had been inseparable. Her father, who was a traveller, explorer, big-game hunter and general sojourner in the lonelier and wilder spots of the world, and paid only infrequent visits to New York, had left her almost entirely in Mr Pett's care and all her pleasantest memories were associated with him. Mr Chester's was in many ways an admirable character, but not a domestic one; and his relations with his daughter were confined for the most part to letters and presents.

In the past few years she had come to regard Mr Pett almost in the light of a father. Hers was a nature swiftly responsive to kindness; and because Mr Pett besides being kind was also pathetic, she pitied as well as loved him.

There was a lingering boyishness in the financier, the boyishness of the boy who muddles along in an unsympathetic world and can never do anything right; and this quality called aloud to the youth in her. She was at the valiant age when we burn to right wrongs and succour the oppressed, and wild rebel schemes for the reformation of her small world came readily to her. From the first she had been a smouldering spectator of the trials of her uncle's married life; and if Mr Pett had ever asked her advice and bound himself to act on it, he would have solved his domestic troubles in explosive fashion. For Ann in her moments of maiden meditation had frequently devised schemes to that end which would have made his grey hair stand erect with horror.

'I've seen a good many boys,' she said, 'but Ogden is in a class by himself. He ought to be sent to a strict boarding-school, of course.'

'He ought to be sent to Sing Sing,' amended Mr Pett.

'Why don't you send him to school?'

'Your aunt wouldn't hear of it. She's afraid of his being kidnapped. It happened last time he went to school. You can't blame her for wanting to keep her eye on him after that.'

Ann ran her fingers meditatively over the keys.

'I've sometimes thought—'

'Yes?'

'Oh, nothing. I must get on with this thing for Aunt Nesta.'

Mr Pett placed the bulk of the Sunday paper on the floor beside him and began to run an appreciative eye over the comic supplement. That lingering boyishness in him which endeared him to Ann always led him to open his Sabbath reading in this fashion. Grey-headed though he was, he still retained both in art and in real life a taste for the slapstick. No one had ever known the pure pleasure it had given him when Raymond Green, his wife's novelist protégé, had tripped over a loose stair-rod one morning and fallen an entire flight.

From some point farther down the corridor came a muffled thudding. Ann stopped her work to listen.

'There's Jerry Mitchell punching the bag.'

'Eh?' said Mr Pett.

'I only said I could hear Jerry Mitchell in the gymnasium.'

'Yes, he's there.'

Ann looked out of the window thoughtfully for a moment. Then she swung round in her swivel chair.

'Uncle Peter!'

Mr Pett emerged slowly from the comic supplement.

'Eh?'

'Did Jerry Mitchell ever tell you about that friend of his who keeps a dogs' hospital down on Long Island somewhere? I forget his name – Smithers or Smethurst or something. People – old ladies, you know, and people – bring him their dogs to be cured when they get sick. He has an infallible remedy, Jerry tells me. He makes a lot of money at it.'

'Money?' Pett, the student, became Pett, the financier, at the magic word. 'There might be something in that if one got behind it. Dogs are fashionable. There would be a market for a really good medicine.'

'I'm afraid you couldn't put Mr Smethurst's remedy on the market. It only works when the dog has been over-eating himself and not taking any exercise.'

'Well, that's all these fancy dogs ever have the matter with them. It looks to me as if I might do business with this man. I'll get his address from Mitchell.'

'It's no use thinking of it, Uncle Peter. You couldn't do business with him – in that way. All Mr Smethurst does when anyone brings him a fat, unhealthy dog, is to feed it next to nothing – just the simplest kind of food, you know – and make it run about a lot. And in about a week the dog's as well and happy and nice as he can possibly be.'

'Oh,' said Mr Pett, disappointed.

Ann touched the keys of her machine softly.

'Why I mentioned Mr Smethurst,' she said, 'was because we had been talking of Ogden. Don't you think his treatment would be just what Ogden needs?'

Mr Pett's eyes gleamed.

'It's a shame he can't have a week or two of it!'

Ann played a little tune with her finger-tips on the desk.

'It would do him good, wouldn't it?'

Silence fell upon the room, broken only by the tapping of the typewriter. Mr Pett, having finished the comic supplement, turned to the sporting section, for he was a baseball fan of no lukewarm order. The claims of business did not permit him to see as many games as he could wish, but he followed the national pastime closely on the printed page and had an admiration for the Napoleonic gifts of Mr McGraw which would have gratified that gentleman had he known of it.

'Uncle Peter,' said Ann, turning round again.

'Eh?'

'It's funny you should have been talking about Ogden getting kidnapped. This story of Aunt Nesta's is all about an angel-child – I suppose it's meant to be Ogden – being stolen and hidden and all that. It's odd that she should write stories like this. You wouldn't expect it of her.'

'Your aunt,' said Mr Pett, 'lets her mind run on that sort of thing a good deal. She tells me there was a time, not so long ago, when half the kidnappers in America were after him. She sent him to school in England – or rather her husband did. They were separated then – and, as far as I can follow the story, the kidnappers all took the next boat and besieged the place.'

'It's a pity somebody doesn't smuggle him away now and keep him till he's a better boy.'

'Ah!' said Mr Pett wistfully.

Ann looked at him fixedly, but his eyes were once more on his paper. She gave a little sigh and turned to her work again.

'It's quite demoralizing, typing Aunt Nesta's stories,' she said. 'They put ideas into one's head.'

Mr Pett said nothing. He was reading an article of medical interest in the magazine section, for he was a man who ploughed steadily through his Sunday paper, omitting nothing. The typewriter began tapping again.

'Great Godfrey!'

Ann swung round and gazed at her uncle in concern. He was staring blankly at the paper.

'What's the matter?'

The page on which Mr Pett's attention was concentrated was decorated with a fanciful picture in bold lines of a young man in evening dress pursuing a young woman similarly clad along what appeared to be a restaurant supper table. An enjoyable time was apparently being had by both. Across the page this legend ran:

PICCADILLY JIM ONCE MORE
The Recent Adventures of Young Mr Crocker of New York and London.

It was not upon the title, however, nor upon the illustration that Mr Pett's fascinated eyes rested. What he was looking at was a small reproduction of a photograph which had been inserted in the body of the article. It was the photograph of a woman in the early forties, rather formidably handsome, beneath which were printed the words:

MRS NESTA FORD PETT
Well-known Society Leader and Authoress.

Ann had risen and was peering over his shoulder. She frowned as she caught sight of the heading of the page. Then her eye fell upon the photograph.

'Good gracious! Why have they got Aunt Nesta's picture there?'

Mr Pett breathed a deep and gloomy breath.

'They've found out she's his aunt. I was afraid they would. I don't know what she will say when she sees this.'

'Don't let her see it.'

'She has the paper downstairs. She's probably reading it now.'

Ann was glancing through the article.

'It seems to be much the same sort of thing that they have published before. I can't understand why the *Chronicle* takes such an interest in Jimmy Crocker.'

'Well, you see he used to be a newspaper man, and the *Chronicle* was the paper he worked for.'

Ann flushed.

'I know,' she said shortly.

Something in her tone arrested Mr Pett's attention.

'Yes, yes, of course,' he said hastily. 'I was forgetting.'

There was an awkward silence. Mr Pett coughed. The matter of young Mr Crocker's erstwhile connection with the *New York Chronicle* was one which they had tacitly decided to refrain from mentioning.

'I didn't know he was your nephew, Uncle Peter.'

'Nephew by marriage,' corrected Mr Pett a little hurriedly. 'Nesta's sister Eugenia married his father.'

'I suppose that makes me a sort of cousin.'

'A distant cousin.'

'It can't be too distant for me.'

There was a sound of hurried footsteps outside the door. Mrs Pett entered, holding a paper in her hand. She waved it before Mr Pett's sympathetic face.

'I know, my dear,' he said, backing. 'Ann and I were just talking about it.'

The little photograph had not done Mrs Pett justice. Seen life-size, she was both handsomer and more formidable than she appeared in reproduction. She was a large woman, with a fine figure and bold and compelling eyes, and her personality crashed disturbingly into the quiet atmosphere of the room. She was the type of woman whom small, diffident men seem to marry instinctively, as unable to help themselves as cockleshell boats sucked into a maelstrom.

'What are you going to do about it?' she demanded, sinking heavily into the chair which her husband had vacated.

This was an aspect of the matter which had not occurred to Mr Pett. He had not contemplated the possibility of actually doing anything. Nature had made him out of office hours essentially a passive organism, and it was his tendency, when he found himself in a sea of troubles, to float plaintively, not to take arms against it. To pick up the slings and arrows of outrageous fortune and fling them back was not a habit of his. He scratched his chin and said nothing. He went on saying nothing.

'If Eugenia had had any sense she would have foreseen what would happen if she took the boy away from New York where he was working too hard to get into mischief and let him run loose in London with too much money and nothing to do. But if she had had any sense she would never have married that impossible Crocker man, as I told her.'

Mrs Pett paused, and her eyes glowed with reminiscent fire. She was recalling the scene which had taken place three years ago between her sister and herself, when Eugenia had told her of her intention to marry an obscure and middle-aged actor named Bingley Crocker. Mrs Pett had never seen Bingley Crocker, but she had condemned the proposed match in terms which had ended definitely and for ever her relations with her sister. Eugenia was not a woman who welcomed criticism of her actions. She was cast in the same formidable mould as Mrs Pett and resembled her strikingly in both appearance and character.

Mrs Pett returned to the present. The past could look after itself. The present demanded surgery.

'One would have thought it would have been obvious even to Eugenia that a boy of twenty-one needed regular work.'

Mr Pett was glad to come out of his shell here. He was the Apostle of work, and this sentiment pleased him.

'That's right,' he said. 'Every boy ought to have work.'

'Look at this young Crocker's record since he went to live in London. He is always doing something to make himself notorious. There was that breach-of-promise case, and that fight at the political meeting, and his escapades at Monte Carlo, and – and everything. And he must be drinking himself to death. I think Eugenia's insane. She seems to have no influence over him at all.'

Mr Pett moaned sympathetically.

'And now the papers have found out that I am his aunt, and I suppose they will print my photograph whenever they publish an article about him.'

She ceased and sat rigid with just wrath. Mr Pett, who always felt his responsibilities as chorus keenly during these wifely monologues, surmised that a remark from him was indicated.

'It's tough!' he said.

Mrs Pett turned on him like a wounded tigress.

'What is the use of saying that? It's no use saying anything.'

'No, no,' said Mr Pett, prudently refraining from pointing out that she had already said a good deal.

'You must do something.'

Ann entered the conversation for the first time. She was not very fond of her aunt, and liked her least when she was bullying Mr Pett. There was something in Mrs Pett's character with which the imperiousness which lay beneath Ann's cheerful attitude towards the world was ever at war.

'What can Uncle Peter possibly do?' she inquired.

'Why, get the boy back to America and make him work. It's the only possible thing.'

'But is it possible?'

'Of course it is.'

'Assuming that Jimmy Crocker would accept an invitation to come over to America, what sort of work could he do here? He couldn't get his place on the *Chronicle* back again, after dropping out for all these years and making a public pest of himself all that while. And outside of newspaper work what is he fit for?'

'My dear child, don't make difficulties.'

'I'm not. These are ready-made.'

Mr Pett interposed. He was always nervously apprehensive of a clash between these two. Ann had red hair and the nature which generally goes with red hair. She was impulsive and quick of tongue, and – as he remembered her father had always been – a little too ready for combat. She was usually as quickly remorseful as she was quickly pugnacious, like most persons of her colour. Her offer to type the story which now lay on her desk had been the *amende honorable* following on just such a scene with her aunt as this promised to be. Mr Pett had no wish to see the truce thus consummated broken almost before it had had time to operate.

'I could give the boy a job in my office,' he suggested.

Giving young men jobs in his office was what Mr Pett liked best to do. There were six brilliant youths living in his house and bursting with his food at that very moment whom he would have been delighted to start addressing envelopes downtown. Notably his wife's nephew, Willie Partridge, whom he looked upon as a specious loafer. He had a stubborn disbelief in the explosive that was to revolutionize war. He knew, as all the world did, that Willie's late father had been a great inventor, but he did not accept the fact that Willie had inherited the dead man's genius. He regarded the experiments on Partridgite, as it was to be called, with the profoundest scepticism, and considered that the only thing Willie had ever invented or was likely to invent was a series of ingenious schemes for living in fatted idleness on other people's money.

'Exactly,' said Mrs Pett, delighted at the suggestion. 'The very thing.'

'Will you write and suggest it?' said Mr Pett, basking in the sunshine of unwonted commendation.

'What would be the use of writing? Eugenia would pay no attention. Besides, I could not say all I wished to in a letter. No, the only thing is to go over to England and see her. I shall speak very plainly to her. I shall point out what an advantage it will be to the boy to be in your office and to live here—'

Ann started.

'You don't mean live here – in this house?'

'Of course. There would be no sense in bringing the boy all the way over from England if he was to be allowed to run loose when he got here.'

Mr Pett coughed deprecatingly.

'I don't think that would be very pleasant for Ann, dear.'

'Why in the name of goodness should Ann object?'

Ann moved toward the door.

'Thank you for thinking of it, Uncle Peter. You're always a dear. But don't worry about me. Do just as you want to. In any case I'm quite certain that you won't be able to get him to come over here. You can see by the paper he's having far too good a time in London. You can call Jimmy Crockers from the vasty deep, but will they come when you call for them?'

Mrs Pett looked at the door as it closed behind her, then at her husband.

'What do you mean, Peter, about Ann? Why wouldn't it be pleasant for her if this Crocker boy came to live with us?'

Mr Pett hesitated.

'Well, it's like this, Nesta. I hope you won't tell her I told you. She's sensitive about it, poor girl. It all happened before you and

I were married. Ann was much younger then. You know what schoolgirls are, kind of foolish and sentimental. It was my fault really. I ought to have—'

'Good Heavens, Peter! What are you trying to tell me?'

'She was only a child—'

Mrs Pett rose in slow horror.

'Peter! Tell me! Don't try to break it gently.'

'Ann wrote a book of poetry and I had it published for her.'

Mrs Pett sank back in her chair.

'Oh!' she said, it would have been hard to say whether with relief or disappointment. 'Whatever did you make such a fuss for? Why did you want to be so mysterious?'

'It was all my fault really,' proceeded Mr Pett. 'I ought to have known better. All I thought of at the time was that it would please the child to see the poems in print and to be able to give the book to her friends. She did give it to her friends,' he went on ruefully, 'and ever since she's been trying to live it down. I've seen her bite a young fellow's head off when he tried to make a grandstand play with her by quoting her poems which he'd found on his sister's bookshelf.'

'But, in the name of goodness, what has all this to do with young Crocker?'

'Why, it was this way: most of the papers just gave Ann's book a mention among Volumes Received, or a couple of lines that didn't amount to anything; but the *Chronicle* saw a Sunday feature in it, as Ann was going about a lot then and was a well-known society girl. They sent this Crocker boy to get an interview from her, all about her methods of work and inspirations and what not. We never suspected it wasn't the straight goods. Why, that very evening I mailed an order for a hundred copies to be sent to me when the thing appeared. And'

– pinkness came upon Mr Pett at the recollection – 'it was just a josh from start to finish. The young hound made a joke of the poems and what Ann had told him about her inspirations, and quoted bits of the poems just to kid the life out of them. I thought Ann would never get over it. Well, it doesn't worry her any more – she's grown out of the schoolgirl stage – but you can bet she isn't going to get up and give three cheers and a tiger if you bring young Crocker to live in the same house.'

'Utterly ridiculous!' said Mrs Pett. 'I certainly do not intend to alter my plans because of a trivial incident that happened years ago. We will sail on Wednesday.'

'Very well, my dear,' said Mr Pett resignedly. 'Just as you say. Er – just you and I?'

'And Ogden, of course.'

Mr Pett controlled a facial spasm with a powerful effort of the will. He had feared this.

'I wouldn't dream of leaving him here while I went away, after what happened when poor dear Elmer sent him to school in England that time.' The late Mr Ford had spent most of his married life either quarrelling with or separated from his wife, but since death he had been canonized as 'poor dear Elmer'. 'Besides, the sea voyage will do the poor darling good. He has not been looking at all well lately.'

'If Ogden's coming, I'd like to take Ann.'

'Why?'

'She can—' He sought for a euphemism. 'Keep in order' was the expression he wished to avoid. To his mind Ann was the only known antidote for Ogden, but he felt it would be impolitic to say so. '—look after him on the boat,' he concluded. 'You know you are a bad sailor.'

'Very well. Bring Ann. Oh, Peter, that reminds me of what I wanted to say to you, which this dreadful thing in the paper drove completely out of my mind. Lord Wisbeach has asked Ann to marry him.'

Mr Pett looked a little hurt.

'She didn't tell me.' Ann usually confided in him.

'She didn't tell me either. Lord Wisbeach told me. He said Ann had promised to think it over and give him his answer later. Meanwhile, he had come to me to assure himself that I approved. I thought that so charming of him.'

Mr Pett was frowning.

'She hasn't accepted him?'

'Not definitely.'

'I hope she doesn't.'

'Don't be foolish, Peter. It would be an excellent match.'

Mr Pett shuffled his feet.

'I don't like him. There's something too darned smooth about that fellow.'

'If you mean that his manners are perfect, I agree with you. I shall do all in my power to induce Ann to accept him.'

'I shouldn't,' said Mr Pett with more decision than was his wont. 'You know what Ann is if you try to force her to do anything. She gets her ears back and won't budge. Her father is just the same. When we were boys together, sometimes—'

'Don't be absurd, Peter – as if I should dream of trying to force Ann to do anything.'

'We don't know anything of this fellow. Two weeks ago we didn't know he was on the earth.'

'What do we need to know beyond his name?'

Mr Pett said nothing, but he was not convinced. The Lord Wisbeach under discussion was a pleasant-spoken and presentable young man who had called at Mr Pett's office a short while before to consult him about investing some money. He had brought a letter of introduction from Hammond Chester, Ann's father, whom he had met in Canada, where the latter was at present engaged in the comparatively mild occupation of bass-fishing. With their business talk the acquaintance would have begun and finished, if Mr Pett had been able to please himself, for he had not taken a fancy to Lord Wisbeach. But he was an American with an American's sense of hospitality, and the young man being a friend of Hammond Chester, he had felt bound to invite him to Riverside Drive, with misgivings which were now, he felt, completely justified.

'Ann ought to marry,' said Mrs Pett. 'She gets her own way too much now. However, it is entirely her own affair, and there is nothing that we can do.' She rose. 'I only hope she will be sensible.'

She went out, leaving Mr Pett gloomier than she had found him. He hated the idea of Ann marrying Lord Wisbeach, who, even if he had had no faults at all, would be objectionable in that he would probably take her to live three thousand miles away in his own country. The thought of losing Ann oppressed Mr Pett sorely.

Ann, meanwhile, had made her way down the passage to the gymnasium, which Mr Pett, in the interests of his health, had caused to be constructed in a large room at the end of the house, a room designed by the original owner, who had had artistic leanings, for a studio. The tap-tap-tap of the leather bag had ceased, but voices from within told her that Jerry Mitchell, Mr Pett's private physical instructor, was still there. She wondered who was his companion, and found on opening the door that it was Ogden. The boy was leaning against the wall and regarding Jerry with a dull and supercilious gaze which the latter was plainly finding it hard to bear.

'Yes, sir!' Ogden was saying as Ann entered. 'I heard Biggs asking her to come for a joyride.'

'I bet she turned him down,' said Jerry Mitchell sullenly.

'I bet she didn't. Why should she? Biggs is an awful good-looking fellow.'

'What are you talking about, Ogden?' said Ann.

'I was telling him that Biggs asked Celestine to go for a ride in the car with him.'

'I'll knock his block off!' muttered the incensed Jerry.

Ogden laughed derisively.

'Yes, you will! Mother would fire you if you touched him. She wouldn't stand for having her chauffeur beaten up.'

Jerry Mitchell turned an appealing face to Ann. Ogden's revelations and especially his eulogy of Biggs' personal appearance had tormented him. He knew that, in his wooing of Mrs Pett's maid, Celestine, he was handicapped by his looks, concerning which he had no illusions. No Adonis to begin with, he had been so edited and re-edited during a long and prosperous ring career by the gloved fists of a hundred foes that in affairs of the heart he was obliged to rely exclusively on moral worth and charm of manner. He belonged to the old school of fighters who looked the part, and in these days of pugilists who resemble matinée idols he had the appearance of an anachronism. He was a stocky man with a round, solid head, small eyes, an undershot jaw, and a nose which ill-treatment had reduced to a mere scenario. A narrow strip of forehead acted as a kind of buffer state, separating his front hair from his eyebrows, and he bore beyond hope of concealment the badge of his late employment, the cauliflower ear. Yet was he a man of worth and a good citizen, and Ann had liked him from their first meeting. As for Jerry, he worshipped Ann and would have done anything she asked him. Ever since he had discovered that Ann was willing to listen to and sympathize with his outpourings on the subject of his troubled wooing he had been her slave.

Ann came to the rescue in characteristically direct fashion.

'Get out, Ogden!' she said.

Ogden tried to meet her eye mutinously, but failed. Why he should be afraid of Ann he had never been able to understand, but it was a fact that she was the only person of his acquaintance whom he respected. She had a bright eye and a calm, imperious stare that never failed to tame him.

'Why?' he muttered. 'You're not my boss.'

'Be quick, Ogden.'

'What's the big idea, ordering a fellow—'

'And close the door gently behind you,' said Ann. She turned to Jerry as the order was obeyed. 'Has he been bothering you, Jerry?'

Jerry Mitchell wiped his forehead.

'Say, if that kid don't quit butting in when I'm working in the gym—. You heard what he was saying about Maggie, Miss Ann?'

Celestine had been born Maggie O'Toole, a name which Mrs Pett stoutly refused to countenance in any maid of hers.

'Why on earth do you pay any attention to him, Jerry? You must have seen that he was making it all up. He spends his whole time wandering about till he finds someone he can torment, and then he enjoys himself. Maggie would never dream of going out in the car with Biggs.'

Jerry Mitchell sighed a sigh of relief.

'It's great for a fellow to have you in his corner, Miss Ann.'

Ann went to the door and opened it. She looked down the passage, then, satisfied as to its emptiness, returned to her seat.

'Jerry, I want to talk to you. I have an idea. Something I want you to do for me.'

'Yes, Miss Ann?'

'We've got to do something about that child Ogden. He's been worrying Uncle Peter again, and I'm not going to have it. I warned him once that if he did it again awful things would happen to him; but he didn't believe me, I suppose. Jerry, what sort of a man is your friend, Mr Smethurst?'

'Do you mean Smithers, Miss Ann?'

'I knew it was either Smithers or Smethurst. The dog man, I mean. Is he a man you can trust?'

'With my last buck. I've known him since we were kids.'

'I don't mean as regards money. I am going to send Ogden to him for treatment, and I want to know if I can rely on him to help me.'

'For the love of Mike!'

Jerry Mitchell, after an instant of stunned bewilderment, was looking at her with worshipping admiration. He had always known that Miss Ann possessed a mind of no common order, but this, he felt, was genius. For a moment the magnificence of the idea took his breath away.

'Do you mean that you're going to kidnap him, Miss Ann?'

'Yes. That is to say, you are – if I can persuade you to do it for me.'

'Sneak him away and send him to Bud Smithers' dog hospital?'

'For treatment. I like Mr Smithers' methods. I think they would do Ogden all the good in the world.'

Jerry was enthusiastic.

'Why, Bud would make him part human. But, say, isn't it taking big chances? Kidnapping's a penitentiary offence.'

'This isn't that sort of kidnapping.'

'Well, it's mighty like it.'

'I don't think you need be afraid of the penitentiary. I can't see Aunt Nesta prosecuting, when it would mean that she would have to charge us with having sent Ogden to a dogs' hospital. She likes publicity, but it has to be the right kind of publicity. No, we do run a risk, but it isn't that one. You run the risk of losing your job here, and I should certainly be sent to my grandmother for an indefinite sentence. You've never seen my grandmother, have you, Jerry? She's the only person in the world I'm afraid of! She lives miles from anywhere and has family prayers at seven-thirty sharp every morning. Well, I'm ready to risk her, if you're ready to risk your job in such a good cause. You know you're just as fond of Uncle Peter as I am, and Ogden is worrying him into breakdown. Surely you won't refuse to help me, Jerry?'

Jerry rose and extended a callused hand.

'When do we start?'

Ann shook the hand warmly.

'Thank you, Jerry. You're a jewel! I envy Maggie. Well, I don't think we can do anything till they come back from England, as Aunt Nesta is sure to take Ogden with her.'

'Who's going to England?'

'Uncle Peter and Aunt Nesta were talking just now of sailing to try to persuade a young man named Crocker to come back here.'

'Crocker? Jimmy Crocker? Piccadilly Jim?'

'Yes. Why, do you know him?'

'I used to meet him sometimes when he was working on the *Chronicle* here. Looks as if he was cutting a wide swath in dear old London. Did you see the paper to-day?'

'Yes, that's what made Aunt Nesta want to bring him over. Of course there isn't the remotest chance that she will be able to make him come. Why should he come?'

'Last time I saw Jimmy Crocker,' said Jerry, 'was a couple of years ago, when I went over to train Eddie Flynn for his go with Porky Jones at the National. I bumped into him at the N.S.C. He was a good deal tanked.'

'He's always drinking, I believe.'

'He took me to supper at some swell joint where they all had the soup-and-fish on but me. I felt like a dirty deuce in a clean deck. He used to be a regular fellow, Jimmy Crocker, but from what you read in the papers it begins to look as if he was hitting it up too swift. It's always the way with those boys when you take them off a steady job and let them run around loose with their jeans full of mazuma.'

'That's exactly why I want to do something about Ogden. If he's allowed to go on as he is at present he will grow up exactly like Jimmy Crocker.'

'Aw, Jimmy Crocker ain't in Ogden's class,' protested Jerry.

'Yes, he is. There's absolutely no difference between them.'

'Say, you've got it in for Jim, haven't you, Miss Ann?' Jerry looked at her wonderingly. 'What's your kick against him?'

Ann bit her lip. 'I object to him on principle,' she said. 'I don't like his type. Well, I'm glad we've settled this about Ogden, Jerry. I knew I could rely on you. But I won't let you do it for nothing. Uncle Peter shall give you something for it – enough to start that health-farm you talk about so much. Then you can marry Maggie and live happily ever afterward.'

'Gee! Is the boss in on this too?'

'Not yet. I'm going to tell him now. Hush, there's somebody coming.'

Mr Pett wandered in. He was still looking troubled.

'Oh, Ann – good morning, Mitchell – your aunt has decided to go to England. I want you to come too.'

'You want me? To help interview Jimmy Crocker!'

'No, no; just to come along and be company on the voyage. You'll be such a help with Ogden, Ann. You can keep him in order. How you do it I don't know. You seem to make another boy of him.'

Ann stole a glance at Jerry, who answered with an encouraging grin. Ann was constrained to make her meaning plainer than by the language of the eye.

'Would you mind just running away for half a moment, Jerry?' she said winningly. 'I want to say something to Uncle Peter.'

'Sure! Sure!'

Ann turned to Mr Pett as the door closed.

'You'd like somebody to make Ogden a different boy, wouldn't you, Uncle Peter?'

'I wish it were possible.'

'He's been worrying you a lot lately, hasn't he?' asked Ann sympathetically.

'Yes,' sighed Mr Pett.

'Then that's all right,' said Ann briskly. 'I was afraid that you might not approve. But if you do I'll go right ahead.'

Mr Pett started violently. There was something in Ann's voice and, as he looked at her, something in her face that made him fear the worst. Her eyes were flashing with an inspired light of a highly belligerent nature, and the sun turned the red hair to which she owed her deplorable want of balance to a mass of flame. There was something in the air. Mr Pett sensed it with every nerve of his apprehensive person. He gazed at Ann, and as he did so the years seemed to slip from him and he was a boy again, about to be urged to lawless courses by the superior will of his boyhood's hero, Hammond Chester. In the boyhood of nearly every man there is a single outstanding figure, some one youthful hypnotic Napoleon whose will was law and at whose bidding his better judgement curled up and died.

In Mr Pett's life Ann's father had filled this rôle. He had dominated Mr Pett at an age when the mind is most malleable. And now – so true is it that though Time may blunt our boyish memories, the traditions of boyhood live on in us and an emotional crisis will bring them to the surface as an explosion brings up the fish that lurk in the nethermost mud – it was as if he were facing the youthful Hammond Chester again and being irresistibly impelled to some course of which he entirely disapproved but which he knew that he was destined to undertake. He watched Ann as a trapped man might watch a ticking bomb, bracing himself for the explosion and knowing that he is helpless. She was Hammond Chester's daughter, and she spoke to him with the voice of Hammond Chester. She was her father's child and she was going to start something.

'I've arranged it all with Jerry,' said Ann. 'He's going to help me smuggle Ogden away to that friend of his I told you about who keeps the dog hospital. And the friend is going to keep him until he reforms. Isn't it a perfectly splendid idea?'

Mr Pett blanched. The frightfulness of reality had exceeded anticipation.

'But, Ann!'

The words came from him in a strangled bleat. His whole being was paralysed by a clammy horror. This was beyond the uttermost limit of his fears. And to complete the terror of the moment, he knew, even while he rebelled against the insane lawlessness of her scheme, that he was going to agree to it, and – worst of all – that deep down in him there was a feeling toward it which did not dare to come to the surface, but which he knew to be approval.

'Of course Jerry would do it for nothing,' said Ann, 'but I promised him that you would give him something for his trouble. You can arrange all that yourselves later.'

'But, Ann! But, Ann! Suppose your aunt finds out who did it!'

'Well, there will be a tremendous row!' said Ann composedly. 'And you will have to assert yourself. It will be a splendid thing for you. You know you are much too kind to everyone, Uncle Peter. I don't think there's anyone who would put up with what you do. Father told me in one of his letters that he used to call you Patient Pete as a boy.'

Mr Pett started. Not for many a day had a nickname which he considered the most distasteful of all possible nicknames risen up from its grave to haunt him. Patient Pete! He had thought the repulsive title buried for ever in the same tomb as his dead youth. Patient Pete! The first faint glimmer of the flame of rebellion began to burn in his bosom.

'Patient Pete!'

'Patient Pete!' said Ann inexorably.

'But, Ann' – there was pathos in Mr Pett's voice – 'I like a peaceful life.'

'You'll never have one if you don't stand up for yourself. You know quite well that Father is right. You do let everyone trample on you. Do you think Father would let Ogden worry him and have his house filled with affected imitation geniuses so that he couldn't find a room to be alone in?'

'But Ann, your father is different. He likes fusses. I've known your father to contradict a man weighing two hundred pounds out of sheer exuberance. There's a lot of your father in you, Ann. I've often noticed it.'

'There is! That's why I'm going to make you put your foot down sooner or later. You're going to turn all these loafers out of the house. And first of all you're going to help us send Ogden away to Mr Smithers.'

There was a long silence.

'It's your red hair!' said Mr Pett at length with the air of a man who has been solving a problem. 'It's your red hair that makes you like this, Ann. Your father has red hair too.'

Ann laughed.

'It's not my fault that I have red hair, Uncle Peter. It's my misfortune.'

Mr Pett shook his head.

'Other people's misfortune too!' he said.

CHAPTER 2

London brooded under a grey sky. There had been rain in the night, and the trees were still dripping. Presently, however, there appeared in the leaden haze a watery patch of blue; and through this crevice in the clouds the sun, diffidently at first but with gradually increasing confidence, peeped down on the fashionable and exclusive turf of Grosvenor Square. Stealing across the square its rays reached the massive stone walls of Drexdale House, until recently the London residence of the earl of that name; then, passing through the window of the breakfast room, played lightly on the partially bald head of Mr Bingley Crocker, late of New York, in the United States of America, as he bent over his morning paper. Mrs Bingley Crocker, busy across the table reading her mail, the rays did not touch. Had they done so she would have rung for Bayliss, the butler, to come and lower the shade, for she endured liberties neither from man nor from Nature.

Mr Crocker was about fifty years of age, clean shaven and of a comfortable stoutness. He was frowning as he read. His smooth, good-humoured face wore an expression that might have been disgust, perplexity, or a blend of both. His wife, on the other hand, was looking happy. She extracted the substance from her correspondence with swift glances of her compelling eyes, just as she would have extracted guilty secrets from Bingley, if he had had any. This was a woman who, like her sister Nesta, had been able all her life to accomplish more with a glance than other women with recrimination and threat. It had been a popular belief among his friends that her late husband, the well-known Pittsburgh millionaire, G. G. van Brunt, had been in the habit of automatically confessing all if he merely caught the eye of her photograph on his dressing table.

From the growing pile of opened envelopes Mrs Crocker looked up, a smile softening the firm line of her lips.

'A card from Lady Corstorphine, Bingley, for her at-home on the twenty-ninth.'

Mr Crocker, still absorbed, snorted absently.

'One of the most exclusive hostesses in England. She has influence with the right sort of people. Her brother, the Duke of Devizes, is the Premier's oldest friend.'

'Uh?'

'The Duchess of Axminster has written to ask me to look after a stall at her bazaar for the Indigent Daughters of the Clergy.'

'Huh?'

'Bingley, you aren't listening! What is that you are reading?'

Mr Crocker tore himself from the paper.

'This? Oh, I was looking at a report of that cricket game you made me go and see yesterday.'

'Oh, I am glad you have begun to take an interest in cricket. It is simply a social necessity in England. Why you ever made such a fuss about taking it up I can't think. You used to be so fond of watching baseball, and cricket is just the same thing.'

A close observer would have marked a deepening of the look of pain on Mr Crocker's face. Women say this sort of thing carelessly, with no wish to wound; but that makes it none the less hard to bear.

From the hall outside came faintly the sound of the telephone, then the measured tones of Bayliss answering it. Mr Crocker returned to his paper. Bayliss entered.

'Lady Corstorphine desires to speak to you on the telephone, madam.'

Half-way to the door Mrs Crocker paused, as if recalling something that had slipped her memory.

'Is Mr James getting up, Bayliss?'

'I believe not, madam. I am informed by one of the house-maids who passed his door a short time back that there were no sounds.'

Mrs Crocker left the room. Bayliss, preparing to follow her example, was arrested by an exclamation from the table.

'Say!' His master's voice. 'Say, Bayliss, come here a minute. Want to ask you something.'

The butler approached the table. It seemed to him that his employer was not looking quite himself this morning. There was something a trifle wild, a little haggard, about his expression. He had remarked on it earlier in the morning in the servants' hall.

As a matter of fact, Mr Crocker's ailment was a perfectly simple one. He was suffering from one of those acute spasms of homesickness which invariably racked him in the earlier summer months. Ever since his marriage, five years previously, and this simultaneous removal from his native land, he had been a chronic victim to the complaint. The symptoms grew less acute in winter and spring, but from May onward he suffered severely.

Poets have dealt feelingly with the emotions of practically every variety except one. They have sung of Ruth, of Israel in bondage, of slaves pining for their native Africa, and of the miner's dream of home. But the sorrows of the baseball enthusiast, compelled by fate to live three thousand miles away from the Polo Grounds, have been neglected in song. Bingley Crocker was such a one, and in summer his agonies were awful. He pined away in a country where they said 'Well played, sir!' when they meant 'At-a-boy!'

'Bayliss, do you play cricket?'

'I am a little past the age, sir. In my younger days—'

'Do you understand it?'

'Yes, sir. I frequently spend an afternoon at Lord's or the Oval when there is a good match.'

Many who enjoyed a merely casual acquaintance with the butler would have looked on this as an astonishingly unexpected revelation of humanity in Bayliss, but Mr Crocker was not surprised. To him, from the very beginning, Bayliss had been a man and a brother, who was always willing to suspend his duties in order to answer questions dealing with the thousand and one problems which the social life of England presented. Mr Crocker's mind had adjusted itself with difficulty to the niceties of class distinction, and though he had cured himself of his early tendency to address the butler as 'Bill', he never failed to consult him as man to man in his moments of perplexity. Bayliss was always eager to be of assistance. He liked Mr Crocker. True, his manner might have struck a more sensitive man than his employer as a shade too closely resembling that of an indulgent father toward a son who was not quite right in the head; but it had genuine affection in it.

Mr Crocker picked up his paper and folded it back at the sporting page, pointing with a stubby forefinger.

'Well, what does all this mean? I've kept out of watching cricket since I landed in England, but yesterday they got the poison needle to work and took me off to see Surrey play Kent at that place, Lord's, where you say you go sometimes.'

'I was there yesterday, sir. A very exciting game.'

'Exciting? How do you make that out? I sat in the bleachers all afternoon, waiting for something to break loose. Doesn't anything ever happen at cricket?'

The butler winced a little, but managed to smile a tolerant smile. This man, he reflected, was but an American, and, as such, more to be pitied than censured. He endeavoured to explain.

'It was a sticky wicket yesterday, sir, owing to the rain.'

'Eh?'

'The wicket was sticky, sir.'

'Come again.'

'I mean that the reason why the game yesterday struck you as slow was that the wicket – I should say the turf – was sticky – that is to say, wet. Sticky is the technical term, sir. When the wicket is sticky the batsmen are obliged to exercise a great deal of caution, as the stickiness of the wicket enables the bowlers to make the ball turn more sharply in either direction as it strikes the turf than when the wicket is not sticky.'

'That's it, is it?'

'Yes, sir.'

'Thanks for telling me.'

'Not at all, sir.'

Mr Crocker pointed to the paper.

'Well, now, this seems to be the boxscore of the game we saw yesterday. If you can make sense out of that, go to it.'

The passage on which his finger rested was headed Final Score, and ran as follows:

SURREY

FIRST INNINGS

Hayward, c Wooley b Carr	67
Hobbs, run out	0
Hayes, st Huish b Fielder	12
Ducat, b Fielder	33
Harrison, not out	11
Sandham, not out	6
Extras	10
Total (for four wickets)	139

Bayliss inspected the cipher gravely.

'What is it you wish me to explain, sir?'

'Why, the whole thing. What's it all about?'

'It's perfectly simple, sir. Surrey won the toss and took first knock. Hayward and Hobbs were the opening pair. Hayward called Hobbs for a short run, but the latter was unable to get across and was thrown out by mid-on. Hayes was the next man in. He went out of his ground and was stumped. Ducat and Hayward made a capital stand considering the stickiness of the wicket, until Ducat was bowled by a good length off-break and Hayward caught at second slip off a googly. Then Harrison and Sandham played out time.'

Mr Crocker breathed heavily through his nose.

'Yes!' he said. 'Yes! I had an idea that was it. But I think I'd like to have it once again slowly. Start with these figures. What does that sixty-seven mean, opposite Hayward's name?'

'He made sixty-seven runs, sir.'

'Sixty-seven! In one game?'

'Yes, sir.'

'Why, Home-Run Baker couldn't do it!'

'I am not familiar with Mr Baker, sir.'

'I suppose you've never seen a ball game?'

'Ball game, sir?'

'A baseball game?'

'Never, sir.'

'Then, Bill,' said Mr Crocker, reverting in his emotion to the bad habit of his early London days, 'you haven't lived. See here!'

Whatever vestige of respect for class distinctions Mr Crocker had managed to preserve during the opening stages of the interview now definitely disappeared. His eyes shone wildly and he snorted like a warhorse. He clutched the butler by the sleeve and drew him closer to the table, then began to move forks, spoons, cups, and even the contents of his plate, about the cloth with an energy little short of feverish.

'Bayliss?'

'Sir?'

'Watch!' said Mr Crocker, with the air of an excitable high priest about to initiate a novice into the mysteries.

He removed a roll from the basket.

'You see this roll? That's the home plate. This spoon is first base. Where I'm putting this cup is second. This piece of bacon is third. There's your diamond for you. Very well then. These lumps of sugar are the infielders and the outfielders. Now we're ready. Batter up! He stands here. Catcher behind him. Umps behind catcher.'

'Umps, I take it, sir, is what we would call the umpire?'

'Call him anything you like. It's part of the game. Now here's the box, where I've put this dab of marmalade, and here's the pitcher winding up.'

'The pitcher would be equivalent to our bowler?'

'I guess so, though why you should call him a bowler gets past me.'

'The box, then, is the bowler's wicket?'

'Have it your own way. Now pay attention. Play ball! Pitcher's winding up. Put it over, Mike, put it over! Some speed, kid! Here it comes right in the groove. Bing! Batter slams it and streaks for first. Outfielder – this lump of sugar – boots it. Bonehead! Batter touches second. Third? No! Get back! Can't be done. Play it safe. Stick round the sack, old pal. Second batter up. Pitcher getting something on the ball now besides the cover. Whiffs him. Back to the bench, Cyril! Third batter up. See him rub his hands in the dirt. Watch this kid. He's good! Lets two alone, then slams the next right on the nose. Whizzes round to second. First guy, the one we left on second, comes home for one run. That's a game! Take it from me, Bill, that's a game!'

Somewhat overcome with the energy with which he had flung himself into his lecture, Mr Crocker sat down and refreshed himself with cold coffee.

'Quite an interesting game,' said Bayliss. 'But I find, now that you have explained it, sir, that it is familiar to me, though I have always known it under another name. It is played a great deal in this country.'

Mr Crocker started to his feet.

'It is? And I've been five years here without finding it out! When's the next game scheduled?'

'It is known in England as rounders, sir. Children play it with a soft ball and a racket, and derive considerable enjoyment from it. I have never heard of it before as a pastime for adults.'

Two shocked eyes stared into the butler's face.

'Children?' The word came in a whisper. 'A racket?'

'Yes, sir.'

'You – you didn't say a soft ball?'

'Yes, sir.'

A sort of spasm seemed to convulse Mr Crocker. He had lived five years in England, but not till this moment had he realized to the full how utterly alone he was in an alien land. Fate had placed him, bound and helpless, in a country where they called baseball rounders and played it with a soft ball.

He sank back in his chair, staring before him. And as he sat the wall seemed to melt and he was gazing upon a green field, in the centre of which a man in a grey uniform was beginning a Salome dance. Watching this person with a cold and suspicious eye stood another uniformed man, holding poised above his shoulder a sturdy club. Two Masked Marvels crouched behind him in attitudes of watchful waiting. On wooden seats all round sat a vast multitude of shirt-sleeved spectators, and the air was full of voices. One voice detached itself from the din.

'Pea-nuts! Get y'r pea-nuts!'

Something that was almost a sob shook Bingley Crocker's ample frame. Bayliss, the butler, gazed down upon him with concern. He was sure the master was unwell.

The case of Mr Bingley Crocker was one that would have provided an admirable instance for a preacher seeking to instil into an impecunious and sceptical flock the lesson that money does not of necessity bring with it happiness. And poetry has crystallized his position in the following stanza:

> An exile from home splendour dazzles in vain,
> Oh give me my lowly thatched cottage again;
> The birds singing gaily, that came at my call,
> Give me them, and that peace of mind dearer than all.

Mr Crocker had never lived in a thatched cottage, nor had his relations with the birds of his native land ever reached the stage of intimacy indicated by the poet; but substitute 'Lambs Club' for the former and 'members' for the latter, and the parallel becomes complete.

Until the time of his second marriage Bingley Crocker had been an actor, a snapper-up of whatever small character parts the gods provided. He had an excellent disposition, no money, and one son, a young man of twenty-one. For forty-five years he had lived a hand-to-mouth existence in which his next meal had generally come as a pleasant surprise; and then, on an Atlantic liner, he met the widow of G. G. van Brunt, the sole heiress to that magnate's immense fortune.

What Mrs van Brunt could have seen in Bingley Crocker to cause her to single him out from all the world passes comprehension; but the eccentricities of Cupid are commonplace. It were best to shun examination into first causes and stick to results. The swift romance began and reached its climax in the ten days which it took one of the smaller Atlantic liners to sail from Liverpool to New York. Mr Crocker was on board because he was returning with a theatrical company from a failure in London, Mrs van Brunt because she had been told that the slow boats were the steadiest. They began the voyage as strangers and ended it as an engaged couple – the affair being expedited, no doubt, by the fact that, even if it ever occurred to Bingley to resist the onslaught on his bachelor peace, he soon realized the futility of doing so, for the cramped conditions of shipboard intensified the always overwhelming effects of his future bride's determined nature.

The engagement was received in a widely differing spirit by the only surviving blood relations of the two principals. Jimmy,

Mr Crocker's son, on being informed that his father had plighted his troth to the widow of a prominent millionaire, displayed the utmost gratification and enthusiasm, and at a little supper, which he gave by way of farewell to a few of his newspaper comrades and which lasted till six in the morning, when it was broken up by the flying wedge of waiters for which the selected restaurant is justly famous, joyfully announced that work and he would from then on be total strangers. He alluded in feeling terms to the Providence that watches over good young men, and saves them from the blighting necessity of offering themselves in the flower of their golden youth as human sacrifices to the Moloch of capitalistic greed; and, having commiserated with his guests in that a similar stroke of luck had not happened to each of them, advised them to drown their sorrows in drink. Which they did.

Far different was the attitude of Mrs Crocker's sister, Nesta Pett. She entirely disapproved of the proposed match. At least, the fact that in her final interview with her sister she described the bridegroom-to-be as a wretched mummer, a despicable fortune hunter, a broken-down tramp, and a sneaking, grafting confidence trickster, lends colour to the supposition that she was not a warm supporter of it. She agreed whole-heartedly with Mrs Crocker's suggestion that they should never speak to each other again as long as they lived; and it was immediately after this that the latter removed husband Bingley, stepson Jimmy, and all her other goods and chattels to London, where they had remained ever since. Whenever Mrs Crocker spoke of America now it was in tones of the deepest dislike and contempt. Her friends were English, and every year more exclusively of England's aristocracy. She intended to become a leading figure in London society, and already her progress had been astonishing. She knew the right people, lived in the right square, said the right things and thought the right thoughts; and in the spring of her third year had succeeded in curing Bingley of his habit of beginning his remarks with the words: 'Say, lemme tell ya something!' Her progress, in short, was beginning to assume the aspect of a walk-over.

Against her complete contentment and satisfaction only one thing militated: that was the behaviour of her stepson, Jimmy. It was of Jimmy that she spoke when, having hung the receiver on its hook, she returned to the breakfast room. Bayliss had silently withdrawn, and Mr Crocker was sitting in sombre silence at the table.

'A most fortunate thing has happened, Bingley,' she said. 'It was most kind of dear Lady Corstorphine to ring me up. It seems that her nephew, Lord Percy Whipple, is back in England. He has been in Ireland for the past three years, on the staff of the Lord Lieutenant, and only arrived in London yesterday afternoon. Lady Corstorphine has promised to arrange a meeting between him and James. I particularly want them to be friends.'

'Eugenia,' said Mr Crocker in a hollow voice, 'do you know they call baseball rounders over here, and children play it with a soft ball?'

'James is becoming a serious problem. It is absolutely necessary that he should make friends with the right kind of young men.'

'And a racket,' said Mr Crocker.

'Please listen to what I am saying, Bingley. I am talking about James. There is a crude American strain in him that seems to grow worse instead of better. I was lunching with the Delafields at the Carlton yesterday, and there, only a few tables away, was

James with an impossible young man in appalling clothes. It was outrageous that James should have been seen in public at all with such a person. The man had a broken nose and talked through it. He was saying in a loud voice that made everybody turn round something about his half-scissors hook – whatever that may have been. I discovered later that he was a low professional pugilist from New York – a man named Spike Dillon, I think Captain Wroxton said. And Jimmy was giving him lunch – at the Carlton!'

Mr Crocker said nothing. Constant practice had made him an adept at saying nothing when his wife was talking.

'James must be made to realize his responsibilities. I shall have to speak to him. I was hearing only the other day of a most deserving man, extremely rich and lavishly generous in his contributions to the party funds, who was given only a knighthood, simply because he had a son who had behaved in a manner that could not possibly be overlooked. The present Court is extraordinarily strict in its views. James cannot be too careful. A certain amount of wildness in a young man is quite proper in the best set, provided that he is wild in the right company. Everyone knows that young Lord Datchet was ejected from the Empire Music Hall on boat-race night every year during his residence at Oxford University; but nobody minds. The family treat it as a joke. But James has such low tastes. Professional pugilists! I believe that many years ago it was not unfashionable for young men in society to be seen about with such persons, but those days are over. I shall certainly speak to James. He cannot afford to call attention to himself in any way. That breach-of-promise case of his three years ago is, I hope and trust, forgotten, but the slightest slip on his part might start the papers talking about it again, and that would be fatal. The eventual successor to a title must be quite as careful as—'

It was not, as has been hinted above, the usual practice of Mr Crocker to interrupt his wife when she was speaking, but he did it now.

'Say!'

Mrs Crocker frowned.

'I wish, Bingley – and I have told you so often – that you would not begin your sentences with the word "Say!" It is such a revolting Americanism. Suppose some day when you are addressing the House of Lords you should make a slip like that! The papers would never let you hear the end of it.'

Mr Crocker was swallowing convulsively, as if testing his larynx with a view to speech. Like Saul of Tarsus, he had been stricken dumb by the sudden bright light which his wife's words had caused to flash upon him. Frequently during his sojourn in London he had wondered just why Eugenia had settled there in preference to her own country. It was not her wont to do things without an object, yet until this moment he had been unable to fathom her motives. Even now it seemed almost incredible. And yet what meaning would her words have other than the monstrous one which had smitten him as a blackjack?

'Say – I mean, Eugenia – you don't want – you aren't trying – you aren't working to – you haven't any idea of trying to get them to make me a lord, have you?'

'It is what I have been working for all these years!'

'But – but why? Why? That's what I want to know. Why?'

Mrs Crocker's fine eyes glittered.

'I will tell you why, Bingley. Just before we were married I had a talk with my sister Nesta. She was insufferably offensive. She referred to you in terms which I shall never forgive. She affected to look down on you, to think I was marrying beneath me. So I am going to make you an English peer and send Nesta a newspaper clipping of the Birthday Honours with your name in it, if I have to keep working till I die! Now you know!'

Silence fell. Mr Crocker drank cold coffee. His wife stared with glittering eyes into the glorious future.

'Do you mean that I shall have to stop on here till they make me a lord?' said Mr Crocker limply.

'Yes.'

'Never go back to America?'

'Not till we have succeeded.'

'Oh, gee! Oh, gosh! Oh, hell!' said Mr Crocker, bursting the bonds of years.

Mrs Crocker, though resolute, was not unkindly. She made allowances for her husband's state of mind. She was willing to permit even American expletives during the sinking-in process of her great idea, much as a broad-minded cowboy might listen indulgently to the squealing of a mustang during the branding process. Docility and obedience would be demanded of him later, but not till the first agony had abated. She spoke soothingly to him.

'I am glad we have had this talk, Bingley. It is best that you should know. It will help you to realize your responsibilities. And that brings me back to James. Thank goodness, Lord Percy Whipple is in town. He is about James' age, and from what Lady Corstorphine tells me will be an ideal friend for him. You understand who he is, of course – the second son of the Duke of Devizes, the Premier's closest friend, the man who can practically dictate the Birthday Honours. If James and Lord Percy can only form a close friendship our battle will be as good as won. It will mean everything. Lady Corstorphine has promised to arrange a meeting. In the meantime I will speak to James and warn him to be more careful.'

Mr Crocker had produced a stump of pencil from his pocket and was writing on the tablecloth:

> *Lord Crocker*
> *Lord Bingley Crocker*
> *Lord Crocker of Crocker*
> *The Marquis of Crocker*
> *Baron Crocker*
> *Bingley, first Viscount Crocker.*

He blanched as he read the frightful words. A sudden thought stung him.

'Eugenia!'

'Well?'

'What will the boys at the Lambs say?'

'I am not interested,' replied his wife, 'in the boys at the Lambs.'

'I thought you wouldn't be,' said the future baron gloomily.

CHAPTER 3

It is a peculiarity of the human mind that, with whatever apprehension it may be regarding the distant future, it must return after a while to face the minor troubles of the future that is immediate. The prospect of a visit to the dentist this afternoon causes us to forget for the moment the prospects of total ruin next year. Mr Crocker, therefore, having tortured himself for about a quarter of an hour with his meditations on the subject of titles, was jerked back to a more imminent calamity than the appearance of his name in the Birthday Honours – the fact that in all probability he would be taken again this morning to watch the continuation of that infernal cricket match, and would be compelled to spend the greater part of to-day, as he had spent the greater part of yesterday, bored to the verge of dissolution in the pavilion at Lord's.

One gleam of hope alone presented itself. Like baseball, this pastime of cricket was apparently affected by rain, if there had been enough of it. He had an idea that there had been a good deal of rain in the night, but had there been sufficient to cause the teams of Surrey and Kent to postpone the second instalment of their serial struggle? He rose from the table and went out into the hall. It was his purpose to sally out into Grosvenor Square and examine the turf in its centre with the heel of his shoe, in order to determine the stickiness or non-stickiness of the wicket. He moved towards the front door, hoping for the best, and just as he reached it the bell rang.

One of the bad habits of which his wife had cured Mr Crocker in the course of the years was the habit of going and answering doors. He had been brought up in surroundings where every man was his own doorkeeper, and it had been among his hardest tasks to learn the lesson that the perfect gentleman does not open doors, but waits for the appropriate menial to come along and do it for him. He had succeeded at length in mastering this great truth, and nowadays seldom offended. But this morning his mind was clouded by his troubles, and instinct, allying itself with opportunity, was too much for him. His fingers had been on the handle when the ring came, so he turned it.

At the top of the steps which connect the main entrance of Drexdale House with the sidewalk three persons were standing. One was tall and a formidably handsome woman in the early forties, whose appearance seemed somehow oddly familiar. The second was a small, fat, blobby, bulging boy who was chewing something. The third, lurking diffidently in the rear, was a little man of about Mr Crocker's own age, grey-haired and thin, with brown eyes that gazed meekly through rimless glasses.

Nobody could have been less obtrusive than this person, yet it was he who gripped Mr Crocker's attention and caused that homesick sufferer's heart to give an almost painful leap. For he was clothed in one of those roomy suits with square shoulders which to the seeing eye are as republican as the Stars and Stripes. His blunt-toed yellow shoes sang gaily of home. And his hat was not so much a hat as an effusive greeting from Gotham. A long time had passed since Mr Crocker had set eyes upon a biped so exhilaratingly American, and rapture held him speechless, as one who after long exile beholds some landmark of his childhood.

The female member of the party took advantage of his dumbness – which, as she had not unnaturally mistaken him for the butler, she took for a silent and respectful query as to her business and wishes – to open the conversation.

'Is Mrs Crocker at home? Please tell her that Mrs Pett wishes to see her.'

There was a rush and scurry in the corridors of Mr Crocker's brain, as about six different thoughts tried to squash simultaneously into that main chamber where there is room for only one at a time. He understood now why this woman's appearance had seemed familiar. She was his wife's sister, and that same Nesta who was some day to be pulverized by the sight of his name in the Birthday Honours. He was profoundly thankful that she had mistaken him for the butler. A chill passed through him as he pictured what would have been Eugenia's reception of the information that he had committed such a bourgeois solecism as opening the front door to Mrs Pett of all people, who already despised him as a low vulgarian. There had been trouble enough when she had found him opening it a few weeks before to a mere collector of subscriptions for a charity. He perceived, with a clarity remarkable in view of the fact that the discovery of her identity had given him a feeling of physical dizziness, that at all costs he must foster this misapprehension on his sister-in-law's part.

Fortunately he was in a position to do so. He knew all about what butlers did and what they said on these occasions, for in his innocently curious way he had often pumped Bayliss on the subject. He bowed silently and led the way to the morning-room, followed by the drove of Petts; then, opening the door, stood aside to allow the procession to march past the given point.

'I will inform Mrs Crocker that you are here, madam.'

Mrs Pett, shepherding the chewing child before her, passed into the room. In the light of her outspoken sentiments regarding her brother-in-law, it is curious to reflect that his manner at this, their first meeting, had deeply impressed her. After many months of smouldering revolt she had dismissed her own butler a day or so before sailing for England, and for the first time envy of her sister Eugenia gripped her. She did not covet Eugenia's other worldly possessions, but she did grudge her this supreme butler.

Mr Pett, meanwhile, had been trailing in the rear with a hunted expression on his face. He wore the unmistakable look of a man about to be present at a row between women, and only a wet cat in a strange back yard bears itself with less jauntiness than a man faced by such a prospect. A millionaire several times over, Mr Pett would cheerfully have given much of his wealth to have been elsewhere at that moment. Such was the agitated state of his mind that, when a hand was laid lightly upon his arm as he was about to follow his wife into the room, he started so violently that his hat flew out of his hand. He turned to meet the eyes of the butler who had admitted him to the house fixed on his in an appealing stare.

'Who's leading in the pennant race?' said this strange butler in a feverish whisper.

It was a question, coming from such a source, which in another than Mr Pett might well have provoked a blank stare of amazement. Such, however, is the almost superhuman intelligence and quickness of mind engendered by the study of

America's national game, that he answered without the slightest hesitation:

'Giants!'

'Wow!' said the butler.

No sense of anything strange or untoward about the situation came to mar the perfect joy of Mr Pett, the overmastering joy of the baseball fan who in a strange land unexpectedly encounters a brother. He thrilled with a happiness which he had never hoped to feel that morning.

'No signs of them slumping?' inquired the butler.

'No; but you never can tell. It's early yet. I've seen those boys lead the league till the end of August and then be nosed out.'

'True enough,' said the butler sadly.

'Matty's in shape.'

'He is? The old arm working well?'

'Like a machine. He shut out the Cubs the day before I sailed!'

'Fine!'

At this point an appreciation of the unusualness of the proceedings began to steal upon Mr Pett. He gaped at this surprising servitor.

'How on earth do you know anything about baseball?' he demanded.

The other seemed to stiffen. A change came over his whole appearance. He had the air of an actor who has remembered his part.

'I beg your pardon, sir. I trust I have not taken a liberty. I was at one time in the employment of a gentleman in New York, and during my stay I became extremely interested in the national game. I picked up a few of the American idioms while in the country.' He smiled apologetically. 'They sometimes slip out.'

'Let 'em slip!' said Mr Pett with enthusiasm. 'You're the first thing that's reminded me of home since I left. Say!'

'Sir?'

'Got a good place here?'

'Er – oh, yes, sir.'

'Well, here's my card. If you ever feel like making a change there's a job waiting for you at that address.'

'Thank you, sir.' Mr Crocker stooped. 'Your hat, sir!'

He held it out, gazing fondly at it the while. It was like being home again to see a hat like that. He followed Mr Pett with an affectionate eye as he went into the morning-room.

Bayliss was coming along the hall, hurrying more than his wont. The ring at the front door had found him deep in an extremely interesting piece of news in his halfpenny morning paper, and he was guiltily aware of having delayed in answering it.

'Bayliss,' said Mr Crocker in a cautious undertone, 'go and tell Mrs Crocker that Mrs Pett is waiting to see her. She's in the morning-room. If you're asked say you let her in. Get me?'

'Yes, sir,' said Bayliss, grateful for this happy solution.

'Oh, Bayliss!'

'Sir?'

'Is the wicket at Lord's likely to be too sticky for them to go on with that game to-day?'

'I hardly think it probable that there will be play, sir. There was a great deal of rain in the night.'

Mr Crocker passed on to his den with a lighter heart.

It was Mrs Crocker's habit, acquired after years of practice and a sedulous study of the best models, to conceal beneath a mask of well-bred indifference any emotion which she might chance to feel. Her dealings with the aristocracy of England had shown her that. Though the men occasionally permitted themselves an outburst, the women never did, and she had schooled herself so rigorously that nowadays she seldom even raised her voice. Her bearing, as she approached the morning-room, was calm and serene, but inwardly curiosity consumed her. It was unbelievable that Nesta could have come to try to effect a reconciliation, yet she could think of no other reason for her visit.

She was surprised to find three persons in the morning-room. Bayliss, delivering his message, had mentioned only Mrs Pett. To Mrs Crocker the assemblage had the appearance of being a sort of Old Home Week of Petts, a kind of Pett family mob scene. Her sister's second marriage having taken place after their quarrel, she had never seen her new brother-in-law, but she assumed that the little man lurking in the background was Mr Pett. The guess was confirmed.

'Good morning, Eugenia,' said Mrs Pett. 'Peter, this is my sister Eugenia. My husband.'

Mrs Crocker bowed stiffly. She was thinking how hopelessly American Mr Pett was; how baggy his clothes looked; what absurdly shaped shoes he wore; how appalling his hat was; how little hair he had; and how deplorably he lacked all those graces of repose, culture, physical beauty, refinement, dignity and mental alertness which raise men above the level of the common cockroach.

Mr Pett, on his side, receiving her cold glance squarely between the eyes, felt as if he were being disembowelled by a clumsy amateur. He could not help wondering what sort of a man this fellow Crocker was whom this sister-in-law of his had married. He pictured him as a handsome, powerful, robust individual, with a strong jaw and a loud voice, for he could imagine no lesser type of man consenting to link his lot with such a woman. He sidled in a circuitous manner toward a distant chair, and having lowered himself into it, kept perfectly still, pretending to be dead, like an opossum. He wished to take no part whatever in the coming interview.

'Ogden, of course, you know,' said Mrs Pett.

She was sitting so stiffly upright on a hard chair and had so much the appearance of having been hewn from the living rock, that every time she opened her mouth it was as if a statue had spoken.

'I know Ogden,' said Mrs Crocker shortly. 'Will you please stop him fidgeting with that vase? It is valuable.'

She directed at little Ogden, who was juggling aimlessly with a handsome *objet d'art* of the early Chinese school, a glance similar to that which had just disposed of his stepfather. But Ogden required more than a glance to divert him from any pursuit in which he was interested. He shifted a deposit of candy from his right cheek to his left cheek, inspected Mrs Crocker for a moment with a pale eye, and resumed his juggling. Mrs Crocker meant nothing in his young life.

'Ogden, come and sit down,' said Mrs Pett.

'Don't want to sit down.'

'Are you making a long stay in England, Nesta?' asked Mrs Crocker coldly.

'I don't know. We have made no plans.'

'Indeed?'

She broke off. Ogden, who had possessed himself of a bronze paperknife, had begun to tap the vase with it. The ringing note thus produced appeared to please his young mind.

'If Ogden really wishes to break that vase,' said Mrs Crocker in a detached voice, 'let me ring for the butler to bring him a hammer.'

'Ogden!' said Mrs Pett.

'Oh, gee! A fellow can't do a thing!' muttered Ogden, and walked to the window. He stood looking out into the square, a slight twitching of the ears indicating that he still made progress with the candy.

'Still the same engaging child!' murmured Mrs Crocker.

'I did not come here to discuss Ogden!' said Mrs Pett.

Mrs Crocker raised her eyebrows. Not even Mrs Otho Lanners, from whom she had learned the art, could do it more effectively.

'I am still waiting to find out why you did come, Nesta!'

'I came here to talk to you about your stepson, James Crocker.'

The discipline to which Mrs Crocker had subjected herself in the matter of the display of emotion saved her from the humiliation of showing surprise. She waved her hand graciously – in the manner of the Duchess of Axminster, a supreme hand-waver – to indicate that she was all attention.

'Your stepson, James Crocker,' repeated Mrs Pett. 'What is it the New York papers call him, Peter?'

Mr Pett, the human opossum, came to life. He had contrived to create about himself such a defensive atmosphere of non-existence that now that he re-entered the conversation it was as if a corpse had popped out of its tomb like a jack-in-the-box. Obeying the voice of authority he pushed the tombstone to one side and poked his head out of the sepulchre.

'Piccadilly Jim!' he murmured apologetically.

'Piccadilly Jim!' said Mrs Crocker. 'It is extremely impertinent of them!'

In spite of his misery, a wan smile appeared on Mr Pett's death-mask at this remark.

'They should worry about—'

'Peter!'

Mr Pett died again, greatly respected.

'Why should the New York papers refer to James at all?' said Mrs Crocker.

'Explain, Peter!'

Mr Pett emerged reluctantly from the cerements. He had supposed that Nesta would do the talking.

'Well, he's a news item.'

'Why?'

'Well, here's a boy that's been a regular fellow – raised in America – done work on a newspaper – suddenly taken off to England to become a London duke, mixing with all the dukes, playing pinochle with the King. Naturally they're interested in him.'

A more agreeable expression came over Mrs Crocker's face.

'Of course that is quite true. One cannot prevent the papers from printing what they wish. So they have published articles about James' doings in English Society?'

'Doings,' said Mr Pett, 'is right!'

'Something has got to be done about it,' said Mrs Pett.

Mr Pett endorsed this.

'Nesta's going to lose her health if these stories go on,' he said.

Mrs Crocker raised her eyebrows, but she had hard work to keep a contented smile off her face.

'If you are not above petty jealousy, Nesta—'

Mrs Pett laughed a sharp, metallic laugh.

'It is the disgrace I object to!'

'The disgrace!'

'What else would you call it, Eugenia? Wouldn't you be ashamed if you opened your Sunday paper and came upon a full-page article about your nephew having got intoxicated at the races and fought a bookmaker, having broken up a political meeting, having been sued for breach of promise by a barmaid?'

Mrs Crocker preserved her well-bred calm, but she was shaken. The episodes to which her sister had alluded were ancient history, horrors of the long dead past, but it seemed that they still lived in print. There and then she registered the resolve to talk to her stepson James, when she got hold of him, in such a manner as would scourge the offending Adam out of him for once and for all.

'And not only that,' continued Mrs Pett. 'That would be bad enough in itself, but somehow the papers have discovered that I am the boy's aunt. Two weeks ago they printed my photograph with one of these articles. I suppose they will always do it now. That is why I have come to you. It must stop. And the only way it can be made to stop is by taking your stepson away from London where he is running wild. Peter has most kindly consented to give the boy a position in his office. It is very good of him, for the boy cannot in the nature of things be of any use for a very long time, but we have talked it over and it seems the only course. I have come this morning to ask you to let us take James Crocker back to America with us and keep him out of mischief by giving him honest work. What do you say?'

Mrs Crocker raised her eyebrows.

'What do you expect me to say? It is utterly preposterous. I have never heard anything so supremely absurd in my life.'

'You refuse?'

'Of course I refuse.'

'I think you are extremely foolish.'

'Indeed!'

Mr Pett cowered in his chair. He was feeling rather like a nervous and peace-loving patron of a wild Western saloon who observes two cowboys reach for their hip pockets. Neither his wife nor his sister-in-law paid any attention to him. The concluding exercises of a duel of the eyes were in progress between them. After some silent, age-long moments Mrs Crocker laughed a light laugh.

'Most extraordinary!' she murmured.

Mrs Pett was in no mood for Anglicisms.

'You know perfectly well, Eugenia,' she said heatedly, 'that James Crocker is being ruined here. For his sake, if not for mine—'

Mrs Crocker laughed another light laugh, one of those offensive, rippling things that cause so much annoyance.

'Don't be so ridiculous, Nesta! Ruined! Really! It is quite true that, a long while ago, when he was much younger and not quite used to the ways of London society, James was a little wild, but all that sort of thing is over now. He knows' – she paused, setting herself as it were for the punch – 'he knows that at any moment the government may decide to give his father a peerage—'

The blow went home. A quite audible gasp escaped her stricken sister.

'What!'

Mrs Crocker placed two ringed fingers before her mouth in order not to hide a languid yawn.

'Yes. Didn't you know? But, of course, you live so out of the world. Oh, yes, it is extremely probable that Mr Crocker's name will appear in the next Honours List. He is very highly thought of by the Powers. So naturally James is quite aware that he must behave in a suitable manner. He is a dear boy! He was handicapped at first by getting into the wrong set, but now his closest friend is Lord Percy Whipple, the second son of the Duke of Devizes, who is one of the most eminent men in the kingdom and a personal friend of the Premier.'

Mrs Pett was in bad shape under this rain of titles, but she rallied herself to reply in kind.

'Indeed?' she said. 'I should like to meet him. I have no doubt he knows our great friend, Lord Wisbeach.'

Mrs Crocker was a little taken aback. She had not supposed that her sister had even this small shot in her locker.

'Do you know Lord Wisbeach?' she said.

'Oh, yes,' replied Mrs Pett, beginning to feel a little better. 'We have been seeing him every day. He always says that he looks on my house as quite a home. He knows so few people in New York. It has been a great comfort to him, I think, knowing us.'

Mrs Crocker had had time now to recover her poise.

'Poor, dear Wizzy!' she said languidly.

Mrs Pett started.

'What!'

'I suppose he is still the same dear, stupid, shiftless fellow? He left here with the intention of travelling round the world, and he has stopped in New York! How like him!'

'Do you know Lord Wisbeach?' demanded Mrs Pett.

Mrs Crocker raised her eyebrows.

'Know him? Why, I suppose, after Lord Percy Whipple, he is James' most intimate friend!'

Mrs Pett rose. She was dignified even in defeat. She collected Ogden and Mr Pett with an eye which even Ogden could see was not to be trifled with. She uttered no word.

'Must you really go?' said Mrs Crocker. 'It was sweet of you to bother to come all the way from America like this. So strange to meet anyone from America nowadays. Most extraordinary!'

The *cortège* left the room in silence. Mrs Crocker had touched the bell, but the mourners did not wait for the arrival of Bayliss. They were in no mood for the formalities of polite society. They wanted to be elsewhere, and they wanted to be there quick. The front door had closed behind them before the butler reached the morning-room.

'Bayliss,' said Mrs Crocker with happy shining face, 'send for the car to come round at once.'

'Very good, madam.'

'Is Mr James up yet?'

'I believe not, madam.'

Mrs Crocker went upstairs to her room. If Bayliss had not been within earshot she would probably have sung a bar or two. Her amiability extended even to her stepson, though she had not altered her intention of speaking eloquently to him on certain matters when she could get hold of him. That, however, could wait. For the moment she felt in vein for a gentle drive in the park.

A few minutes after she had disappeared there was a sound of slow footsteps on the stairs, and a young man came down into the hall. Bayliss, who had finished telephoning to the garage for Mrs Crocker's limousine and was about to descend to those lower depths where he had his being, turned, and a grave smile of welcome played over his face.

'Good morning, Mr James,' he said.

CHAPTER 4

Jimmy Crocker was a tall and well-knit young man, who later on in the day would no doubt be at least passably good-looking. At the moment an unbecoming pallor marred his face, and beneath his eyes were marks that suggested that he had slept little and ill. He stood at the foot of the stairs, yawning cavernously.

'Bayliss,' he said, 'have you been painting yourself yellow?'

'No, sir.'

'Strange! Your face looks a bright gamboge to me, and your outlines wobble. Bayliss, never mix your drinks. I say this to you as a friend. Is there any one in the morning-room?'

'No, Mr James.'

'Speak softly, Bayliss, for I am not well. I am conscious of a strange weakness. Lead me to the morning-room then, and lay me gently on a sofa. These are the times that try men's souls.'

The sun was now shining strongly through the windows of the morning-room. Bayliss lowered the shades. Jimmy Crocker sank on to the sofa and closed his eyes.

'Bayliss.'

'Sir?'

'A conviction is stealing over me that I am about to expire.'

'Shall I bring you a little breakfast, Mr James?'

A strong shudder shook Jimmy.

'Don't be flippant, Bayliss,' he protested. 'Try to cure yourself of this passion for being funny at the wrong time. Your comedy is good, but tact is a finer quality than humour. Perhaps you think I have forgotten that morning when I was feeling just as I do to-day, and you came to my bedside and asked me if I would like a nice rasher of ham. I haven't and I never shall. You may bring me a brandy-and-soda. Not a large one. A couple of bath-tubsful will be enough.'

'Very good, Mr James.'

'And now leave me, Bayliss, for I would be alone. I have to make a series of difficult and exhaustive tests to ascertain whether I am still alive.'

When the butler had gone Jimmy adjusted the cushions, closed his eyes, and remained for a space in a state of coma. He was trying, as well as an exceedingly severe headache would permit, to recall the salient events of the previous night. At present his memories refused to solidify. They poured about in his brain in a fluid and formless condition, exasperating to one who sought for hard facts.

It seemed strange to Jimmy that the shadowy and inchoate vision of a combat, a fight, a brawl of some kind persisted in flitting about in the recesses of his mind, always just far enough away to elude capture. The absurdity of the thing annoyed him. A man has either indulged in a fight overnight or he has not indulged in a fight overnight. There can be no middle course. That he should be uncertain on the point was ridiculous. Yet try as he would he could not be sure. There were moments when he seemed on the verge of settling the matter, and then some invisible person would meanly insert a red-hot corkscrew in the top of his head and begin to twist it, and this would interfere with calm thought. He was still in a state of uncertainty when Bayliss returned, bearing healing liquids on a tray.

'Shall I set it beside you, sir?'

Jimmy opened one eye.

'Indubitably. No mean word that, Bayliss, for the morning after. Try it yourself next time. Bayliss, who let me in this morning?'

'Let you in, sir?'

'Precisely. I was out and now I am in. Obviously I must have passed the front door somehow. This is logic.'

'I fancy you let yourself in, Mr James, with your key.'

'That would seem to indicate that I was in a state of icy sobriety. Yet, if such is the case, how is it that I can't remember whether I murdered somebody or not last night. It isn't the sort of thing your sober man would lightly forget. Have you ever murdered anybody, Bayliss?'

'No, sir.'

'Well, if you had, you would remember it next morning?'

'I imagine so, Mr James.'

'Well, it's a funny thing, but I can't get rid of the impression that at some point in my researches into the night life of London yestreen I fell upon some person to whom I had never been introduced and committed mayhem upon his person.'

It seemed to Bayliss that the time had come to impart to Mr James a piece of news which he had supposed would require no imparting. He looked down upon his young master's recumbent form with a grave commiseration. It was true that he had never been able to tell with any certainty whether Mr James intended the statements he made to be taken literally or not; but on the present occasion he seemed to have spoken seriously, and to be genuinely at a loss to recall an episode over the printed report of which the entire domestic staff had been gloating ever since the arrival of the halfpenny morning paper to which they had subscribed.

'Do you really mean it, Mr James?' he inquired cautiously.

'Mean what?'

'You have really forgotten that you were engaged in a fracas last night at the Six Hundred Club?'

Jimmy sat up with a jerk, staring at this omniscient man. Then, the movement having caused a renewal of the operations of the red-hot corkscrew, he fell back again with a groan.

'Was I! How on earth did you know? Why should you know all about it when I can't remember a thing? It was my fault, not yours.'

'There is quite a long report of it in to-day's *Daily Sun*, Mr James.'

'A report? In the *Sun*?'

'Half a column, Mr James. Would you like me to fetch the paper? I have it in my pantry.'

'I should say so. Trot a quick heat back with it. This wants looking into.'

Bayliss retired, to return immediately with the paper. Jimmy took it, gazed at it and handed it back.

'I overestimated my powers. It can't be done. Have you any important duties at the moment, Bayliss?'

'No, sir.'

'Perhaps you wouldn't mind reading me the bright little excerpt then?'

'Certainly, sir.'

'It will be good practice for you. I am convinced I am going to be a confirmed invalid for the rest of my life, and it will be part of your job to sit at my bedside and read to me. By the way, does the paper say who the party of the second part was? Who was the citizen with whom I went to the mat?'

'Lord Percy Whipple, Mr James.'

'Lord who?'

'Lord Percy Whipple.'

'Never heard of him. Carry on, Bayliss.'

Jimmy composed himself to listen, yawning.

CHAPTER 5

Bayliss took a spectacle case from the recesses of his costume, opened it, took out a pair of gold-rimmed glasses, dived into the jungle again, came out with a handkerchief, polished the spectacles, put them on his nose, closed the case, restored it to its original position, replaced the handkerchief and took up the paper.

'Why the hesitation, Bayliss? Why the coyness?' inquired Jimmy, lying with closed eyes. 'Begin!'

'I was adjusting my glasses, sir.'

'All set now?'

'Yes, sir. Shall I read the headlines first?'

'Read everything.'

The butler cleared his throat.

'Good heavens, Bayliss,' moaned Jimmy, starting; 'don't gargle! Have a heart! Go on!'

Bayliss began to read,

FRACAS IN FASHIONABLE NIGHT CLUB

SPRIGS OF NOBILITY BRAWL

Jimmy opened his eyes, interested.

'Am I a sprig of nobility?'

'It is what the paper says, sir.'

'We live and learn. Carry on.'

The butler started to clear his throat, but checked himself.

SENSATIONAL INTERNATIONAL CONTEST

BATTLING PERCY

(England)

v.

CYCLONE JIM

(America)

Full Description by Our Expert

Jimmy sat up.

'Bayliss, you're indulging that distorted sense of humour of yours again. That isn't in the paper?'

'Yes, sir. Very large headlines.'

Jimmy groaned.

'Bayliss, I'll give you a piece of advice which may be useful to you when you grow up. Never go about with newspaper men. It all comes back to me. Out of pure kindness of heart I took young Bill Blake, of the *Sun*, to supper at the Six Hundred last night. This is my reward. I suppose he thinks it funny. Newspaper men are a low lot, Bayliss.'

'Shall I go on, sir?'

'Most doubtless. Let me hear all.'

Bayliss resumed. He was one of those readers who, whether their subject be a murder case or a funny anecdote, adopt a measured and sepulchral delivery which gives a suggestion of tragedy and horror to whatever they read. At the church he attended on Sundays, of which he was one of the most influential and respected members, children would turn pale and snuggle up to their mothers when Bayliss read the lessons. Young Mr Blake's account of the overnight proceedings at the Six Hundred Club he rendered with a gloomy gusto more marked even than his wont. It had a topical interest for him which urged him to extend himself.

'At an early hour this morning, when our myriad readers were enjoying that refreshing and brain-restoring sleep so necessary to the proper appreciation of the *Daily Sun* at the breakfast table, one of the most interesting sporting events of the season was being pulled off at the Six Hundred Club, in Regent Street, where, after three rounds of fast exchanges, James B. Crocker, the well-known American middle-weight scrapper, succeeded in stopping Lord Percy Whipple, second son of the Duke of Devizes, better known as the Pride of Old England. Once again the superiority of the American over the English style of boxing was demonstrated. Battling Percy has a kind heart, but Cyclone Jim packs the punch.

'The immediate cause of the encounter had to do with a disputed table, which each gladiator claimed to have engaged in advance over the telephone.'

'I begin to remember,' said Jimmy meditatively. 'A pill with butter-coloured hair tried to jump my claim. Honeyed words proving fruitless, I socked him on the jaw. It may be that I was not wholly myself. I seem to remember an animated session at the Empire earlier in the evening, which may have impaired my self-control. Proceed!'

'One word leading to others, which in their turn led to several more, Cyclone Jim struck Battling Percy on what our rude forefathers were accustomed to describe as the mazzard, and the gong sounded for

ROUND ONE

'Both men came up fresh and eager to mix things, though it seems only too probable that they had already been mixing more things than was good for them. Battling Percy tried a right swing, which got home on a waiter. Cyclone Jim put in a rapid one-two punch, which opened a large gash in the atmosphere. Both men sparred cautiously, being hampered in their movements by the fact, which neither had at this stage of the proceedings perceived, that they were on opposite sides of the disputed table. A clever Fitzsimmons shift on the part of the Battler removed this obstacle, and some brisk work ensued in neutral territory. Percy landed twice without a return. The Battler's round by a shade.

ROUND TWO

'The Cyclone came out of his corner with a rush, getting home on the Battler's shirt front and following it up with a right to the chin. Percy swung wildly and upset a bottle of champagne on a neighbouring table. A good rally followed, both men doing impressive in-fighting. The Cyclone landed three without a return. The Cyclone's round.

ROUND THREE

'Percy came up weak, seeming to be overtrained. The Cyclone waded in, using both hands effectively. The Battler fell into a clinch, but the Cyclone broke away and, measuring his distance, picked up a haymaker from the floor and put it over. Percy down and out.

'Interviewed by our representative after the fight, Cyclone Jim said: "The issue was never in doubt. I was handicapped at the outset by the fact that I was under the impression that I was fighting three twin brothers, and I missed several opportunities of putting over the winning wallop by attacking the outside ones. It was only in the second round that I decided to concentrate my assault on the one in the middle, when the affair speedily came to a conclusion. I shall not adopt pugilism as a profession. The prizes are attractive, but it is too much like work."'

Bayliss ceased, and silence fell upon the room.

'Is that all?'

'That is all, sir.'

'And about enough.'

'Very true, sir.'

'You know, Bayliss,' said Jimmy thoughtfully, rolling over on the couch, 'life is peculiar, not to say odd. You never know what is waiting for you round the corner. You start the day with the fairest prospects, and before nightfall everything is as rocky and ding-basted as stig tossed full of doodle-gammon. Why is this, Bayliss?'

'I couldn't say, sir.'

'Look at me. I go out to spend a happy evening, meaning no harm to any one, and I come back all blue with the blood of the aristocracy. We now come to a serious point. Do you think my lady stepmother has read that sporting chronicle?'

'I fancy not, Mr James.'

'On what do you base these words of comfort?'

'Mrs Crocker does not read the halfpenny papers, sir.'

'True! She does not. I had forgotten. On the other hand, the probability that she will learn about the little incident from other sources is great. I think the merest prudence suggests that I keep out of the way for the time being, lest I be fallen upon and questioned. I am not equal to being questioned this morning. I have a headache that starts at the soles of my feet and gets worse all the way up. Where is my stepmother?'

'Mrs Crocker is in her room, Mr James. She ordered the car to be brought round at once. It should be here at any moment now, sir. I think Mrs Crocker intends to visit the park before luncheon.'

'Is she lunching out?'

'Yes, sir.'

'Then if I pursue the excellent common-sense tactics of the lesser sand eel, which, as you doubtless know, buries itself tail upward in the mud on hearing the baying of the eel hounds and remains in that position until the danger is past, I shall be able to postpone an interview. Should you be questioned as to my whereabouts, inflate your chest and reply in a clear and manly voice that I have gone out, you know not where. May I rely on your benevolent neutrality, Bayliss?'

'Very good, Mr James.'

'I think I will go and sit in my father's den. A man may lie hid there with some success as a rule.'

Jimmy heaved himself painfully off the sofa, blinked, and set out for the den, where his father, in a deep armchair, was smoking a restful pipe and reading the portions of the daily papers which did not deal with the game of cricket.

Mr Crocker's den was a small room at the back of the house. It was not luxurious, and it looked out on to a blank walk, but it was the spot he liked best in all that vast pile which had once echoed to the tread of titled shoes; for, as he sometimes observed to his son, it had the distinction of being the only room on the ground floor where a fellow could move without stubbing his toe on a countess or an honourable. In this peaceful backwater he could smoke a pipe, put his feet up, take off his coat and generally indulge in that liberty and pursuit of happiness to which the Constitution entitles a free-born American. Nobody ever came there except Jimmy and himself.

He did not suspend his reading at his son's entrance. He muttered a welcome through the clouds, but he did not raise his eyes. Jimmy took the other armchair, and began to smoke silently. It was the unwritten law of the den that soothing silence rather than aimless chatter should prevail. It was not until a quarter of an hour had passed that Mr Crocker dropped his paper and spoke:

'Say, Jimmy, I want to talk to you.'

'Say on. You have our ear.'

'Seriously.'

'Continue – always, however, keeping before you the fact that I am a sick man. Last night was a wild night on the moors, Dad.'

'It's about your stepmother. She was talking at breakfast about you. She's sore at you for giving Spike Dillon lunch at the Carlton. You oughtn't to have taken him there, Jimmy. That's what got her goat. She was there with a bunch of swells, and they had to sit and listen to Spike talking about his half-scissors hook.'

'What's their kick against Spike's half-scissors hook? It's a darned good one.'

'She said she was going to speak to you about it. I thought I'd let you know.'

'Thanks, Dad. But was that all?'

'All?'

'All that she was going to speak to me about? Sure there was nothing else?'

'She didn't say anything about anything else.'

'Then she doesn't know! Fine!'

Mr Crocker's feet came down from the mantelpiece with a crash.

'Jimmy! You haven't been raising Cain again?'

'No, no, Dad. Nothing serious. High-spirited Young Patrician stuff, the sort of thing that's expected of a fellow in my position.'

Mr Crocker was not to be comforted.

'Jimmy, you've got to pull up. Honest, you have. I don't care for myself. I like to see a boy having a good time. But your stepmother says you're apt to queer us with the people up top, the way you're going on. Lord knows I wouldn't care if things were different, but I'll tell you exactly how I stand. I didn't get wise till this morning. Your stepmother sprang it on me suddenly. I've often wondered what all this stuff was about, this living in London and trailing the swells. I couldn't think what was your stepmother's idea. Now I know. Jimmy, she's trying to get them to make me a peer.'

'What!'

'Just that. And she says—'

'But, Dad, this is rich! This is comedy of a high order! A peer! Good heavens, if it comes off, what shall I be? This title business is all so complicated. I know I should have to change my name to Hon. Rollo Cholmondeley or the Hon. Aubrey Majoribanks, but what I want to know is, which? I want to be prepared for the worst.'

'And you see, Jimmy, these people up top, the guys who arrange the giving of titles, are keeping an eye on you, because you would have the title after me, and naturally they don't want to get stung. I gathered all that from your stepmother. Say, Jimmy, I'm not saving a lot of you, but there is just one thing you can do for me without putting yourself out too much.'

'I'll do it, Dad, if it kills me. Slip me the info!'

'Your stepmother's friend, Lady Corstorphine's nephew—'

'It's not the sort of story to ask a man with a headache to follow. I hope it gets simpler as it goes along.'

'Your stepmother wants you to be a good fellow and make friends with this boy. You see, his father is in right with the Premier and has the biggest kind of a pull when it comes to handing out titles.'

'Is that all you want? Leave it to me. Inside of a week I'll be playing kiss-in-the-ring with him. The whole force of my sunny personality shall be directed toward making him love me. What's his name?'

'Lord Percy Whipple.'

Jimmy's pipe fell with a clatter.

'Dad, pull yourself together! Reflect! You know you don't seriously mean Lord Percy Whipple.'

'Eh?'

Jimmy laid a soothing hand on his father's shoulder.

'Dad, prepare yourself for the big laugh. This is where you throw your head back and roar with honest mirth. I met Lord Percy Whipple last night at the Six Hundred Club. Words ensued. I fell upon Percy and beat his block off! How it started, except that we both wanted the same table, I couldn't say. "Why, that I cannot tell, said he, but 'twas a famous victory!" If I had known, Dad, nothing would have induced me to lay a hand upon

Perce, save in the way of kindness, but not even knowing who he was, it would appear from contemporary accounts of the affair that I just naturally sailed in and expunged the poor dear boy!'

The stunning nature of this information had much the same effect on Mr Crocker that the announcement of his ruin had upon the Good Old Man in melodrama. He sat clutching the arms of his chair and staring into space, saying nothing. Dismay was written upon his anguished countenance.

His collapse sobered Jimmy. For the first time he perceived that the situation had another side than the humorous one which had appealed to him. He had anticipated that Mr Crocker, who as a general thing shared his notions of what was funny and could be relied on to laugh in the right place, would have been struck, like himself, by the odd and pleasing coincidence of his having picked on for purposes of assault and battery the one young man with whom his stepmother wished him to form a firm and lasting friendship. He perceived now that his father was seriously upset. Neither Jimmy nor Mr Crocker possessed a demonstrative nature, but there had always existed between them the deepest affection. Jimmy loved his father as he loved nobody else in the world and the thought of having hurt him was like a physical pain. His laughter died away, and he set himself with a sinking heart to try to undo the effect of his words.

'I'm awfully sorry, Dad; I had no idea you would care. I wouldn't have done a fool thing like that for a million dollars if I'd known. Isn't there anything I can do? Gee whiz! I'll go right round to Percy now and apologize. I'll lick his boots. Don't you worry, Dad, I'll make it all right.'

The whirl of words roused Mr Crocker from his thoughts.

'It doesn't matter, Jimmy. Don't worry yourself. It's only a little unfortunate, because your stepmother says she won't think of our going back to America till these people here have given me a title. She wants to put one over on her sister. That's all that's troubling me – the thought that this affair will set us back, this Lord Percy being in so strong with the guys who give the titles. I guess it will mean my staying on here for a while longer, and I'd have liked to have seen another ball game. Jimmy, do you know they call baseball rounders in this country, and children play it with a soft ball!'

Jimmy was striding up and down the little room. Remorse had him in its grip.

'What a damn fool I am!'

'Never mind, Jimmy. It's unfortunate, but it wasn't your fault. You couldn't know.'

'It was my fault. Nobody but a fool like me would go about beating people up. But don't worry, Dad; it's going to be all right. I'll fix it. I'm going right round to this fellow Percy now to make things all right. I won't come back till I've squared him. Don't you bother yourself about it any longer, Dad. It's going to be all right.'

Jimmy removed himself sorrowfully from the doorstep of the Duke of Devizes' house in Cleveland Row. His mission had been a failure. In answer to his request to be permitted to see Lord Percy Whipple, the butler had replied that Lord Percy was confined to his bed and was seeing nobody. He eyed Jimmy, on receiving his name, with an interest which he failed to conceal, for he, too, like Bayliss, had read and heartily enjoyed Bill Blake's version of the affair of last night which had appeared in the *Daily Sun*. Indeed, he had clipped the report out and had been engaged in pasting it in an album when the bell rang.

In face of this repulse Jimmy's campaign broke down. He was at a loss to know what to do next. He ebbed away from the Duke's front door like an army that has made an unsuccessful frontal attack on an impregnable fortress. He could hardly force his way in and search for Lord Percy.

He walked along Pall Mall, deep in thought. It was a beautiful day. The rain which had fallen in the night, and relieved Mr Crocker from the necessity of watching cricket, had freshened London up. The sun was shining now from a turquoise sky. A gentle breeze blew from the south. Jimmy made his way into Piccadilly, and found that thoroughfare a-roar with happy automobiles and cheery pedestrians. Their gaiety irritated him. He resented their apparent enjoyment of life.

Jimmy's was not a nature that lent itself readily to introspection, but he was putting himself now through a searching self-examination which was revealing all kinds of unsuspected flaws in his character. He had been having too good a time for years past to have leisure to realize that he possessed any responsibilities. He had lived each day as it came in the spirit of the monks of Thelema. But his father's reception of the news of last night's escapade and the few words he had said had given him pause. Life had taken on of a sudden a less simple aspect. Dimly, for he was not accustomed to thinking along these lines, he perceived the numbing truth that we human beings are merely as many pieces in a jig-saw puzzle, and that our every movement affects the fortunes of some other piece. Just so, faintly at first and taking shape by degrees, must the germ of a civic spirit have come to prehistoric man. We are all individualists till we wake up.

The thought of having done anything to make his father unhappy was bitter to Jimmy Crocker. They had always been more like brothers than father and son. Hard thoughts about himself surged through Jimmy's mind. With a dejectedness to which it is possible that his headache contributed he put the matter squarely to himself. His father was longing to return to America – he, Jimmy, by his idiotic behaviour, was putting obstacles in the way of return. What was the answer? The answer, to Jimmy's way of thinking, was that all was not well with James Crocker; that, when all the evidence was weighed, James Crocker would appear to be a fool, a worm, a selfish waster and a hopeless, lowdown skunk.

Having come to this conclusion Jimmy found himself so low in spirit that the cheerful bustle of Piccadilly was too much for him. He turned and began to retrace his steps. Arriving in due course at the top of the Haymarket he hesitated, then turned down it till he reached Cockspur Street. Here the transatlantic steamship companies have their offices, and so it came about that Jimmy, chancing to look up as he walked, perceived before him, riding gallantly on a cardboard ocean behind a plate-glass window, the model of a noble vessel. He stopped, conscious of a curious thrill. There is a superstition in all of us. When an accidental happening chances to fit smoothly in with a mood, seeming to come as a direct commentary on that mood, we are apt to accept it in defiance of our pure reason as an omen. Jimmy strode to the window and inspected the model narrowly. The sight of it had started a new train of thought. His heart began to race. Hypnotic influences were at work on him.

Why not? Could there be a simpler solution of the whole trouble?

Inside the office he could see a man with whiskers buying a ticket for New York. The simplicity of the process fascinated him. All you had to do was to walk in, bend over the counter while the clerk behind it made dabs with a pencil at the illustrated plate of the ship's interior organs, and hand over your money. A child could do it, if in funds. At this thought his hand strayed to his trousers pocket. A musical crackling of banknotes proceeded from the depths. His quarterly allowance had been paid to him only a short while before, and, though a willing spender, he still retained a goodly proportion of it. He rustled the notes again. There was enough in that pocket to buy three tickets to New York. Should he? Or, on the other hand – always look on both sides of a question – should he not?

It would certainly seem to be the best thing for all parties if he did follow the impulse. By remaining in London he was injuring everybody, himself included. Well, there was no harm in making inquiries. Probably the boat was full up anyway. He walked into the office.

'Have you anything left on the *Atlantic* this trip?'

The clerk behind the counter was quite the wrong sort of person for Jimmy to have had dealings with in his present mood. What Jimmy needed was a grave, sensible man who would have laid a hand on his shoulder and said: 'Do nothing rash, my boy!' The clerk fell short of this ideal in practically every particular. He was about twenty-two, and he seemed perfectly enthusiastic about the idea of Jimmy's going to America. He beamed at Jimmy.

'Plenty of room,' he said. 'Very few people crossing. Give you excellent accommodation.'

'When does the boat sail?'

'Eight to-morrow morning from Liverpool. Boat train leaves Paddington six to-night.'

Prudence came at the eleventh hour to check Jimmy. This was not a matter, he perceived, to be decided recklessly, on the spur of a sudden impulse. Above all, it was not a matter to be decided before lunch. An empty stomach breeds imagination. He had ascertained that he could sail on the *Atlantic* if he wished to. The sensible thing to do now was to go and lunch and see how he felt about it after that. He thanked the clerk, and started to walk up the Haymarket, feeling hard-headed and practical, yet with a strong premonition that he was going to make a fool of himself just the same.

It was half-way up the Haymarket that he first became conscious of the girl with red hair. Plunged in thought, he had not noticed her before. And yet she had been walking a few paces in front of him most of the way. She had come out of Panton Street, walking briskly, as one going to keep a pleasant appointment. She carried herself admirably, with a jaunty swing.

Having become conscious of this girl, Jimmy, ever a warm admirer of the sex, began to feel a certain interest stealing over him. With interest came speculation. He wondered who she was. He wondered where she had bought that excellently fitting suit of tailor-made grey. He admired her back, and wondered whether her face, if seen, would prove a disappointment. Thus musing, he drew near to the top of the Haymarket, where it ceases to be a street and becomes a whirlpool of rushing traffic. And here the girl, having paused and looked over her shoulder, stepped off the sidewalk. As she did so a taxicab rounded the corner quickly from the direction of Coventry Street.

The agreeable surprise of finding the girl's face fully as attractive as her back had stimulated Jimmy, so that he was keyed up for the exhibition of swift presence of mind. He jumped forward and caught her arm, and swung her to one side as the cab rattled past, its driver thinking hard thoughts to himself. The whole episode was an affair of seconds.

'Thank you,' said the girl.

She rubbed the arm which he had seized, with rather a rueful expression. She was a little white and her breath came quickly.

'I hope I didn't hurt you,' said Jimmy.

'You did. Very much. But the taxi would have hurt me more.'

She laughed. She looked very attractive when she laughed. She had a small, piquant, vivacious face. Jimmy, as he looked at it, had an odd feeling that he had seen her before – when and where he did not know. That mass of red-gold hair seemed curiously familiar. Somewhere in the hinterland of his mind there lurked a memory, but he could not bring it into the open. As for the girl, if she had ever met him before she showed no signs of recollecting it. Jimmy decided that, if he had seen her, it must have been in his reporter days. She was plainly an American, and he occasionally had the feeling that he had seen everyone in America when he had worked for the *Chronicle*.

'That's right,' he said approvingly. 'Always look on the bright side.'

'I arrived in London only yesterday,' said the girl, 'and I haven't got used to your keeping-to-the-left rules. I don't suppose I shall ever get back to New York alive. Perhaps, as you have saved my life, you wouldn't mind doing me another service. Can you tell me which is the nearest and safest way to a restaurant called the Regent Grill?'

'It's just over there, at the corner of Regent Street. As to the safest way, if I were you I would cross over at the top of the street there and then work round westward. Otherwise you will have to cross Piccadilly Circus.'

'I absolutely refuse even to try to cross Piccadilly Circus. Thank you very much. I will follow your advice. I hope I shall get there. It doesn't seem at all likely.'

She gave him a little nod, and moved away. Jimmy turned into that drug store at the top of the Haymarket at which so many Londoners have found healing and comfort on the morning after, and bought the pink drink for which his system had been craving since he rose from bed. He wondered why, as he drained it, he should feel ashamed and guilty.

A few minutes later he found himself with mild surprise going down the steps of the Regent Grill. It was the last place he had had in his mind when he had left the steamship company's offices in quest of lunch. He had intended to seek out some quiet, restful nook where he could be alone with his thoughts. If anybody had told him then that five minutes later he would be placing himself of his own free will within range of a restaurant orchestra playing 'My Little Grey Home in the West' – and the orchestra at the Regent played little else – he would not have believed him.

Restaurants in all large cities have their ups and downs. At this time the Regent Grill was enjoying one of those bursts of popularity for which restaurateurs pray to whatever strange gods they worship. The more prosperous section of London's Bohemia flocked to it daily. When Jimmy had deposited his hat with the robber band who had their cave just inside the main entrance, and had entered the grillroom, he found it congested. There did not appear to be a single unoccupied table.

From where he stood he could see the girl of the red-gold hair. Her back was toward him, and she was sitting at a table against one of the pillars with a little man with eye-glasses, a handsome woman in the forties, and a small stout boy who was skirmishing with the olives. As Jimmy hesitated, the vigilant head waiter, who knew him well, perceived him and hurried up.

'In one moment, Mister Crockaire!' he said, and began to scatter commands among the underlings. 'I will place a table for you in the aisle.'

'Next to that pillar, please,' said Jimmy.

The underlings had produced a small table, apparently from up their sleeves, and were draping it in a cloth. Jimmy sat down and gave his order. Ordering was going on at the other table. The little man seemed depressed at the discovery that corn on the cob and soft-shelled crabs were not to be obtained, and his wife's reception of the news that clams were not included in the Regent's bill of fare was so indignant, that one would have said that she regarded the fact as evidence that Great Britain was going to pieces and would shortly lose her place as a world power.

A selection having finally been agreed upon, the orchestra struck up 'My Little Grey Home in the West', and no attempt was made to compete with it. When the last lingering strains had died away, and the violinist leader, having straightened out the kinks in his person which the rendition of the melody never failed to produce, had bowed for the last time, a clear, musical voice spoke from the other side of the pillar:

'Jimmy Crocker is a worm!'

Jimmy spilled his cocktail. It might have been the voice of Conscience.

'I despise him more than anyone on earth. I hate to think that he's an American.'

Jimmy drank the few drops that remained in his glass, partly to make sure of them, partly as a restorative. It is an unnerving thing to be despised by a red-haired girl whose life you have just saved. To Jimmy it was not only unnerving, it was uncanny. This girl had not known him when they met on the street a few moments before. How then was she able to display such intimate acquaintance with his character now as to describe him – justly enough – as a worm? Mingled with the mystery of the thing was its pathos. The thought that a girl could be as pretty as this one and yet dislike him so much was one of the saddest things Jimmy had ever come across. It was like one of those Things Which Make Me Weep in This Great City so dear to the hearts of the sob-writers of his late newspaper.

A waiter bustled up with a highball. Jimmy thanked him with his eyes. He needed it. He raised it to his lips.

'He's always drinking—'

He set it down hurriedly.

'—and making a disgraceful exhibition of himself in public! I always think Jimmy Crocker—'

Jimmy began to wish that somebody would stop this girl. Why couldn't the little man change the subject to the weather, or that stout child start prattling about some general topic? Surely a boy of that age, newly arrived in London, must have all sorts of things to prattle about? But the little man was dealing strenuously with a breaded cutlet, while the stout boy, grimly silent, surrounded fish pie in the forthright manner of a starving python. As for the elder woman, she seemed to be wrestling with unpleasant thoughts, beyond speech.

'I always think that Jimmy Crocker is the worst case I know of the kind of American young man who spends all his time in Europe and tries to become an imitation Englishman. Most of them are the sort any country would be glad to get rid of; but he used to work once, so you can't excuse him on the ground that he hasn't the sense to know what he's doing. He's deliberately chosen to loaf about London and make a pest of himself. He went to pieces with his eyes open. He's a perfect, utter, hopeless worm!'

Jimmy had never been very fond of the orchestra at the Regent Grill, holding the view that it interfered with conversation and made for an unhygienic rapidity of mastication; but he was profoundly grateful to it now for bursting suddenly into 'La Bohème', the loudest item in its repertory. Under cover of that protective din he was able to toy with a steaming dish which his waiter had brought. Probably that girl was saying all sorts of things about him still, but he could not hear them.

The music died away. For a moment the tortured air quivered in comparative silence; then the girl's voice spoke again. She had, however, selected another topic of conversation.

'I've seen all I want to of England,' she said. 'I've seen Westminster Abbey and the Houses of Parliament and His Majesty's Theatre and the Savoy and the Cheshire Cheese, and I've developed a frightful homesickness. Why shouldn't we go back to-morrow?'

For the first time in the proceedings the elder woman spoke. She cast aside her mantle of gloom long enough to say 'Yes,' then wrapped it round her again. The little man, who had apparently been waiting for her vote before giving his own, said that the sooner he was on board a New York-bound boat, the better he would be pleased. The stout boy said nothing. He had finished his fish pie and was now attacking jam roll with a sort of morose resolution.

'There's certain to be a boat,' said the girl.

'There always is. You've got to say that for England – it's an easy place to get back to America from.' She paused. 'What I can't understand is how, after having been in America and knowing what it was like, Jimmy Crocker could stand living—'

The waiter had come to Jimmy's side, bearing cheese; but Jimmy looked at it with dislike and shook his head in silent negation. He was about to depart from this place. His capacity for absorbing home truths about himself was exhausted. He placed a noiseless sovereign on the table, caught the waiter's eye, registered renunciation and departed soft-footed down the aisle. The waiter, a man who had never been able to bring himself to believe in miracles, revised the views of a lifetime. He looked at the sovereign, then at Jimmy, then at the sovereign again. Then he took up the coin and bit it furtively.

A few minutes later a hat-check boy, untipped for the first time in his predatory career, was staring at Jimmy with equal intensity but with far different feelings. Speechless concern was limned on his young face.

The commissionaire at the Piccadilly entrance of the restaurant touched his hat ingratiatingly, with the smug confidence of a man who is accustomed to getting sixpence a time for doing it.

'Taxi, Mr Crocker?'

'A worm,' said Jimmy.

'Beg pardon, sir?'

'Always drinking,' explained Jimmy, 'and making a pest of himself.'

He passed on. The commissionaire stared after him as intently as the waiter and the hat-check boy. He had sometimes known Mr Crocker like this after supper, but never before during the luncheon hour.

Jimmy made his way to his club in Northumberland Avenue. For perhaps an hour he sat in a condition of coma in the smoking-room; then, his mind made up, he went to one of the writing-tables. He sat awaiting inspiration for some minutes, then began to write. The letter he wrote was to his father:

'DEAR DAD, – I have been thinking over what we talked about this morning, and it seems to me the best thing I can do is to drop out of sight for a brief space. If I stay on in London I am likely at any moment to pull some bone like last night's which will spill the beans for you once more. The least I can do for you is to give you a clear field and not interfere, so I am off to New York by to-night's boat. I went round to Percy's to try to grovel in the dust before him, but he wouldn't see me. It's no good grovelling in the dust of the front steps for the benefit of a man who's in bed on the second floor, so I withdrew in more or less good order. I then got the present idea. Mark how all things work together for good. When they come to you and say "No title for you. Your son slugged our pal Percy," all you have to do is to come back at them with: "I know my son slugged Percy, and believe me I didn't do a thing to him! I packed him off to America within twenty-four hours. Get me right, boys! I'm anti-Jimmy and pro-Percy." To which their reply will be: "Oh, well, in that case arise, Lord Crocker!" or whatever they say when slipping a title to a deserving guy. So you will see that by making this getaway I am doing the best I can to put things straight. I shall give this to Bayliss to give to you. I am going to call him up on the phone in a minute to have him pack a few simple toothbrushes, and so on, for me. On landing in New York I shall instantly proceed to the Polo Grounds to watch a game of rounders, and will cable you the full score. Well, I think that's about all. So good-bye – or even farewell – for the present. J.

'P.S. – I know you'll understand, Dad. I'm doing what seems to me the only possible thing. Don't worry about me. I shall be all right. I'll get back my old job and be a terrific success all round. You go ahead and get that title and then meet me at the entrance of the Polo Grounds. I'll be looking out for you.

'P.P.S. – I'm a worm.'

The young clerk at the steamship offices appeared rejoiced to see Jimmy once more. With a sunny smile he snatched a pencil from his ear and plunged it into the vitals of the *Atlantic*.

'How about E a hundred and eight?'

'Suits me.'

'You're too late to go in the passenger list, of course.'

Jimmy did not reply. He was gazing rigidly at a girl who had just come in, a girl with red hair and a friendly smile.

'So you're sailing on the *Atlantic* too!' she said with a glance at the chart on the counter. 'How odd! We have just decided to go back on her too. There's nothing to keep us here and we're all homesick. Well, you see I wasn't run over after I left you.'

A delicious understanding relieved Jimmy's swimming brain as thunder relieves the tense and straining air. The feeling that he was going mad left him, as the simple solution of his mystery came to him. This girl must have heard of him in New York, perhaps she knew people whom he knew, and it was on hearsay, not on personal acquaintance, that she based that dislike of him which she had expressed with such freedom and conviction so short a while before at the Regent Grill. She did not know who he was! Into this soothing stream of thought cut the voice of the clerk.

'What name, please?'

Jimmy's mind rocked again. Why were these things happening to him to-day of all days, when he needed the tenderest treatment, when he had a headache already? The clerk was eyeing him expectantly. He had laid down his pencil and was holding aloft a pen. Jimmy gulped. Every name in the English language had passed from his mind. And then from out of the dark came inspiration.

'Bayliss,' he croaked.

The girl held out her hand.

'Then we can introduce ourselves at last. My name is Ann Chester. How do you do, Mr Bayliss?'

'How do you do, Miss Chester?'

The clerk had finished writing the ticket, and was pressing labels and a pink paper on him. The paper, he gathered dully, was a form and had to be filled up. He examined it, and found it to be a searching document. Some of its questions could be answered off-hand, others required thought.

'Height?' Simple. Five feet eleven.

'Hair?' Simple. Brown.

'Eyes?' Simple again. Blue.

Next, queries of a more offensive kind.

'Are you a polygamist?'

He could answer that. Decidedly no. One wife would be ample, provided she had red-gold hair, brown-gold eyes, the right kind of mouth and a dimple. Whatever doubts there might be in his mind on other points, on that one he had none whatever.

'Have you ever been in prison?'

Not yet.

And then a very difficult one. 'Are you a lunatic?'

Jimmy hesitated. The ink dried on his pen. He was wondering.

In the dim cavern of Paddington Station the boat train snorted impatiently, varying the process with an occasional sharp shriek. The hands of the station clock pointed to ten minutes to six. The platform was a confused mass of travellers, porters, baggage, trucks, boys with buns and fruit, boys with magazines, friends, relatives and Bayliss the butler, standing like a faithful watchdog beside a large suit case. To the human surf that broke and swirled about him he paid no attention. He was looking for the young master.

Jimmy clove the crowd like a one-man flying-wedge. Two fruit-and-bun boys who impeded his passage drifted away like leaves on an autumn gale.

'Good man!' He possessed himself of the suit case. 'I was afraid you might not be able to get here.'

'The mistress is dining out, Mr James. I was able to leave the house.'

'Have you packed everything I shall want?'

'Within the scope of a suit case, yes, sir.'

'Splendid! Oh, by the way, give this letter to my father, will you?'

'Very good, sir.'

'I'm glad you were able to manage. I thought your voice sounded doubtful over the phone.'

'I was a good deal taken aback, Mr James. Your decision to leave was so extremely sudden.'

'So was Columbus'. You know about him? He saw an egg standing on its head and whizzed off like a jack rabbit.'

'If you will pardon the liberty, Mr James, is it not a little rash—'

'Don't take the joy out of life, Bayliss. I may be a chump, but try to forget it. Use your will power.'

'Good evening, Mr Bayliss,' said a voice behind them. They both turned. The butler was gazing rather coyly at a vision in a grey tailor-made suit.

'Good evening, miss,' he said doubtfully.

Ann looked at him in astonishment, then broke into a smile.

'How stupid of me! I meant this Mr Bayliss – your son! We met at the steamship offices. And before that he saved my life. So we are old friends.'

Bayliss, gaping perplexedly and feeling unequal to the intellectual pressure of the conversation, was surprised further to perceive a warning scowl on the face of his Mr James. Jimmy had not foreseen this thing, but he had a quick mind and was equal to it.

'How are you, Miss Chester? My father has come down to see me off. This is Miss Chester, Dad.'

A British butler is not easily robbed of his poise, but Bayliss was frankly unequal to the sudden demand on his presence of mind. He lowered his jaw an inch or two, but spoke no word.

'Dad's a little upset at my going,' whispered Jimmy confidentially. 'He's not quite himself.'

Ann was a girl possessed not only of ready tact, but of a kind heart. She had summed up Mr Bayliss at a glance. Every line of him proclaimed him a respectable upper servant. No girl on earth could have been freer than she of snobbish prejudice, but she could not check a slight thrill of surprise and disappointment at this discovery of Jimmy's humble origin. She understood everything, and there were tears in her eyes as she turned away to avoid intruding on the last moments of the parting of father and son.

'I'll see you on the boat, Mr Bayliss,' she said.

'Eh?' said Bayliss.

'Yes, yes,' said Jimmy. 'Good-bye till then.'

Ann walked on to her compartment. She felt as if she had just read a whole long novel, one of those chunky younger-English-novelist things. She knew the whole story as well as if it had been told to her in detail. She could see the father, the honest steady butler, living his life with but one aim, to make a gentleman of his beloved only son. Year by year he had saved. Probably he had sent the son to college. And now, with a father's blessing and the remains of a father's savings, the boy was setting out for the new world, where dollar bills grew on trees and no one asked or cared who anyone else's father might be.

There was a lump in her throat. Bayliss would have been amazed if he could have known what a figure of pathetic fineness he seemed to her. And then her thoughts turned to Jimmy, and she was aware of a glow of kindliness towards him. His father had succeeded in his life's ambition. He had produced a gentleman! How easily and simply, without a trace of snobbish shame, the young man had introduced his father. There was the right stuff in him. He was not ashamed of the humble man who had given him his chance in life. She found herself liking Jimmy amazingly.

The hands of the clock pointed to three minutes to the hour. Porters skimmed to and fro like water beetles.

'I can't explain,' said Jimmy. 'It wasn't temporary insanity; it was necessity.'

'Very good, Mr James. I think you had better be taking your seat now.'

'Quite right, I had. It would spoil the whole thing if they left me behind. Bayliss, did you ever see such eyes? Such hair! Look after my father while I am away. Don't let the dukes worry him. Oh, and Bayliss' – Jimmy drew his hand from his pocket – 'as one pal to another—'

Bayliss looked at the crackling piece of paper.

'I couldn't, Mr James, I really couldn't! A five-pound note! I couldn't!'

'Nonsense! Be a sport!'

'Begging your pardon, Mr James, I really couldn't. You cannot afford to throw away your money like this. You cannot have a great deal of it, if you will excuse me for saying so.'

'I won't do anything of the sort. Grab it! Oh, Lord, the train's starting! Good-bye, Bayliss!'

The engine gave a final shriek of farewell. The train began to slide along the platform, pursued to the last by optimistic boys offering buns for sale. It gathered speed. Jimmy, leaning out of the window, was amazed at a spectacle so unusual as practically to amount to a modern miracle – the spectacle of Bayliss running. The butler was not in the pink of condition, but he was striding out gallantly. He reached the door of Jimmy's compartment and raised his hand.

'Begging your pardon, Mr James,' he panted, 'for taking the liberty, but I really couldn't!'

He reached up and thrust something into Jimmy's hand, something crisp and crackling: then, his mission performed, fell back and stood waving a snowy handkerchief. The train plunged into the tunnel.

Jimmy stared at the five-pound note. He was aware, like Ann farther along the train, of a lump in his throat. He put the note slowly into his pocket. The train moved on.

CHAPTER 7

Rising waters and a fine flying scud that whipped stingingly over the side had driven most of the passengers on the *Atlantic* to the shelter of their staterooms or to the warm stuffiness of the library. It was the fifth evening of the voyage. For five days and four nights the ship had been racing through a placid ocean on her way to Sandy Hook; but in the early hours of this afternoon the wind had shifted to the north, bringing heavy seas. Darkness had begun to fall now. The sky was a sullen black. The white crest of the rollers gleamed faintly in the dusk, and the wind sang in the ropes.

Jimmy and Ann had had the boat deck to themselves for half an hour. Jimmy was a good sailor. It exhilarated him to fight the wind and to walk a deck that heaved and dipped and shuddered beneath his feet; but he had not expected to have Ann's company on such an evening. She had come out of the saloon entrance, her small face framed in a hood and her slim body shapeless beneath a great cloak, and joined him in his walk.

Jimmy was in a mood of exaltation. He had passed the last few days in a condition of intermittent melancholy, consequent on the discovery that he was not the only man on board the *Atlantic* who desired the society of Ann as an alleviation of the tedium of an ocean voyage. The world, when he embarked on this venture, had consisted so exclusively of Ann and himself, that, until the ship was well on its way to Queenstown, he had not conceived the possibility of intrusive males forcing their unwelcome attentions on her. And it had added bitterness to the bitter awakening that their attentions did not appear to be at all unwelcome. Almost immediately after breakfast on the very first day a creature, with a small black moustache and shining teeth, had descended upon Ann and, vocal with surprise and pleasure at meeting her again – he claimed, damn him, to have met her before at Palm Beach, Bar Harbour, and a dozen other places – had carried her off to play an idiotic game known as shuffleboard.

Nor was this an isolated case. It began to be borne in upon Jimmy that Ann, whom he had looked upon purely in the light of an Eve playing opposite his Adam in an exclusive Garden of Eden, was an extremely well-known and popular character. The clerk at the shipping office had lied absurdly when he had said that very few people were crossing on the *Atlantic* this voyage. The vessel was crammed till its sides bulged. It was loaded down, in utter defiance of the Plimsoll Law, with Rollos and Clarences and Dwights and Twombleys who had known and golfed and ridden and driven and motored and swum and danced with Ann for years. A ghastly being, entitled Edgar Something or Teddy Something, had beaten Jimmy by a short head in the race for the deck steward, the prize of which was the placing of his deck chair next to Ann's. Jimmy had been driven from the promenade deck by the spectacle of this beastly creature lying swathed in rugs reading best sellers to her.

He had scarcely seen her to speak to since the beginning of the voyage. When she was not walking with Rollo or playing shuffleboard with Twombley, she was down below ministering to the comfort of a chronically seasick aunt, referred to in conversation as 'Poor Aunt Nesta'. Sometimes Jimmy saw the little man – presumably her uncle – in the smoking-room, and once he came upon the stout boy recovering from the effects of a cigar in a quiet corner of the boat deck. But apart from these meetings the family was as distant from him as if he had never seen Ann at all, let alone saved her life.

And now she had dropped down on him from heaven. They were alone together with a good clean wind and the bracing scud. Rollo, Clarence, Dwight and Twombley, not to mention Edgar or possibly Teddy, were down below – he hoped, dying. They had the world to themselves.

'I love rough weather,' said Ann, lifting her face to the wind. Her eyes were very bright. She was beyond any doubt or question the only girl on earth. 'Poor Aunt Nesta doesn't. She was bad enough when it was quite calm, but this storm has finished her. I've just been down below trying to cheer her up.'

Jimmy thrilled at the picture. Always fascinating, Ann seemed to him at her best in the rôle of ministering angel. He longed to tell her so, but found no words. They reached the end of the deck and turned. Ann looked up at him.

'I've hardly seen anything of you since we sailed,' she said. She spoke almost reproachfully. 'Tell me all about yourself, Mr Bayliss. Why are you going to America?'

Jimmy had had an impassioned indictment of the Rollos on his tongue, but she had closed the opening for it as quickly as she had made it. In face of her direct demand for information he could not hark back to it now. After all, what did the Rollos matter? They had no part in this little wind-swept world. They were where they belonged, in some nether hell on the C or D deck, moaning for death.

'To make my fortune, I hope,' he said.

Ann was pleased at this confirmation of her diagnosis. She had deduced this from the evidence at Paddington Station.

'How pleased your father will be if you do!'

The slight complexity of Jimmy's affairs caused him to pause for a moment to sort out his fathers, but an instant's reflection told him that she must be referring to Bayliss, the butler.

'Yes.'

'He's a dear old man,' said Ann. 'I suppose he's very proud of you?'

'I hope so.'

'You must do tremendously well in America, so as not to disappoint him. What are you thinking of doing?'

Jimmy considered for a moment.

'Newspaper work, I think.'

'Oh? Why, have you had any experience?'

'A little.'

Ann seemed to grow a little aloof, as if her enthusiasm had been damped.

'Oh, well, I suppose it's a good enough profession. I'm not very fond of it myself. I've only met one newspaper man in my life, and I dislike him very much, so I suppose that has prejudiced me.'

'Who was that?'

'You wouldn't have met him. He was on an American paper. A man named Crocker.'

A sudden gust of wind drove them back a step, rendering talk impossible. It covered a gap when Jimmy could not have spoken. The shock of the information that Ann had met him before made him dumb. This thing was beyond him. It baffled him. Her next words supplied a solution. They were under shelter of one of the boats now and she could make herself heard.

'It was five years ago, and I only met him for a very short while, but the prejudice has lasted.'

Jimmy began to understand. Five years ago! It was not so strange, then, that they should not recognize each other now. He stirred up his memory. Nothing came to the surface. Not a gleam of recollection of that early meeting rewarded him. And yet something of importance must have happened then for her to remember it. Surely his mere personality could not have been so unpleasant as to have made such a lasting impression on her!

'I wish you could do something better than newspaper work,' said Ann. 'I always think the splendid part about America is that it is such a land of adventure. There are such millions of chances. It's a place where anything may happen. Haven't you an adventurous soul, Mr Bayliss?'

No man lightly submits to a charge, even a hinted charge, of being deficient in the capacity for adventure.

'Of course I have,' said Jimmy indignantly. 'I'm game to tackle anything that comes along.'

'I'm glad of that.'

Her feeling of comradeship toward this young man deepened. She loved adventure and based her estimate of any member of the opposite sex largely on his capacity for it. She moved in a set, when at home, which was more polite than adventurous, and had frequently found the atmosphere enervating.

'Adventure,' said Jimmy, 'is everything.' He paused. 'Or a good deal,' he concluded weakly.

'Why qualify it like that? It sounds so tame. Adventure is the biggest thing in life.'

It seemed to Jimmy that he had received an excellent cue for a remark of a kind that had been waiting for utterance ever since he had met her. Often and often in the watches of the night, smoking endless pipes and thinking of her, he had conjured up just such a vision as this – they two walking the deserted deck alone, and she innocently giving him an opening for some low-voiced, tender speech, at which she would start, look at him quickly, and then ask him haltingly if the words had any particular application. And after that – oh, well, all sorts of things might happen. And now the moment had come. It was true that he had always pictured the scene as taking place by moonlight, and at present there was a half gale blowing out of an inky sky; also, on the present occasion anything in the nature of a low-voiced speech was absolutely out of the question owing to the uproar of the elements. Still, taking these drawbacks into consideration, the chance was far too good to miss. Such an opening might never happen again. He waited till the ship had steadied herself after an apparently suicidal dive into an enormous roller, then, staggering back to her side, spoke.

'Love is the biggest thing in life!' he roared.

'What is?' shrieked Ann.

'Love!' bellowed Jimmy.

He wished a moment later that he had postponed his statement of faith, for their next steps took them into a haven of comparative calm, where some dimly seen portion of the vessel's anatomy jutted out and formed a kind of nook where it was possible to hear the ordinary tones of the human voice. He halted here, and Ann did the same, though unwillingly. She was conscious of a feeling of disappointment and of a modification of her mood of comradeship toward her companion. She held strong views, which she believed to be unalterable, on the subject under discussion.

'Love!' she said. It was too dark to see her face, but her voice sounded unpleasantly scornful. 'I shouldn't have thought that you would have been so conventional as that. You seemed different.'

'Eh?' said Jimmy blankly.

'I hate all this talk about love, as if it were something wonderful that was worth everything else in life put together. Every book you read and every song that you see in the shop windows is all about love. It's as if all the people in the world were in conspiracy to persuade themselves that there's a wonderful something just round the corner which they can get if they try hard enough. And they hypnotize themselves into thinking of nothing else, and miss all the splendid things of life.'

'That's Shaw, isn't it?' said Jimmy.

'What is Shaw?'

'What you were saying. It's out of one of Bernard Shaw's things, isn't it?'

'It is not.' A note of acidity had crept into Ann's voice. 'It is perfectly original.'

'I'm certain I've heard it before somewhere.'

'If you have that simply means that you must have associated with some sensible person.'

Jimmy was puzzled.

'But why the grouch?' he asked.

'I don't understand you.'

'I mean, why do you feel that way about it?'

Ann was quite certain now that she did not like this young man nearly so well as she had supposed. It is trying for a strong-minded, clear-thinking girl to have her philosophy described as a grouch.

'Because I've had the courage to think about it for myself, and not let myself be blinded by popular superstition. The whole world has united in making itself imagine that there is something called love which is the most wonderful happening in life. The poets and novelists have simply hounded them on to believe it. It's a gigantic swindle.'

A wave of tender compassion swept over Jimmy. He understood it all now. Naturally a girl who had associated all her life with the Rollos, Clarences, Dwights and Twombleys would come to despair of the possibility of falling in love with anyone.

'You haven't met the right man,' he said. She had, of course, but only recently; and, anyway, he could point that out later.

'There is no such thing as the right man,' said Ann resolutely, 'if you are suggesting that there is a type of man in existence who is capable of inspiring what is called romantic love. I believe in marriage—'

'Good work!' said Jimmy, well satisfied.

'But not as the result of a sort of delirium. I believe in it as a sensible partnership between two friends who know each other well and trust each other. The right way of looking at marriage is to realize, first of all, that there are no thrills, no romances, and then to pick out someone who is nice and kind and amusing and full of life and willing to do things to make you happy.'

'Ah!' said Jimmy, straightening his tie. 'Well, that's something.'

'How do you mean – that's something? Are you shocked at my views?'

'I don't believe they are your views. You've been reading one of these stern, soured fellows who analyse things.'

Ann stamped. The sound was inaudible, but Jimmy noticed the movement.

'Cold?' he said. 'Let's walk on.'

Ann's sense of humour reasserted itself. It was not often that it remained dormant for so long. She laughed.

'I know exactly what you are thinking,' she said. 'You believe that I am posing, that these aren't my real opinions.'

'They can't be. But I don't think you are posing. It's getting on to dinner time, and you've got that wan, sinking feeling that makes you look upon the world and find it a hollow fraud. The bugle will be blowing in a few minutes, and half an hour after that you will be yourself again.'

'I'm myself now. I suppose you can't realize that a pretty girl can hold such views.'

Jimmy took her arm.

'Let me help you,' he said. 'There's a knot-hole in the deck. Watch your step. Now listen to me. I'm glad you've brought up this subject – I mean the subject of your being the prettiest girl in the known world—'

'I never said that.'

'Your modesty prevented you. But it's a fact, nevertheless. I'm glad, I say, because I have been thinking a lot along those lines myself, and I have been anxious to discuss the point with you. You have the most glorious hair I have ever seen!'

'Do you like red hair?'

'Red-gold.'

'It's nice of you to put it like that. When I was a child all except a few of the other children called me Carrots.'

'They have undoubtedly come to a bad end by this time. If bears were sent to attend to the children who criticized Elisha your little friends were in line for a troupe of tigers. But there were some of a finer fibre? There were a few who didn't call you Carrots?'

'One or two. They called me Brick-Top.'

'They have probably been electrocuted since. Your eyes are perfectly wonderful!'

Ann withdrew her arm. An extensive acquaintance of young men told her that the topic of conversation was now due to be changed.

'You will like America,' she said.

'We are not discussing America.'

'I am. It is a wonderful country for a man who wants to succeed. If I were you I should go out West.'

'Do you live out West?'

'No.'

'Then why suggest my going there? Where do you live?'

'I live in New York.'

'I shall stay in New York then.'

Ann was wary, but amused. Proposals of marriage – and Jimmy seemed to be moving swiftly toward one – were no novelty in her life. In the course of several seasons at Bar Harbour, Tuxedo, Palm Beach, and in New York itself, she had spent much of her time foiling and discouraging the ardour of a series of sentimental youths who had laid their unwelcome hearts at her feet.

'New York is open for staying in about this time, I believe.'

Jimmy was silent. He had done his best to fight the tendency to become depressed and had striven by means of a light tone to keep himself resolutely cheerful, but the girl's apparently total indifference to him was too much for his spirits. One of the young men who had had to pick up the heart he had flung at Ann's feet and carry it away for repairs had once confided to an intimate friend, after the sting had to some extent passed, that the feelings of a man who made love to Ann might be likened to the emotions which hot chocolate might be supposed to entertain on contact with vanilla ice cream. Jimmy, had the comparison been presented to him, would have endorsed its perfect accuracy. The wind from the sea, until now keen and bracing, had become merely infernally cold. The song of the wind in the rigging, erstwhile melodious, had turned into a depressing howling.

'I used to be as sentimental as anyone a few years ago,' said Ann, returning to the dropped subject. 'Just after I left college I was quite maudlin. I dreamed of moons and Junes and loves and doves all the time. Then something happened which made me see what a little fool I was. It wasn't pleasant at the time, but it had a very bracing effect. I have been quite different ever since. It was a man, of course, who did it. His method was quite simple. He just made fun of me, and Nature did the rest.'

Jimmy scowled in the darkness. Murderous thoughts toward the unknown brute flooded his mind.

'I wish I could meet him!' he growled.

'You aren't likely to,' said Ann. 'He lives in England. His name is Crocker – Jimmy Crocker. I spoke about him just now.'

Through the howling of the wind cut the sharp notes of a bugle. Ann turned to the saloon entrance.

'Dinner!' she said brightly. 'How hungry one gets on board ship!' She stopped. 'Aren't you coming down, Mr Bayliss?'

'Not just yet,' said Jimmy thickly.

CHAPTER 8

The noonday sun beat down on Park Row. Hurrying mortals, released from a thousand offices, congested the sidewalks, their thoughts busy with the vision of lunch. Up and down the cañon of Nassau Street the crowds moved more slowly. Candy-selling aliens jostled newsboys, and huge dray horses endeavoured to the best of their ability not to grind the citizenry beneath their hoofs. Eastward, pressing on to the City Hall, surged the usual dense army of happy lovers on their way to buy marriage licences. Men popped in and out of the subway entrances like rabbits. It was a stirring, bustling scene, typical of this nerve centre of New York's vast body.

Jimmy Crocker, standing in the doorway, watched the throngs enviously. There were men in that crowd who chewed gum; there were men who wore white-satin ties with imitation diamond stickpins; there were men who, having smoked seven-tenths of a cigar, were eating the remainder; but there was not one with whom he would not at that moment willingly have exchanged identities. For these men had jobs. And in his present frame of mind it seemed to him that no further ingredient was needed for the recipe of the ultimate human bliss.

The poet has said some very searching and unpleasant things about the man 'whose heart hath ne'er within him burn'd as home his footsteps he hath turned from wandering on a foreign strand', but he might have excused Jimmy for feeling just then not so much a warmth of heart as a cold and clammy sensation of dismay. He would have had to admit that the words, 'High though his titles, proud his name, boundless his wealth as wish can claim,' did not apply to Jimmy Crocker. The latter may have been 'concentred all on self', but his wealth consisted of one hundred and thirty-three dollars and forty cents; and his name was so far from being proud, that the mere sight of it in the files of the New York *Sunday Chronicle*, the record room of which he had just been visiting, had made him consider the fact that he had changed it to Bayliss, the most sensible act of his career.

The reason for Jimmy's lack of enthusiasm as he surveyed the portion of his native land visible from his doorway is not far to seek. The *Atlantic* had docked on Saturday night, and Jimmy, having driven to an excellent hotel and engaged an expensive room therein, had left instructions at the desk that breakfast should be served to him at ten o'clock and with it the Sunday issue of the *Chronicle*. Five years had passed since he had seen the dear old rag for which he had reported so many fires, murders, street accidents and weddings; and he looked forward to its perusal as a formal taking seisin of his long-neglected country. Nothing could be more fitting and symbolic than that the first morning of his return to America should find him propped up in bed reading the good old *Chronicle*. Among his final meditations as he dropped off to sleep was a gentle speculation as to who was city editor now, and whether the comic supplement was still featuring the sprightly adventures of the Doughnut Family.

A wave of not unmanly sentiment passed over him on the following morning as he reached out for the paper. The skyline of New York, seen as the boat comes up the bay, has its points;

and the rattle of the elevated trains and the quaint odour of the subway extend a kindly welcome; but the thing that really convinces the returned traveller that he is back on Manhattan Island is the first Sunday paper. Jimmy, like everyone else, began by opening the comic supplement; and as he scanned it a chilly discomfort, almost a premonition of Evil, came upon him. The Doughnut Family was no more. He knew that it was unreasonable of him to feel as if he had just been informed of the death of a dear friend, for Pa Doughnut and his associates had been having their adventures five years before he had left the country, and even the toughest comic supplementary hero rarely endures for a decade. But, nevertheless, the shadow did fall upon his morning optimism, and he derived no pleasure whatever from the artificial rollickings of a degraded creature called Old Pop Dill-Pickle, who was offered as a substitute.

But this, he was to discover almost immediately, was a trifling disaster. It distressed him, but it did not affect his material welfare. Tragedy really began when he turned to the magazine section. Scarcely had he started to glance at it when this headline struck him like a bullet:

PICCADILLY JIM AT IT AGAIN

And beneath it his own name.

Nothing is so capable of diversity as the emotion we feel on seeing our name unexpectedly in print. We may soar to the heights or we may sink to the depths. Jimmy did the latter. A mere cursory first inspection of the article revealed the fact that it was no eulogy. With an unsparing hand the writer had muckraked his eventful past, the text on which he hung his remarks being that ill-fated encounter with Lord Percy Whipple at the Six Hundred Club. This the scribe had recounted at a length and with a boisterous vim which outdid even Bill Blake's effort in the London *Daily Sun*. Bill Blake had been handicapped by consideration of space and the fact that he had turned in his copy at an advanced hour when the paper was almost made up. The present writer was shackled by no restrictions. He had plenty of room to spread himself in, and he had spread himself. So liberal had been the editor's views in that respect that, in addition to the letter-press, the pages contained an unspeakably offensive picture of a burly young man, in an obviously advanced condition of alcoholism, raising his first to strike a monocled youth in evening dress who had so little chin that Jimmy was surprised that he had ever been able to hit it. The only gleam of consolation that he could discover in this repellent drawing was the fact that the artist had treated Lord Percy even more scurvily than himself. Among other things, the second son of the Duke of Devizes was depicted as wearing a coronet – a thing which would have excited remark even in a London night club.

Jimmy read the thing through in its entirety three times before he appreciated a *nuance* which his disordered mind had at first failed to grasp – to wit, that this character sketch of himself was no mere isolated outburst, but apparently one of a series. In several places the writer alluded unmistakably to other theses on the same subject. Jimmy's breakfast congealed on its tray, untouched. That boon which the gods so seldom bestow – of seeing ourselves as others see us – had been accorded to him in full measure. By the time he had completed his third reading he was regarding himself in a purely objective fashion, not unlike the attitude of a naturalist toward some strange and loathsome manifestation of insect life. So this was the sort of fellow he was! He wondered they had let him in at a reputable hotel.

The rest of the day he passed in a state of such humility that he could have wept when the waiters were civil to him. On the Monday morning he made his way to Park Row to read the files of the *Chronicle* – a morbid enterprise, akin to the eccentric behaviour of those priests of Baal who gashed themselves with knives, or of authors who subscribe to press-clipping agencies.

He came upon another of the articles almost at once, in an issue not a month old. Then there was a gap of several weeks, and hope revived that things might not be so bad as he had feared – only to be crushed by another trenchant screed. After that he set about his excavations methodically, resolved to know the worst. He knew it in just under two hours. There it all was – his row with the bookie, his bad behaviour at the political meeting, his breach-of-promise case. It was a complete biography.

And the name they called him. Piccadilly Jim! Ugh!

He went out into Park Row, and sought a quiet doorway where he could brood upon these matters. It was not immediately that the practical or financial aspect of the affair came to scourge him. For an appreciable time he suffered in his self-esteem alone. It seemed to him that all these bustling persons who passed knew him; that they were casting sidelong glances at him and laughing derisively; that those who chewed gum chewed it sneeringly; and that those who ate their cigars ate them with thinly veiled disapproval and scorn. Then, the passage of time blunting sensitiveness, he found that there were other and weightier things to consider.

As far as he had any connected plan of action in his sudden casting-off of the fleshpots of London, he had determined as soon as possible after landing to report at the office of his old paper and apply for his ancient position. So little thought had been given to the minutiæ of his future plans, that it had not occurred to him that he had anything to do but walk in, slap the gang on the back and announce that he was ready to work. Work! On the staff of a paper whose chief diversion appeared to be the satirizing of his escapades! Even had he possessed the moral courage – or gall – to make the application, what good would it be? He was a byword in a world where he had once been a worthy citizen. What paper would trust Piccadilly Jim with an assignment? What paper would consider Piccadilly Jim even on space rates? A chill dismay crept over him. He seemed to hear the grave voice of Bayliss, the butler, speaking in his ear as he had spoken so short a while before at Paddington Station:

'Is it not a little rash, Mr James?'

Rash was the word. Here he stood, in a country that had no possible use for him, a country where competition was keen and jobs for the unskilled infrequent. What on earth was there that he could do?

Well, he could go home. No, he couldn't. His pride revolted at that solution. Prodigal Son stuff was all very well in its way, but it lost its impressiveness if you turned up again at home two weeks after you had left. A decent interval among the husks and swine was essential. Besides, there was his father to consider. He might be a poor specimen of a fellow, as witness the *Sunday Chronicle passim*, but he was not so poor as to come slinking back to upset things for his father just when he had done the only decent thing by removing himself. No, that was out of the question.

What remained? The air of New York is bracing and healthy, but a man cannot live on it. Obviously he must find a job. But what job?

What could he do?

A gnawing sensation in the region of the waistcoat answered the question. The solution which it put forward was, it was true, but a temporary one, yet it appealed strongly to Jimmy. He had found it admirable at many crises. He would go and lunch, and it might be that food would bring inspiration.

He moved from his doorway and crossed to the entrance of the subway. He caught a timely express, and a few minutes later emerged into the sunlight again at Grand Central. He made his way westward along Forty-second Street to the hotel which he thought would meet his needs. He had scarcely entered it when in a chair by the door he perceived Ann Chester, and at the sight of her all his depression vanished and he was himself again.

'Why, how do you do, Mr Bayliss? Are you lunching here?'

'Unless there is some other place that you would prefer,' said Jimmy. 'I hope I haven't kept you waiting.'

Ann laughed. She was looking very delightful in something soft and green.

'I'm not going to lunch with you. I'm waiting for Mr Ralstone and his sister. Do you remember him? He crossed over with us. His chair was next to mine on the promenade deck.'

Jimmy was shocked. When he thought how narrowly she had escaped, poor girl, from lunching with that insufferable pill Teddy – or was it Edgar? – he felt quite weak. Recovering himself, he spoke firmly:

'When were they to have met you?'

'At one o'clock.'

'It is now five past. You are certainly not going to wait any longer. Come with me, and we will whistle for a cab.'

'Don't be absurd!'

'Come along. I want to talk to you about my future.'

'I shall certainly do nothing of the kind,' said Ann, rising. She went with him to the door. 'Teddy would never forgive me.' She got into the cab. 'It's only because you have appealed to me to help you discuss your future,' she said, as they drove off. 'Nothing else would have induced me—'

'I know,' said Jimmy. 'I felt that I could rely on your womanly sympathy. Where shall we go?'

'Where do you want to go? Oh, I forget that you have never been in New York before. By the way, what are your impressions of our glorious country?'

'Most gratifying, if only I could get a job.'

'Tell him to drive to Delmonico's. It's just round the corner on Forty-fourth Street.'

'There are some things round the corner, then?'

'That sounds cryptic. What do you mean?'

'You've forgotten our conversation that night on the ship. You refused to admit the existence of wonderful things just round the corner. You said some very regrettable things that night. About love, if you remember.'

'You can't be going to talk about love at one o'clock in the afternoon! Talk about your future.'

'Love is inextricably mixed up with my future.'

'Not with your immediate future. I thought you said that you were trying to get a job. Have you given up the idea of newspaper work then?'

'Absolutely.'

'Well, I'm rather glad.'

The cab drew up at the restaurant door, and the conversation was interrupted. When they were seated at their table, and Jimmy had given an order to the waiter of absolutely inexcusable extravagance, Ann returned to the topic.

'Well, now the thing is to find something for you to do.'

Jimmy looked round the restaurant with appreciative eyes. The summer exodus from New York was still several weeks distant, and the place was full of prosperous-looking lunchers, not one of whom appeared to have a care or an unpaid bill in the world. The atmosphere was redolent of substantial bank balances. Solvency shone from the closely shaven faces of the men and reflected itself in the dresses of the women. Jimmy sighed.

'I suppose so,' he said. 'Though for choice I'd like to be one of the Idle Rich. To my mind the ideal profession is strolling into the office and touching the old dad for another thousand.'

Ann was severe.

'You revolt me!' she said. 'I never heard anything so thoroughly disgraceful. You need work!'

'One of these days,' said Jimmy plaintively, 'I shall be sitting by the roadside with my dinner pail, and you will come by in your limousine, and I shall look up at you and say: "You hounded me into this!" How will you feel then?'

'Very proud of myself.'

'In that case there is no more to be said. I'd much rather hang about and try to get adopted by a millionaire, but if you insist on my working— Waiter!'

'What do you want?' asked Ann.

'Will you get me a Classified Telephone Directory?' said Jimmy.

'What for?' asked Ann.

'To look for a profession. There is nothing like being methodical.'

The waiter returned, bearing a red book. Jimmy thanked him and opened it at the A's.

'The boy, what will he become?' he said. He turned the pages. 'How about an Auditor? What do you think of that?'

'Do you think you could audit?'

'That I could not say till I had tried. I might turn out to be very good at it. How about an Adjuster?'

'An adjuster of what?'

'The book doesn't say. It just remarks broadly – in a sort of spacious way – "Adjusters". I take it that, having decided to become an Adjuster, you then sit down and decide what you wish to adjust. One might, for example, become an Asparagus Adjuster.'

'A what?'

'Surely you know? Asparagus Adjusters are the fellows who sell those rope-and-pulley affairs by means of which the Smart Set lower asparagus into their mouths – or rather Francis the footman does it for them, of course. The diner leans back in his chair, and the menial works the apparatus in the background. It is entirely superseding the old-fashioned method of picking the vegetable up and taking a snap at it. But I suspect that to be a successful Asparagus Adjuster requires capital. We now come to Awning Crank and Spring Rollers. I don't think I should like that. Rolling awning cranks seems to me a sorry way of spending life's springtime. Let's try the B's.'

'Let's try this omelette. It looks delicious.' Jimmy shook his head.

'I will toy with it – but absently and in a *distrait* manner, as becomes a man of affairs. There's nothing in the B's. I might devote my ardent youth to Bar-room Glassware and Bottlers' Supplies. On the other hand, I might not. Similarly, while there is no doubt a bright future for somebody in Celluloid, Fibreloid, and Other Factitious Goods, instinct tells me that there is none for' – he pulled up on the verge of saying 'James Braithwaite Crocker', and shuddered at the nearness of the pitfall – 'for' – he hesitated again – 'for Algernon Bayliss,' he concluded.

Ann smiled delightedly. It was so typical that his father should have called him something like that. Time had not dimmed her regard for the old man she had seen for that brief moment at Paddington Station. He was an old dear, and she thoroughly approved of this latest manifestation of his supposed pride in his offspring.

'Is that really your name – Algernon?'

'I cannot deny it.'

'I think your father is a darling,' said Ann inconsequently.

Jimmy had buried himself in the directory again.

'The D's,' he said. 'Is it possible that posterity will know me as Bayliss the Dermatologist? Or as Bayliss the Drop Forger? I don't quite like that last one. It may be a respectable occupation, but it sounds rather criminal to me. The sentence for forging drops is probably about twenty years with hard labour.'

'I wish you would put that book away and go on with your lunch,' said Ann.

'Perhaps,' said Jimmy, 'my grandchildren will cluster round my knee some day and say in their piping, childish voices: "Tell us how you became the Elastic Stocking King, Grandpa!" What do you think?'

'I think you ought to be ashamed of yourself. You are wasting your time, when you ought to be either talking to me or else thinking very seriously about what you mean to do.'

Jimmy was turning the pages rapidly.

'I will be with you in a moment,' he said. 'Try to amuse yourself somehow till I am at leisure. Ask yourself a riddle. Tell yourself an anecdote. Think of life. No, it's no good.

I don't see myself as a Fan Importer, a Glass Beveller, a Hotel Broker, an Insect Exterminator, a Junk Dealer, a Kalsomine Manufacturer, a Laundryman, a Mausoleum Architect, a Nurse, an Oculist, a Paper Hanger, a Quilt Designer, a Roofer, a Ship Plumber, a Tinsmith, an Undertaker, a Veterinarian, a Wig Maker, an X-ray Apparatus Manufacturer, a Yeast Producer or a Zinc Spelter.' He closed the book. 'There is only one thing to do. I must starve in the gutter. Tell me – you know New York better than I do – where is there a good gutter?'

At this moment there entered the restaurant an Immaculate Person. He was a young man attired in faultlessly fitting clothes, with shoes of flawless polish and a perfectly proportioned floweret in his buttonhole. He surveyed the room through a monocle. He was a pleasure to look upon, but Jimmy, catching sight of him, started violently and felt no joy at all – for he had recognized him. It was a man he knew well and who knew him well, a man whom he had last seen a bare two weeks ago at the Bachelors' Club in London. Few things are certain in this world, but one was that, if Bartling – such was the Vision's name – should see him, he would come over and address him as Crocker. He braced himself to the task of being Bayliss, the whole Bayliss, and nothing but Bayliss. It might be that stout denial would carry him through. After all, Reggie Bartling was a man of notoriously feeble intellect, who could believe in anything.

The monocle continued its sweep. It rested on Jimmy's profile.

'By Gad!' said the Vision.

Reginald Bartling had landed in New York that morning, and already the loneliness of a strange city had begun to oppress him. He had come over on a visit of pleasure, his suit case stuffed with letters of introduction, but these he had not yet used. There was a feeling of homesickness upon him, and he ached for a pal. And there before him sat Jimmy Crocker, one of the best. He hastened to the table.

'I say, Crocker, old chap, I didn't know you were over here. When did you arrive?'

Jimmy was profoundly thankful that he had seen this pest in time to be prepared for him. Suddenly assailed in this fashion, he would undoubtedly have incriminated himself by recognition of his name. But, having anticipated the visitation, he was able to say a whole sentence to Ann before showing himself aware that it was he who was addressed.

'I say! Jimmy Crocker!'

Jimmy achieved one of the blankest stares of modern times. He looked at Ann. Then he looked at Bartling again.

'I think there's some mistake,' he said. 'My name is Bayliss.'

Before his stony eye the immaculate Bartling wilted. All that he had ever heard and read about doubles came to him. He was confused. He blushed. It was deuced bad form going up to a perfect stranger like this and pretending you know him. Probably the chappie thought he was some kind of a confidence Johnnie or something. It was absolutely rotten! He continued to blush till one could have fancied him scarlet to the ankles. He backed away, apologizing in ragged mutters. Jimmy was not insensible to the pathos of his suffering acquaintance's position; he knew Reggie and his devotion to good form sufficiently well to enable him to appreciate the other's horror at having spoken to a fellow to whom he had never been introduced. But necessity forbade any other course. However Reggie's soul might writhe and however sleepless Reggie's nights might become as a result of this encounter, he was prepared to fight it out on those lines if it took all summer. And, anyway, it was darned good for Reggie to get a jolt like that every once in a while. Kept him bright and lively.

So thinking, he turned to Ann again, while the crimson Bartling tottered off to restore his nerve centres to their normal tone at some other hostelry. He found Ann staring amazedly at him, eyes wide and lips parted.

'Odd, that!' he observed, with a light carelessness which he admired extremely, and of which he would not have believed himself capable. 'I suppose I must be somebody's double. What was the name he said?'

'Jimmy Crocker!' cried Ann.

Jimmy raised his glass, sipped, and put it down.

'Oh, yes, I remember. So it was. It's a curious thing, too, that it sounds familiar. I've heard the name before somewhere.'

'I was talking about Jimmy Crocker on the ship – that evening on deck.'

Jimmy looked at her doubtfully.

'Were you? Oh, yes, of course; I've got it now. He is the man you dislike so.'

Ann was still looking at him as if he had undergone a change into something new and strange.

'I hope you aren't going to let the resemblance prejudice you against me?' said Jimmy. 'Some are born Jimmy Crockers, others have Jimmy Crockers thrust upon them. I hope you'll bear in mind that I belong to the latter class.'

'It's such an extraordinary thing.'

'Oh, I don't know. You often hear of doubles. There was a man in England a few years ago who kept getting sent to prison for things some genial stranger who happened to look like him had done.'

'I don't mean that. Of course there are doubles. But it is curious that you should have come over here and that we should have met like this at just this time. You see the reason I went over to England at all was to try to get Jimmy Crocker to come back here.'

'What!'

'I don't mean that I did. I mean that I went with my uncle and aunt, who wanted to persuade him to come and live with them.'

Jimmy was now feeling completely out of his depth.

'Your uncle and aunt? Why?'

'I ought to have explained that they are his uncle and aunt too. My aunt's sister married his father.'

'But—'

'It's quite simple, though it doesn't sound so. Perhaps you haven't read the *Sunday Chronicle* lately? It has been publishing articles about Jimmy Crocker's disgusting behaviour in London – they call him Piccadilly Jim, you know—'

In print that name had shocked Jimmy. Spoken, and by Ann, it was loathly. Remorse for his painful past tore at him.

'There was another one printed yesterday.'

'I saw it,' said Jimmy, to avert description.

'Oh, did you? Well, just to show you what sort of a man Jimmy Crocker is, the Lord Percy Whipple whom he attacked in the club was his very best friend. His stepmother told my aunt so. He seems to be absolutely hopeless.' She smiled. 'You're looking quite sad, Mr Bayliss. Cheer up! You may look like him, but you aren't him – he? – him? – no, "he" is right. The soul is what counts. If you've got a good, virtuous, Algernonish soul, it doesn't matter if you're so like Jimmy Crocker that his friends come up and talk to you in restaurants. In fact, it's rather an advantage really. I'm sure that if you were to go to my aunt and pretend to be Jimmy Crocker, who had come over after all in a fit of repentance, she would be so pleased that there would be nothing she wouldn't do for you. You might realize your ambition of being adopted by a millionaire. Why don't you try it? I won't give you away.'

'Before they found me out and hauled me off to prison I should have been near you for a time. I should have lived in the same house with you, spoken to you—!' Jimmy's voice shook.

Ann turned her head to address an imaginary companion.

'You must listen to this, my dear,' she said in an undertone. 'He speaks wonderfully! They used to call him the Boy Orator in his home town. Sometimes that, and sometimes Eloquent Algernon!'

Jimmy eyed her fixedly. He disapproved of this frivolity.

'One of these days you will try me too high—'

'Oh, you didn't hear what I was saying to my friend, did you?' she said in concern. 'But I meant it, every word. I love to hear you talk. You have such feeling!'

Jimmy attuned himself to the key of the conversation.

'Have you no sentiment in you?' he demanded. 'I was just warming up too! In another minute you would have heard something worth while. You've damped me now. Let's talk about my lifework again.'

'Have you thought of anything?'

'I'd like to be one of those fellows who sit in offices and sign cheques, and tell the office boy to tell Mr Rockefeller they can give him five minutes. But, of course, I should need a cheque book, and I haven't got one. Oh, well, I shall find something to do all right. Now tell me something about yourself. Let's drop the future for a while.'

An hour later Jimmy turned into Broadway. He walked pensively, for he had much to occupy his mind. How strange that the Petts should have come over to England to try to induce him to return to New York, and how galling that, now that he was in New York, this avenue to a prosperous future was closed by the fact that something which he had done five years ago – that he could remember nothing about it was quite maddening – had caused Ann to nurse this abiding hatred of him. He began to dream tenderly of Ann, bumping from pedestrian to pedestrian in a gentle trance.

From this trance the seventh pedestrian aroused him by uttering his name, the name which circumstances had compelled him to abandon.

'Jimmy Crocker!'

Surprise brought Jimmy back from his dreams to the hard world – surprise and a certain exasperation. It was ridiculous to be incognito in a city which he had not visited in five years, and to be instantly recognized in this way by every second man he met. He looked sourly at the man. The other was a sturdy, square-shouldered, battered young man, who wore on his homely face a grin of recognition and regard. Jimmy was not particularly good at remembering faces, but this person's was of a kind which the poorest memory might have recalled. It was, as the advertisements say, distinctively individual. The broken nose, the exiguous forehead and the enlarged ears all clamoured for recognition. The last time Jimmy had seen Jerry Mitchell had been two years before at the National Sporting Club in London, and, placing him at once, he braced himself, as a short while ago he had braced himself to confound immaculate Reggie.

'Hello!' said the battered one.

'Hello, indeed!' said Jimmie courteously. 'In what way can I brighten your life?'

The grin faded from the other's face. He looked puzzled.

'You're Jimmy Crocker, ain't you?'

'No. My name chances to be Algernon Bayliss.'

Jerry Mitchell reddened.

'Scuse me. My mistake.'

He was moving off, but Jimmy stopped him. Parting from Ann had left a large gap in his life, and he craved human society.

'I know you now,' he said. 'You're Jerry Mitchell. I saw you fight Kid Burke four years ago in London.'

The grin returned to the pugilist's face, wider than ever. He beamed with gratification.

'Gee! Think of that! I've quit since then. I'm working for an old guy named Pett. Funny thing, he's Jimmy Crocker's uncle that I mistook you for. Say, you're a dead ringer for that guy! I could have sworn it was him when you bumped into me. Say, are you doing anything?'

'Nothing in particular.'

'Come and have a yarn. There's a place I know just round by here.'

'Delighted.'

They made their way to the place.

'What's yours?' said Jerry Mitchell. 'I'm on the wagon myself,' he added apologetically.

'So am I,' said Jimmy. 'It's the only way. No sense in always drinking and making a disgraceful exhibition of yourself in public!'

Jerry Mitchell received this homily in silence. It disposed definitely of the lurking doubt in his mind as to the possibility of this man being Jimmy Crocker. Though outwardly convinced by the other's denial he had not been able to rid himself till now of a nebulous suspicion. But this convinced him. Jimmy Crocker would never have said a thing like that, nor would he have refused the offer of alcohol. He fell into pleasant conversation with him, his mind eased.

CHAPTER 9

At five o'clock in the afternoon, some ten days after her return to America, Mrs Pett was at home to her friends in the house on Riverside Drive. The proceedings were on a scale that amounted to a reception, for they were not only a sort of official notification to New York that one of its most prominent hostesses was once more in its midst, but were also designed to entertain and impress Mr Hammond Chester, Ann's father, who had been spending a couple of days in the metropolis preparatory to departing for South America on one of his frequent trips. He was very fond of Ann in his curious, detached way, though he never ceased in his private heart to consider it injudicious of her not to have been born a boy, and he always took in New York for a day or so on his way from one wild and lonely spot to another, if he could manage it.

The large drawing-room overlooking the Hudson was filled almost to capacity with that strange mixture of humanity which Mrs Pett chiefly affected. She prided herself on the Bohemian element in her parties, and had become during the past two years a human dragon, scooping genius from its hiding-places and bringing it into the open. At different spots in the room stood the six resident geniuses to whose presence in the home Mr Pett had such strong objections, and in addition to these she had collected so many more of a like breed from the environs of Washington Square that the air was clamorous with the hoarse cries of futurist painters, esoteric Buddhists, *vers libre* poets, interior decorators and stage reformers, sifted in among the more conventional members of society who had come to listen to them. Men with new religions drank tea with women with new hats. Apostles of free love expounded their doctrines to persons who had been practising them for years without realizing it. All over the room throats were being strained and minds broadened.

Mr Chester, standing near the door with Ann, eyed the assemblage with the genial contempt of a large dog for a voluble pack of small ones. He was a massive, weather-beaten man, who looked very like Ann in some ways and would have looked more like her but for the misfortune of having had some of his face clawed away by an irritable jaguar with whom he had had a difference some years back in the jungles of Peru.

'Do you like this sort of thing?' he asked.

'I don't mind it,' said Ann.

'Well, I shall be very sorry to leave you, Ann, but I'm glad I'm pulling out of here this evening. Who are all these people?'

Ann surveyed the gathering.

'That's Ernest Wisden, the playwright, over there, talking to Lora Delane Porter, the feminist writer. That's Clara What's-Her-Name, the sculptor, with the bobbed hair. Next to her—'

Mr Chester cut short the catalogue with a stifled yawn.

'Where's old Pete? Doesn't he come to these jamborees?'

Ann laughed.

'Poor Uncle Peter! If he gets back from the office before these people leave he will sneak up to his room and stay there till it's safe to come out. The last time I made him come to one of these parties he was pounced on by a woman who talked to him for an hour about the morality of finance and seemed to think that millionaires were the scum of the earth.'

'He never would stand up for himself.' Mr Chester's gaze hovered about the room and paused. 'Who's that fellow? I believe I've seen him before somewhere.'

A constant eddying swirl was animating the multitude. Wherever the mass tended to congeal something always seemed to stir it up again. This was due to the restless activity of Mrs Pett, who held it to be the duty of a good hostess to keep her guests moving. From the moment when the room began to fill till the moment when it began to empty she did not cease to plough her way to and fro in a manner equally reminiscent of a hawk swooping on chickens and an earnest collegian bucking the line. Her guests were as a result perpetually forming new *ententes* and combinations, finding themselves bumped about like those little moving figures which one sees in shop windows on Broadway, which revolve on a metal disc until urged by impact with another little figure they scatter to regroup themselves elsewhere. It was a fascinating feature of Mrs Pett's at-homes and one that assisted that mental broadening process already alluded to, that one never knew, when listening to a discussion on the sincerity of Oscar Wilde, whether it would not suddenly change in the middle of a sentence to an argument on the inner meaning of the Russian Ballet.

Plunging now into a group dominated for the moment by an angular woman who was saying loud and penetrating things about the suffrage, Mrs Pett had seized and removed a tall blond young man with a mild, vacuous face. For the past few minutes this young man had been sitting bolt upright on a chair with his hands on his knees, so exactly in the manner of an end-man at a minstrel show that one would hardly have been surprised had he burst into song or asked a conundrum.

Ann followed her father's gaze.

'Do you mean the man talking to Aunt Nesta? There, they've gone over to speak to Willie Partridge. Do you mean that one?'

'Yes. Who is he?'

'Well, I like that!' said Ann, 'considering that you introduced him to us! That's Lord Wisbeach, who came to Uncle Peter with a letter of introduction from you. You met him in Canada.'

'I remember now, I ran across him in British Columbia. We camped together one night. I'd never seen him before and I didn't see him again. He said he wanted a letter to old Peter for some reason, so I scribbled him one in pencil on the back of an envelope. I've never met anyone who played a better game of draw poker. He cleaned me out. There's a lot in that fellow, in spite of his looking like a musical comedy dude. He's clever.'

Ann looked at him meditatively.

'It's odd that you should be discovering hidden virtues in Lord Wisbeach, Father. I've been trying to make up my mind about him. He wants me to marry him.'

'He does! I suppose a good many of these young fellows here want the same thing, don't they, Ann?' Mr Chester looked at his daughter with interest. Her growing up and becoming a beauty had always been a perplexity to him. He could never rid himself of the impression of her as a long-legged child in short skirts. 'I suppose you're refusing them all the time?'

'Every day from ten to four, with an hour off for lunch. I keep regular office hours. Admission on presentation of visiting-card.'

'And how do you feel about this Lord Wisbeach?'

'I don't know,' said Ann frankly. 'He's very nice. And – what is more important – he's different. Most of the men I know are all turned out of the same mould. Lord Wisbeach, and one other man, are the only two I've met who might not be the brothers of all the rest.'

'Who is the other?'

'A man I hardly know. I met him on board ship.' Mr Chester looked at his watch.

'It's up to you, Ann,' he said. 'There's one comfort in being your father – I don't mean that exactly, I mean that it is a comfort to me as your father to know that I need feel no paternal anxiety about you. I don't have to give you advice. You've not only got three times the sense that I have, but you're not the sort of girl who would take advice. You've always known just what you wanted ever since you were a kid. Well, if you're going to take me down to the boat we'd better be starting. Where's the car?'

'Waiting outside. Aren't you going to say goodbye to Aunt Nesta?'

'What! Plunge into that pack of coyotes and fight my way through to her!' exclaimed Mr Chester in honest concern. 'I'd be torn to pieces by wild poets. Besides, it seems silly to make a fuss saying good-bye when I'm only going to be away a short time. I shan't go any farther than Columbia this trip.'

'You'll be able to run back for week-ends,' said Ann.

She paused at the door to cast a fleeting glance over her shoulder at the fair-haired Lord Wisbeach, who was now in animated conversation with her aunt and Willie Partridge, then she followed her father down the stairs. She was a little thoughtful as she took her place at the wheel of her automobile. It was not often that her independent nature craved outside support, but she was half-conscious of wishing at the present juncture that she possessed a somewhat less casual father. She would have liked to ask him to help her decide a problem which had been vexing her for nearly three weeks now, ever since Lord Wisbeach had asked her to marry him and she had promised to give him his answer on her return from England. She had been back in New York several days now, but she had not been able to make up her mind. This annoyed her, for she was a girl who liked swift decisiveness of thought and action both in others and in herself. She was fond of Mr Chester in much the same unemotional, detached way that he was fond of her but she was perfectly well aware of the futility of expecting counsel from him.

She said good-bye to him at the boat, fussed over his comfort for a while in a motherly way, and then drove slowly back. For the first time in her life she was feeling uncertain of herself. When she had left for England she had practically made up her mind to accept Lord Wisbeach, and had only deferred actual acceptance of him because in her cool way she wished to re-examine the position at her leisure. Second thoughts had brought no revulsion of feeling. She had not wavered until her arrival in New York. Then, for some reason which baffled her, the idea of marrying Lord Wisbeach had become vaguely distasteful. And now she found herself fluctuating between this mood and her former one.

She reached the house on Riverside Drive, but did not slacken the speed of the machine. She knew that Lord Wisbeach would be waiting for her there, and she did not wish to meet him just yet. She wanted to be alone. She was feeling depressed. She wondered if this was because she had just parted from her father, and decided that it was. His swift entrances into and exits from her life always left her temporarily restless. She drove on up the river. She meant to decide her problem one way or the other before she returned home.

Lord Wisbeach, meanwhile, was talking to Mrs Pett and Willie, its inventor, about Partridgite. Willie, on hearing himself addressed, had turned slowly with an air of absent self-importance, the air of a great thinker disturbed in mid-thought. He always looked like that when spoken to, and there were those – Mr Pett belonged to this school of thought – who held that there was nothing to him beyond that look, and that he had built up his reputation as a budding master-mind on a foundation that consisted entirely of a vacant eye, a mop of hair through which he could run his fingers, and the fame of his late father.

Willie Partridge was the son of the undeniably great inventor, Dwight Partridge, and it was generally understood that the explosive, Partridgite, was to be the result of a continu-ation of experiments which his father had been working upon at the time of his death. That Dwight Partridge had been trying experiments in the direction of a new and powerful explosive during the last year of his life was common knowledge in those circles which are interested in such things. Foreign governments were understood to have made tentative overtures to him. But a sudden illness, ending fatally, had finished the budding career of Partridgite abruptly, and the world had thought no more of it until an interview in the *Sunday Chronicle*, that storehouse of information about interesting people, announced that Willie was carrying on his father's experiments at the point where he had left off. Since then there had been vague rumours of possible sensational developments, which Willie had neither denied nor confirmed. He preserved the mysterious silence which went so well with his appearance.

Having turned slowly so that his eyes rested on Lord Wisbeach's ingenuous countenance, Willie paused, and his face assumed the expression of his photograph in the *Chronicle*.

'Ah, Wisbeach!' he said.

Lord Wisbeach did not appear to resent the patronage of his manner. He plunged cheerily into talk. He had a pleasant, simple way of comporting himself which made people like him.

'I was just telling Mrs Pett,' he said, 'that I shouldn't be surprised if you were to get an offer for your stuff from our fellows at home before long. I saw a lot of our War Office men when I was in England, don't you know. Several of them mentioned the stuff.'

Willie resented Partridgite being referred to as 'the stuff', but he made allowances. All Englishmen talked that way, he supposed.

'Indeed?' he said.

'Of course,' said Mrs Pett, 'Willie is a patriot and would have to give our own authorities the first chance—'

'Rather!'

'But you know what officials are all over the world. They are so sceptical and they move so slowly.'

'I know. Our men at home are just the same, as a rule. I've got a pal who invented something-or-other, I forget what, but it was a most decent little contrivance and very useful and all that, and he simply can't get them to say Yes or No about it. But, all the same, I wonder you didn't have some of them trying to put out feelers to you when you were in London.'

'Oh, we were only in London a few hours. By the way, Lord Wisbeach, my sister' – Mrs Pett paused. She disliked to have to mention her sister or to refer to this subject at all, but curiosity impelled her – 'my sister said that you are a great friend of her stepson, James Crocker. I didn't know that you knew him.'

Lord Wisbeach seemed to hesitate for a moment.

'He's not coming over, is he? Pity! It would have done him a world of good. Yes, Jimmy Crocker and I have always been great pals. He's a bit of a nut, of course – I beg your pardon! I mean—' He broke off confusedly, and turned to Willie again to cover himself. 'How are you getting on with the jolly old stuff?' he asked.

If Willie had objected to Partridgite being called 'the stuff', he was still less in favour of its being termed 'the jolly old stuff'. He replied coldly:

'I have ceased to get along with the jolly old stuff.'

'Struck a snag?' inquired Lord Wisbeach sympathetically.

'On the contrary, my experiments have been entirely successful. I have enough Partridgite in my laboratory to blow New York to bits!'

'Willie!' exclaimed Mrs Pett. 'Why didn't you tell me before? You know I am so interested.'

'I only completed my work last night.'

He moved off with an important nod. He was tired of Lord Wisbeach's society. There was something about the young man which he did not like. He went to find more congenial company in a group by the window.

Lord Wisbeach turned to his hostess. The vacuous expression had dropped from his face like a mask. A pair of keen and intelligent eyes met Mrs Pett's.

'Mrs Pett, may I speak to you seriously?'

Mrs Pett's surprise at the alteration in the man prevented her from replying. Much as she liked Lord Wisbeach, she had never given him credit for brains, and it was a man with brains and keen ones who was looking at her now. She nodded.

'If your nephew has really succeeded in his experiments you should be awfully careful. That stuff ought not to lie about in his laboratory, though no doubt he has hidden it as carefully as possible. It ought to be in a safe somewhere – in that safe in your library. News of this kind moves like lightning. At this very moment there may be people watching for a chance of getting at the stuff.'

Every nerve in Mrs Pett's body, every cell of a brain which had for years been absorbing and giving out sensational fiction, quivered irrepressibly at these words, spoken in a low tense voice which gave them additional emphasis. Never had she misjudged a man as she had misjudged Lord Wisbeach.

'Spies?' she quavered.

'They wouldn't call themselves that,' said Lord Wisbeach. 'Secret Service agents. Every country has its men whose only duty it is to handle this sort of work.'

'They would try to steal Willie's—' Mrs Pett's voice failed.

'They would not look on it as stealing. Their motives would be patriotic. I tell you, Mrs Pett, I have heard stories from friends of mine in the English Secret Service which would amaze you. Perfectly straight men in private life, but absolutely unscrupulous when at work. They stick at nothing – nothing. If I were you I should suspect everyone, especially every stranger.' He smiled engagingly. 'You are thinking that is odd advice from one like myself who is practically a stranger. Never mind. Suspect me, too, if you like. Be on the safe side.'

'I would not dream of doing such a thing, Lord Wisbeach,' said Mrs Pett, horrified. 'I trust you implicitly. Even supposing such a thing were possible, would you have warned me like this if you had been—'

'That's true,' said Lord Wisbeach. 'I never thought of that. Well, let me say, suspect everybody but me.' He stopped abruptly. 'Mrs Pett,' he whispered, 'don't look round for a moment. Wait.' The words were almost inaudible. 'Who is that man behind you? He has been listening to us. Turn slowly.'

With elaborate carelessness Mrs Pett turned her head. At first she thought her companion must have alluded to one of a small group of young men who, very improperly in such sur-roundings, were discussing with raised voices the prospects of the clubs competing for the National League Baseball Pennant. Then, extending the sweep of her gaze, she saw that she had been mistaken. Midway between her and this group stood a single figure, the figure of a stout man in a swallow-tail suit, who bore before him a tray with cups on it. As she turned this man caught her eye, gave a guilty start and hurried across the room.

'You saw?' said Lord Wisbeach. 'He was listening. Who is that man? Your butler apparently. What do you know of him?'

'He is my new butler. His name is Skinner.'

'Ah, your new butler? He hasn't been with you long then?'

'He arrived from England only three days ago.'

'From England? How did he get in here? I mean, on whose recommendation?'

'Mr Pett offered him the place when we met him at my sister's in London. We went over there to see my sister Eugenia – Mrs Crocker. This man was the butler who admitted us. He asked Mr Pett something about baseball, and Mr Pett was so pleased that he offered him a place here if he wanted to come over. The man did not give any definite answer then, but apparently he sailed on the next boat, and came to the house a few days after we had returned.'

Lord Wisbeach laughed softly.

'Very smart. Of course they had him planted there for the purpose.'

'What ought I to do?' asked Mrs Pett agitatedly.

'Do nothing. There is nothing that you can do, for the present, except keep your eyes open. Watch this man Skinner. See if he has any accomplices. It is hardly likely that he is working alone. Suspect everybody. Believe me—'

At this moment, apparently from some upper region, there burst forth an uproar so sudden and overwhelming that it might well have been taken for a premature testing of a large sample of Partridgite, until a moment later it began to resemble more nearly the shrieks of some partially destroyed victim of that death-dealing invention. It was a bellow of anguish, and it poured through the house in a cascade of sound, advertising to all beneath the roof the twin facts that some person unknown was suffering, and that whoever the sufferer might be he had excellent lungs.

The effect on the gathering in the drawing-room was immediate and impressive. Conversation ceased as if it had been turned off with a tap. Twelve separate and distinct discussions on twelve highly intellectual topics died instantaneously. It was as if the last trump had sounded. Futurist painters stared pallidly at *vers libre* poets, speech smitten from their lips, and stage reformers looked at esoteric Buddhists with a wild surmise.

The sudden silence had the effect of emphasizing the strange noise and rendering it more distinct, thus enabling it to carry its message to one at least of the listeners. Mrs Pett, after a moment of strained attention in which time seemed to her to stand still, uttered a wailing cry and leaped for the door.

'Ogden!' she shrilled; and passed up the stairs two at a time, gathering speed as she went. A boy's best friend is his mother.

CHAPTER 10

While the feast of reason and flow of soul had been in progress in the drawing-room, in the gymnasium on the top floor Jerry Mitchell, awaiting the coming of Mr Pett, had been passing the time in improving with strenuous exercise his already impressive physique. If Mrs Pett's guests had been less noisily concentrated on their conversation they might have heard the muffled tap-tap-tap that proclaimed that Jerry Mitchell was punching the bag upstairs.

It was not till he had punched it for perhaps five minutes that, desisting from his labours, he perceived that he had the pleasure of the company of little Ogden Ford. The stout boy was standing in the doorway, observing him with an attentive eye.

'What are you doing?' inquired Ogden.

Jerry passed a gloved fist over his damp brow.

'Punchin' the bag.'

He began to remove his gloves, eyeing Ogden the while with a disapproval which he made no attempt to conceal. An extremist on the subject of keeping in condition, the spectacle of the bulbous stripling was a constant offence to him. Ogden, in pursuance of his invariable custom on the days when Mrs Pett entertained, had been lurking on the stairs outside the drawing-room for the past hour, levying toll on the foodstuffs that passed his way. He wore a congested look, and there was jam about his mouth.

'Why?' he said, retrieving a morsel of jam from his right cheek with the tip of his tongue.

'To keep in condition.'

'Why do you want to keep in condition?'

Jerry flung the gloves into their locker.

'Fade!' he said wearily. 'Fade!'

'Huh?'

'Beat it!'

'Huh?' Much pastry seemed to have clouded the boy's mind.

'Run away!'

'Don't want to run away.'

The annoyed pugilist sat down and scrutinized his visitor critically.

'You never do anything you don't want to, I guess?'

'No,' said Ogden simply. 'You've got a funny nose,' he added dispassionately. 'What did you do to it to make it like that?'

Mr Mitchell shifted restlessly on his chair. He was not a vain man, but he was a little sensitive about that particular item in his make-up.

'Lizzie says it's the funniest nose she ever saw. She says it's like something out of a comic supplement.'

A dull flush, such as five minutes with the bag had been unable to produce, appeared on Jerry Mitchell's peculiar countenance. It was not that he looked on Lizzie Murphy, herself no Lilian Russell, as an accepted authority on the subject of facial beauty; but he was aware that in this instance she spoke not without reason, and he was vexed, moreover, as many another had been before him, by the note of indulgent patronage in

Ogden's voice. His fingers twitched a little eagerly, and he looked sullenly at his tactless junior.

'Get out!'

'Huh?'

'Get outa here!'

'Don't want to get out of here,' said Ogden with finality. He put his hand in his trousers pocket and pulled out a sticky mass which looked as if it might once have been a cream puff or a meringue. He swallowed it contentedly. 'I'd forgotten I had that,' he explained. 'Mary gave it to me on the stairs. Mary thinks you've a funny nose too,' he proceeded, as one relating agreeable gossip.

'Can it! Can it!' exclaimed the exasperated pugilist.

'I'm only telling you what I heard her say.'

Mr Mitchell rose convulsively and took a step toward his persecutor, breathing noisily through the criticized organ. He was a chivalrous man, a warm admirer of the sex, but he was conscious of a wish that it was in his power to give Mary what he would have described as 'hers'. She was one of the parlour-maids, a homely woman with a hard eye, and it was part of his grievance against her that his Maggie, alias Celestine, Mrs Pett's maid, had formed an enthusiastic friendship with her. He had no evidence to go on, but he suspected Mary of using her influence with Celestine to urge the suit of his leading rival for the latter's hand, Biggs the chauffeur. He disliked Mary intensely even on general grounds. Ogden's revelation added fuel to his aversion. For a moment he toyed with the fascinating thought of relieving his feelings by spanking the boy, but restrained himself reluctantly at the thought of the inevitable ruin which would ensue. He had been an inmate of the house long enough to know, with a completeness which would have embarrassed that gentleman, what a cipher Mr Pett was in the home and how little his championship would avail in the event of a clash with Mrs Pett. And to give Ogden that physical treatment which should long since have formed the main plank in the platform of his education would be to invite her wrath as nothing else could. He checked himself and reached out for the skipping rope, hoping to ease his mind by further exercise.

Ogden, chewing the remains of the cream puff, eyed him with languid curiosity.

'What are you doing that for?'

Mr Mitchell skipped grimly on.

'What are you doing that for? I thought only girls skipped.'

Mr Mitchell paid no heed. Ogden, after a moment's silent contemplation, returned to his original train of thought.

'I saw an advertisement in a magazine the other day of a sort of machine for altering the shape of noses. You strap it on when you go to bed. You ought to get Pop to blow you to one.'

Jerry Mitchell breathed in a laboured way.

'You want to look nice about the face, don't you? Well, then! There's no sense in going round looking like that if you don't have to, is there? I heard Mary talking about your nose to Biggs and Celestine. She said she had to laugh every time she saw it.'

The skipping rope faltered in its sweep, caught in the skipper's legs, and sent him staggering across the room. Ogden threw back his head and laughed merrily. He liked free entertainments, and this struck him as a particularly enjoyable one.

There are moments in the life of every man when the impulse attacks him to sacrifice his future to the alluring gratification of the present. The strong man resists such impulses. Jerry Mitchell was not a weak man, but he had been sorely tried.

The annoyance of Ogden's presence and conversation had sapped his self-restraint as dripping water will wear away a rock. A short while before he had fought down the urgent temptation to massacre this exasperating child, but now, despised love adding its sting to that of injured vanity, he forgot the consequences. Bounding across the room he seized Ogden in a powerful grip, and the next instant the latter's education – in the true sense of the word so long postponed – had begun, and with it that avalanche of sound which, rolling down into the drawing-room, hurled Mrs Pett so violently and with such abruptness from the society of her guests.

Disposing of the last flight of stairs with the agility of the chamois which leaps from crag to crag of the snow-topped Alps, Mrs Pett finished with a fine burst of speed along the passage on the top floor, and rushed into the gymnasium just as Jerry's avenging hand was descending for the eleventh time.

CHAPTER 11

It was less than a quarter of an hour later – such was the speed
with which Nemesis, usually slow, had overtaken him – that
Jerry Mitchell, carrying a grip and walking dejectedly, emerged
from the back premises of the Pett home and started down
Riverside Drive in the direction of his boarding house, a
cheap, clean and respectable establishment situated on Ninety-
seventh Street between the drive and Broadway. His usually
placid nervous system was ruffled and aquiver from the events
of the afternoon, and his cauliflower ears still burned reminis-
cently at the recollection of the uncomplimentary words shot at
them by Mrs Pett before she expelled him from the house.

Moreover, he was in a mild panic at the thought of having to
see Ann later on and try to explain the disaster to her. He knew
how the news would affect her. She had set her heart on removing Ogden to more disciplinary surroundings, and she could not
possibly do it now that her ally was no longer an inmate of the
house. He was an essential factor in the scheme, and now, to
gratify the desire of the moment, he had eliminated himself.
Long before he reached the brownstone house which looked
exactly like all the other brownstone houses in all the other side
streets of uptown New York the first fine careless rapture of his
mad outbreak had passed from Jerry Mitchell, leaving nervous

apprehension in its place. Ann was a girl whom he worshipped respectfully, but he feared her in her wrath.

Having entered the boarding house, Jerry, seeking company in his hour of sorrow, climbed the stairs till he reached a door on the second floor. Sniffing and detecting the odour of tobacco, he knocked, and was bidden to enter.

'Hello, Bayliss!' he said sadly, having obeyed the call.

He sat down on the end of the bed and heaved a deep sigh.

The room which he had entered was airy but small, so small, indeed, that the presence of any furniture in it at all was almost miraculous, for at first sight it seemed incredible that the bed did not fill it from side to side. There were, however, a few vacant spots, and in these had been placed a washstand, a chest of drawers and a midget rocking-chair. The window, which the thoughtful architect had designed at least three sizes too large for the room and which admitted the evening air in pleasing profusion, looked out on to a series of forlorn backyards. In boarding houses it is only the windows of the rich and haughty that face the street.

On the bed, a corncob pipe between his teeth, lay Jimmy Crocker. He was shoeless and in his shirt sleeves. There was a crumpled evening paper on the floor beside the bed. He seemed to be taking his rest after the labours of a trying day.

At the sound of Jerry's sigh he raised his head, but, finding the attitude too severe a strain on the muscles of the neck, restored it to the pillow.

'What's the matter, Jerry? You seem perturbed. You have the aspect of one whom Fate has smitten in the spiritual solar plexus, or of one who has been searching for the leak in life's gaspipe with a lighted candle. What's wrong?'

'Curtains!'

Jimmy, through long absence from his native land, was not always able to follow Jerry's thoughts when concealed in the wrappings of the peculiar dialect which he affected.

'I get you not, friend. Supply a few footnotes.'

'I've been fired.'

Jimmy sat up. This was no imaginary trouble, no mere *malaise* of the temperament. It was concrete, and called for sympathy.

'I'm awfully sorry,' he said. 'No wonder you aren't rollicking. How did it happen?'

'That half-portion Bill Taft came joshing me about my beezer till it got something fierce,' explained Jerry. 'William J. Bryan couldn't have stood for it.'

Once again Jimmy lost the thread. The wealth of political allusion baffled him.

'What's Taft been doing to you?'

'It wasn't Taft. He only looks like him. It was that kid Ogden up where I work. He came butting into the gym, joshing me about – makin' pers'nal remarks till I kind of lost my goat, and the next thing I knew I was giving him his!' A faint gleam of pleasure lightened the gloom of his face. 'I cert'nly give him his!' The gleam faded. 'And after that – well, here I am!'

Jimmy understood now. He had come to the boarding house the night of his meeting with Jerry Mitchell on Broadway, and had been there ever since, and frequent conversations with the pugilist had put him abreast of affairs at the Pett home. He was familiar with the personnel of the establishment on Riverside Drive, and knew precisely how great was the crime of administering correction to Ogden Ford, no matter what the cause. Nor did he require explanation of the phenomenon of Mrs Pett dismissing one who was in her husband's private employment. Jerry had his sympathy freely.

'You appear,' he said, 'to have acted in a thoroughly capable and praiseworthy manner. The only point in your conduct that I would permit myself to criticize is your omission to slay the kid. That, however, was due, I take it, to the fact that you were interrupted. We will now proceed to examine the future. I cannot see that it is altogether murky. You have lost a good job, but there are others equally good for a man of your calibre. New York is crammed with dyspeptic millionaires who need an efficient physical instructor to look after them. Cheer up, Cuthbert, for the sun is still shining!'

Jerry Mitchell shook his head. He refused to be comforted.

'It's Miss Ann,' he said. 'What am I going to say to her?'

'What has she got to do with it?' asked Jimmy, interested.

For a moment Jerry hesitated, but the desire for sympathy and advice was too strong for him. And after all there was no harm in confiding in a good comrade like Jimmy.

'It's like this,' he said. 'Miss Ann and me had got it all fixed up to kidnap the kid!'

'What!'

'Say, I don't mean ordinary kidnapping. It's this way. Miss Ann come to me and we agree that the kid's a pest that had ought to have some strong arm keep him in order, so we decide to get him away to a friend of mine who keeps a dogs' hospital down on Long Island. Bud Smithers is the guy to handle that kid. You ought to see him take hold of a dog that's all grouch and ugliness and make it over into a dog that it's a pleasure to have round. I thought a few weeks with Bud was what the doctor ordered for Ogden, and Miss Ann guessed I was right, so we had it all framed. And now this happens and balls everything up! She can't do nothing with a husky kid like that without me to help her. And how am I going to help her if I'm not allowed in the house?'

Jimmy was conscious of a renewed admiration for a girl whom he had always considered a queen among women. How rarely in this world did one find a girl who combined every feminine charm of mind and body with a resolute determination to raise Cain at the slightest provocation!

'What an absolutely corking idea!'

Jerry smirked modestly at the approbation, but returned instantly to his gloom.

'You get me now? What am I to say to her? She'll be sore!'

'The problem,' Jimmy had begun, 'is one which, as you suggest, presents certain—' when there was a knock at the door, and the head of the boarding house's maid of all works popped in.

'Mr Bayliss, is Mr Mitchell— Oh, say, Mr Mitchell, there's a lady down below to see you. Says her name's Chester.'

Jerry looked at Jimmy appealingly.

'What'll I do?'

'Do nothing,' said Jimmy, rising and reaching for his shoes. 'I'll go down and see her. I can explain for you.'

'It's mighty good of you—'

'It will be a pleasure. Rely on me.'

Ann, who had returned from her drive shortly after the Ogden disaster and had instantly proceeded to the boarding house, had been shown into the parlour. Jimmy found her staring in a rapt way at a statuette of the Infant Samuel that stood near a bowl of wax fruit on the mantelpiece. She was feeling aggrieved with Fate and extremely angry with Jerry Mitchell, and she turned at the sound of the opening door with a militant expression in her eyes, which changed to one of astonishment on perceiving who it was that had come in.

'Mr Bayliss!'

'Good evening, Miss Chester. We, so to speak, meet again. I have come as an intermediary. To be brief, Jerry Mitchell didn't dare face you, so I offered to come down instead.'

'But how – but why are you here?'

'I live here.' He followed her gaze. It rested on a picture of cows in a field. 'Late American school,' he said. 'Attributed to the landlady's niece, a graduate of the Wissahickon, PA, Correspondence School of Pictorial Art. Said to be genuine.'

'You live here?' repeated Ann. She had been brought up all her life among the carefully thought-out effects of eminent interior decorators, and the room seemed more dreadful to her than it actually was. 'What an awful room!'

'Awful? You must be overlooking the piano. Can't you see the handsome plush cover from where you are standing? Move a little to the south-east and shade your eyes. We get music here of an evening – when we don't see it coming and side-step.'

'Why in the name of goodness do you live here, Mr Bayliss?'

'Because, Miss Chester, I am infernally hard up! Because the Bayliss bank roll has been stricken with a wasting sickness.'

Ann was looking at him incredulously.

'But – but – then did you really mean all that at lunch the other day? I thought you were joking. I took it for granted that you could get work whenever you wanted to or you wouldn't have made fun of it like that! Can't you really find anything to do?'

'Plenty to do. But I'm not paid for it. I walk a great number of blocks and jump into a great number of cars and dive into elevators and dive out again and open doors and say "Good morning!" when people tell me they haven't a job for me. My days are quite full – but my pocket-book isn't!'

Ann had forgotten all about her errand in her sympathy.

'I'm so sorry. Why, it's terrible! I should have thought you could have found something.'

'I thought the same till the employers of New York in a body told me I couldn't. Men of widely differing views on religion, politics and a hundred other points were unanimous on that. The nearest I came to being a financial Titan was when I landed a job in a store on Broadway, demonstrating a patent collar-clip at ten dollars a week. For a while all Nature seemed to be shouting: "Ten per! Ten per!" than which there are few sweeter words in the language. But I was fired half-way through the second day, and Nature changed her act.'

'But why?'

'It wasn't my fault. Just Fate. This contrivance was called Klipstone's Kute Kollar-Klip, and it was supposed to make it easy for you to fasten your tie. My job was to stand in the window in my shirt sleeves, gnashing my teeth and registering baffled rage when I tried the old, obsolete method, and beaming on the multitude when I used the Klip. Unfortunately I got the cards mixed. I beamed when I tried the old obsolete method, and nearly burst myself with baffled fury just after I had exhibited the card bearing the words "I will now try Klipstone's Kute Klip." I couldn't think what the vast crowd outside the window was laughing at till the boss, who chanced to pause on the outskirts of the gathering on his way back from lunch, was good enough to tell me. Nothing that I could say would convince him that I was not being intentionally humorous. I was sorry to lose the job, though it did make me feel like a goldfish. But talking of being fired brings us back to Jerry Mitchell.'

'Oh, never mind Jerry Mitchell now—'

'On the contrary, let us discuss his case and the points arising from it with care and concentration. Jerry Mitchell has told me all!'

Ann was startled.

'What do you mean?'

'The word "all",' said Jimmy, 'is slang for "everything". You see in me a confidant. In a word, I am hep.'

'You know—'

'Everything. A colloquialism,' explained Jimmy, 'for "all". About Ogden, you know. The scheme. The plot. The enterprise.'

Ann found nothing to say.

'I am thoroughly in favour of the plan. So much so that I propose to assist you by taking Jerry's place.'

'I don't understand.'

'Do you remember at lunch that day, after that remarkable person had mistaken me for Jimmy Crocker, you suggested in a light, casual way that if I were to walk into your uncle's office and claim to be Jimmy Crocker I should be welcomed without a question? I'm going to do it. Then, once aboard the lugger – once in the house – I am at your orders. Use me exactly as you would have used Jerry Mitchell.'

'But – but—'

'Jerry!' said Jimmy scornfully. 'Can't I do everything that he could have done? And more. A bonehead like Jerry would have been certain to have bungled the thing somehow. I know him well. A good fellow, but in matters requiring intellect and swift thought dead from the neck up. It's a very lucky thing he is out of the running. I love him like a brother, but his dome is of ivory. This job requires a man of tact, sense, shrewdness, initiative, *esprit* and *verve*.' He paused. 'Me!' he concluded.

'But it's ridiculous! It's out of the question!'

'Not at all. I must be extraordinarily like Jimmy Crocker, or that fellow at the restaurant wouldn't have taken me for him. Leave this in my hands. I can get away with it.'

'I shan't dream of allowing you—'

'At nine o'clock to-morrow morning,' said Jimmy firmly, 'I present myself at Mr Pett's office. It's all settled.'

Ann was silent. She was endeavouring to adjust her mind to the idea. Her first startled revulsion from it had begun to wane. It was an idea peculiarly suited to her temperament, an idea that she might have suggested herself if she had thought of it. Soon, from being disapproving, she found herself glowing with admiration for its author. He was a young man of her own sort!

'You asked me on the boat, if you remember,' said Jimmy, 'if I had an adventurous soul. I am now submitting my proofs. You also spoke highly of America as a land where there were adventures to be had. I now see that you were right.'

Ann thought for a moment.

'If I consent to your doing this insane thing, Mr Bayliss, will you promise me something?'

'Anything.'

'Well, in the first place I absolutely refuse to let you risk all sorts of frightful things by coming into this kidnapping plot.' She waved him down and went on. 'But I see where you can help me very much. As I told you at lunch, my aunt would do anything for Jimmy Crocker if he were to appear in New York now. I want you to promise that you confine your activities to asking her to let Jerry Mitchell come back.'

'Never!'

'You said you would promise me anything.'

'Anything but that.'

'Then it is all off!'

Jimmy pondered.

'It's terribly tame that way.'

'Never mind. It's the only way I will consider.'

'Very well. I protest though.'

Ann sat down.

'I think you're splendid, Mr Bayliss. I'm much obliged!'

'Not at all.'

'It will be such a splendid thing for Ogden, won't it?'

'Admirable.'

'Now the only thing to do is just to see that we have got everything straight. How about this, for instance? They will ask you when you arrived in New York. How are you going to account for your delay in coming to see them?'

'I've thought of that. There's a boat that docks to-morrow – the *Caronia*, I think. I've got a paper upstairs. I'll look it up. I can say I came by her.'

'That seems all right. It's lucky you and Uncle Peter never met on the *Atlantic*.'

'And now as to my demeanour on entering the home? How should I behave? Should I be jaunty or humble? What would a long-lost nephew naturally do?'

'A long-lost nephew with a record like Jimmy Crocker's would crawl in with a white flag, I should think.'

A bell clanged in the hall.

'Supper!' said Jimmy. 'To go into painful details, New England boiled dinner, or my senses deceive me, and prunes.'

'I must be going.'

'We shall meet at Philippi.'

He saw her to the door, and stood at the top of the steps watching her trim figure vanish into the dusk. She passed from his sight. Jimmy drew a deep breath, and, thinking hard, went down the passage to fortify himself with supper.

CHAPTER 12

When Jimmy arrived at Mr Pett's office on Pine Street at ten-thirty the next morning – his expressed intention of getting up early enough to be there by nine having proved an empty boast – he was in a high state of preparedness. He had made ready for what might be a trying interview by substituting a combination of well-chosen dishes at an expensive hotel for the less imaginative boarding-house breakfast with which he had of late been insulting his interior. His suit was pressed, his shoes gleamed brightly and his chin was smoothly shaven. These things, combined with the perfection of the morning, and that vague exhilaration which a fine day in down-town New York brings to the man who has not got to work, increased his natural optimism. Something seemed to tell him that all would be well. He would have been the last person to deny that his position was a little complicated – he had to use a pencil and a sheet of paper to show himself just where he stood – but what of that? A few complications in life are an excellent tonic for the brain. It was with a sunny geniality which startled that unaccustomed stripling consider-ably, and indeed caused him to swallow his chewing gum, that he handed in his card to Mr Pett's watchfully waiting office boy.

'This to the boss, my open-faced lad!' he said. 'Get swiftly off the mark.'

The boy departed dumbly.

From where he stood, outside the barrier which separated visitors to the office from the workers within, Jimmy could see a vista of efficient-looking young men with paper protectors round their cuffs working away at mysterious jobs that seemed to involve the use of a great deal of paper. One in particular was so surrounded by it that he had the appearance of a bather in surf. Jimmy eyed these toilers with a comfortable and kindly eye. All this industry made him feel happy. He liked to think of this sort of thing going on all round him.

The office boy returned.

'This way, please.'

The respectfulness of the boy's manner had increased notice-ably. Mr Pett's reception of the visitor's name had impressed him. It was an odd fact that the financier, a cipher in his own home, could impress all sorts of people at the office.

To Mr Pett the announcement that Mr James Crocker was waiting to see him had come like the announcement of a miracle. Not a day had passed since their return to America without lamentations from Mrs Pett on the subject of their failure to secure the young man's person. The occasion of Mrs Pett's reading of the article in the *Sunday Chronicle* descriptive of the Lord Percy Whipple affair had been unique in the little man's domestic history. For the first time since he had known her the indomitable woman had completely broken down. 'Of all sad words of tongue or pen, the saddest are these: "It might have been!"' The thought that, if she had only happened to know it, she had had in her hands during that interview with her sister in London a weapon which would have turned defeat into triumph was more than even Mrs Pett's strong spirit could endure. When she looked back on that scene, and recalled the airy way in which Mrs Crocker had spoken of her stepson's 'best friend, Lord Percy Whipple', and realized that at that very moment Lord Percy had been recovering in bed from the effects of his first meeting with Jimmy Crocker, the iron entered into her soul and she refused to be comforted. In the first instant of realization she thought of six separate and distinct things she could have said to her sister, each more crushing than the last, things that now she would never be able to say.

And now, suddenly and unaccountably, the means was at hand for restoring her to her tranquil self-esteem. Jimmy Crocker, despite what his stepmother had said, probably in active defiance of her commands, had come to America after all. Mr Pett's first thought was that his wife would, as he expressed it to himself, be 'tickled to death about this'. Scarcely waiting for the office boy to retire, he leaped toward Jimmy like a gambolling lamb and slapped him on the back, with every evidence of joy and friendliness.

'My dear boy!' he cried. 'My dear boy! I'm delighted to see you!'

Jimmy was surprised, relieved and pleased. He had not expected this warmth. A civil coldness had been the best he had looked for. He had been given to understand that in the Pett home he was regarded as the black sheep; and, though one may admit a black sheep into the fold, it does not follow that one must of necessity fawn upon him.

'You're very kind,' he said, rather startled.

They inspected each other for a brief moment. Mr Pett was thinking that Jimmy was a great improvement on the picture his imagination had drawn of him. He had looked for something tougher, something flashy and bloated. Jimmy, for his part, had taken an instant liking to the financier. He, too, had been misled by imagination. He had always supposed that these millionaires down Wall Street way were keen, aggressive fellows, with gimlet eyes and sharp tongues. On the boat he had only seen Mr Pett from afar, and had had no means of estimating his character. He found him an agreeable little man.

'We had given up all hope of your coming,' said Mr Pett.

A little manly penitence seemed to Jimmy to be in order.

'I never expected you would receive me like this. I thought I must have made myself rather unpopular.'

Mr Pett buried the past with a gesture.

'When did you land?' he asked.

'This morning. On the *Caronia*.'

'Good passage?'

'Excellent.'

There was a silence. It seemed to Jimmy that Mr Pett was looking at him rather more closely than was necessary for the actual enjoyment of his style of beauty. He was just about to throw out some light remark about the health of Mrs Pett, or something about porpoises on the voyage to add local colour and verisimilitude, when his heart missed a beat, as he perceived that he had made a blunder. Like many other amateur plotters, Ann and he had made the mistake of being too elaborate. It had struck him as an ingenious idea for Jimmy to pretend that he had arrived that morning, and superficially it was a good idea. But he now remembered for the first time that if he had seen Mr Pett on the *Atlantic* the probability was that Mr Pett had seen him. The next moment the other had confirmed this suspicion.

'I've an idea I've seen you before. Can't think where.'

'Everybody well at home?' said Jimmy.

'I'm sure of it.'

'I'm looking forward to seeing them all.'

'I've seen you some place.'

'I'm often there.'

'Eh?'

Mr Pett seemed to be turning this remark over in his mind a trifle suspiciously. Jimmy changed the subject.

'To a young man like myself,' he said, 'with life opening out before him, there is something singularly stimulating in the sight of a modern office. How busy those fellows seem.'

'Yes,' said Mr Pett. 'Yes.' He was glad that this conversational note had been struck. He was anxious to discuss the future with this young man.

'Everybody works but Father!' said Jimmy.

Mr Pett started.

'Eh?'

'Nothing.'

Mr Pett was vaguely ruffled. He suspected insult, but could not pin it down. He abandoned his cheeriness, however, and became the man of business.

'I hope you intend to settle down, now that you are here, and work hard,' he said, in the voice which he vainly tried to use on Ogden at home.

'Work!' said Jimmy blankly.

'I shall be able to make a place for you in my office. That was my promise to your stepmother, and I shall fulfil it.'

'But wait a minute! I don't get this! Do you mean to put me to work?'

'Of course. I take it that that was why you came over here, because you realized how you were wasting your life and wanted a chance of making good in my office.'

A hot denial trembled on Jimmy's tongue. Never had he been so misjudged. And then the thought of Ann checked him. He must do nothing that would interfere with Ann's plans. Whatever the cost, he must conciliate this little man. For a moment he mused sentimentally on Ann. He hoped she would understand what he was going through for her sake. To a man with his ingrained distaste for work in any shape the sight of those wage slaves outside there in the outer office had, as he had told Mr Pett, been stimulating; but only because it filled him with a sort of spiritual uplift to think that he had not got to do that sort of thing. Consider them in the light of fellow-workers, and the spectacle ceased to stimulate and became nauseating. And for her sake he was about to become one of them! Had any knight of old ever done anything as big as that for his lady? He very much doubted it.

'All right,' he said. 'Count me in. I take it that I shall have a job like one of those out there?'

'Yes.'

'Not presuming to dictate, I suggest that you give me something that will take some of the work off that fellow who's swimming in paper. Only the tip of his nose was above the surface as I passed through. I never saw so many fellows working so hard at the same time in my life. All trying to catch the boss's eye, too, I suppose? It must make you feel like a snipe.'

Mr Pett replied stiffly. He disliked this levity on the sacred subject of office work. He considered that Jimmy was not approaching his new life in the proper spirit. Many young men had discussed with him in that room the subject of working in his employment, but none in quite the same manner.

'You are at a serious point in your career,' he said. 'You will have every opportunity of rising.'

'Yes. At seven in the morning, I suppose?'

'A spirit of levity—' began Mr Pett.

'I laugh that I may not weep,' explained Jimmy. 'Try to think what this means to a bright young man who loathes work. Be kind to me. Instruct your floor-walkers to speak gently to me at first. It may be a far, far better thing that I do than I have ever done, but don't ask me to enjoy it! It's all right for you. You're the boss. Any time you want to call it a day and go off and watch a ball game, all you have to do is to leave word that you have an urgent date to see Mr Rockefeller. Whereas I shall have to submerge myself in paper, and only come up for air when the danger of suffocation becomes too great.'

It may have been the mention of his favourite game that softened Mr Pett. The frostiness which had crept into his manner thawed.

'It beats me,' he said, 'why you ever came over at all, if you feel like that.'

'Duty!' said Jimmy. 'Duty! There comes a time in the life of every man when he must choose between what is pleasant and what is right.'

'And that last fool game of yours, that Lord Percy Whipple business, must have made London pretty hot for you?' suggested Mr Pett.

'Your explanation is less romantic than mine, but there is something in what you say.'

'Had it occurred to you, young man, that I am taking a chance putting a fellow like you to work in my office?'

'Have no fear. The little bit of work I shall do won't make any difference.'

'I've half a mind to send you straight back to London.'

'Couldn't we compromise?'

'How?'

'Well, haven't you some snug secretarial job you could put me into? I have an idea that I should make an ideal secretary.'

'My secretaries work.'

'I get you. Cancel the suggestion.'

Mr Pett rubbed his chin thoughtfully.

'You puzzle me. And that's the truth.'

'Always speak the truth,' said Jimmy approvingly.

'I'm darned if I know what to do with you. Well, you'd better come home with me now, anyway, and meet your aunt, and then we can talk things over. After all, the main thing is to keep you out of mischief.'

'You put things crudely, but no doubt you are right.'

'You'll live with us, of course.'

'Thank you very much. This is the right spirit.'

'I'll have to talk to Nesta about you. There may be something you can do.'

'I shouldn't mind being a partner,' suggested Jimmy helpfully.

'Why don't you get work on a paper again? You used to do that well.'

'I don't think my old paper would welcome me now. They regard me rather an entertaining news item than a worker.'

'That's true. Say, why on earth did you make such a fool of yourself over on the other side? That breach-of-promise case with the barmaid!' said Mr Pett reproachfully.

'Let bygones be bygones,' said Jimmy. 'I was more sinned against than sinning. You know how it is, Uncle Pete!' Mr Pett started violently, but said nothing. 'You try out of pure goodness of heart to scatter light and sweetness and protect the poor working-girl and brighten up her lot, and so on, and she turns right round and soaks it to you good! And, anyway, she wasn't a barmaid. She worked in a florist's shop.'

'I don't see that that makes any difference.'

'All the difference in the world, all the difference between the sordid and the poetical. I don't know if you have ever experienced the hypnotic intoxication of a florist's shop? Take it from me, Uncle Pete, any girl can look an angel as long as she is surrounded by choice blooms. I couldn't help myself. I wasn't responsible. I only woke up when I met her outside. But all that sort of thing is different now. I am another man. Sober, steady, serious-minded!'

Mr Pett had taken the receiver from the telephone and was talking to someone. The buzzing of a feminine voice came to Jimmy's ears. Mr Pett hung up the receiver.

'Your aunt says we are to come up at once.'

'I'm ready. And it will be a good excuse for you to knock off work. I bet you're glad I came! Does the carriage wait or shall we take the subway?'

'I guess it will be quicker to take the subway. Your aunt's very surprised that you are here, and very pleased.'

'I'm making everybody happy to-day.'

Mr Pett was looking at him in a meditative way. Jimmy caught his eye.

'You're registering something, Uncle Peter, and I don't know what it is. Why the glance?'

'I was just thinking of something.'

'Jimmy,' prompted his nephew.

'Eh?'

'Add the word Jimmy to your remarks. It will help me to feel at home and enable me to overcome my shyness.'

Mr Pett chuckled.

'Shyness! If I had your nerve—' He broke off with a sigh and looked at Jimmy affectionately. 'What I was thinking was that you're a good boy. At least, you're not, but you're different from that gang of – of – that crowd uptown.'

'What crowd?'

'Your aunt is literary, you know. She's filled the house with poets and that sort of thing. It will be a treat having you round. You're human! I don't see that we're going to make much of you now that you're here, but I'm darned glad you're here, Jimmy!'

'Put it there, Uncle Pete!' said Jimmy. 'You're all right. You're the finest Captain of Industry I ever met!'

CHAPTER 13

Mr Pett and Jimmy Crocker left the subway at Ninety-sixth Street and walked up the drive. Jimmy, like everyone else who saw it for the first time, experienced a slight shock at the sight of the Pett mansion, but, rallying, followed his uncle up the flagged path to the front door.

'Your aunt will be in the drawing-room, I guess,' said Mr Pett, opening the door with his key.

Jimmy was looking round him appreciatively. Mr Pett's house might be an eyesore from without, but inside it had had the benefit of the skill of the best interior decorator in New York.

'A man could be very happy in a house like this, if he didn't have to poison his days with work,' said Jimmy.

Mr Pett looked alarmed.

'Don't go saying anything like that to your aunt!' he urged. 'She thinks you have come to settle down.'

'So I have. I'm going to settle down like a limpet. I hope I shall be living in luxury on you twenty years from now. Is this the room?'

Mr Pett opened the drawing-room door. A small hairy object sprang from a basket and stood yapping in the middle of the room. This was Aïda, Mrs Pett's Pomeranian. Mr Pett, avoiding the animal coldly, for he disliked it, ushered Jimmy into the room.

'Here's Jimmy Crocker, Nesta.'

Jimmy was aware of a handsome woman of middle age, so like his stepmother that for an instant his self-possession left him and he stammered –

'How – how do you do?'

His demeanour made a favourable impression on Mrs Pett. She took it for the decent confusion of remorse.

'I was very surprised when your uncle telephoned me,' she said. 'I had not the slightest idea that you were coming over. I am very glad to see you.'

'Thank you.'

'This is your cousin, Ogden.'

Jimmy perceived a fat boy lying on a settee. He had not risen on Jimmy's entrance, and he did not rise now. He did not even lower the book he was reading.

'Hello,' he said.

Jimmy crossed over to the settee and looked down on him. He had got over his momentary embarrassment, and, as usual with him, the reaction led to a fatal breeziness. He prodded Ogden in his well-covered ribs, producing a yelp of protest from that astonished youth.

'So this is Ogden! Well, well, well! You don't grow up, Ogden, but you do grow out. What are you – a perfect sixty-six?'

The favourable impression which Mrs Pett had formed of her nephew waned. She was shocked by this disrespectful attitude toward the child she worshipped.

'Please do not disturb Ogden, James,' she said stiffly. 'He is not feeling very well to-day. His stomach is weak.'

'Been eating too much?' said Jimmy cheerfully. 'I was just the same at his age. What he wants is half rations and plenty of exercise.'

'Say!' protested Ogden.

'Just look at this,' proceeded Jimmy, grasping a handful of superfluous tissue round the boy's ribs. 'All that ought to come off. I'll tell you what I'll do. I'll buy a pair of flannel trousers and a sweater and some sneakers, and I'll take him for a run up Riverside Drive this evening. Do him no end of good. And a good skipping rope too. Nothing like it. In a couple of weeks I'll have him as fit as a—'

'Ogden's case,' said Mrs Pett coldly, 'which is very complicated, is in the hands of Doctor Briginshaw, in whom we have every confidence.'

There was a silence, the paralysing effects of which Mr Pett vainly tried to mitigate by shuffling his feet and coughing. Mrs Pett spoke:

'I hope that, now that you are here, James, you intend to settle down and work hard.'

'Indubitably. Like a beaver,' said Jimmy, mindful of Mr Pett's recent warning. 'The only trouble is that there seems to be a little uncertainty as to what I am best fitted for. We talked it over in Uncle Pete's office and arrived at no conclusion.'

'Can't you think of anything?' said Mr Pett.

'I looked right through the telephone classified directory the other day—'

'The other day? But you only landed this morning.'

'I mean this morning. When I was looking up your address so that I could go and see you,' said Jimmy glibly. 'It seems a long time ago. I think the sight of all those fellows in your office has aged me. I think the best plan would be for me to settle down here and learn how to be an electrical engineer or something by mail. I was reading an advertisement in a magazine as we came up on the subway. I see they guarantee to teach you anything, from sheet-metal working to poultry raising. The thing began: "You are standing still because you lack training." It seemed to me to apply to my case exactly. I had better drop them a line to-night asking for a few simple facts about chickens.'

Whatever comment Mrs Pett might have made on this suggestion was checked by the entrance of Ann. From the window of her room Ann had observed the arrival of Jimmy and her uncle, and now, having allowed sufficient time to elapse for the former to make Mrs Pett's acquaintance, she came down to see how things were going.

She was well satisfied with what she saw. A slight strain which she perceived in the atmosphere she attributed to embarrassment natural to the situation.

She looked at Jimmy inquiringly. Mrs Pett had not informed her of Mr Pett's telephone call, so Jimmy, she realized, had to be explained to her. She waited for some one to say something.

Mr Pett undertook the introduction.

'Jimmy, this is my niece, Ann Chester. This is Jimmy Crocker, Ann.'

Jimmy could not admire sufficiently the start of surprise which she gave. It was artistic and convincing.

'Jimmy Crocker!'

Mr Pett was on the point of mentioning that this was not the first time Ann had met Jimmy, but refrained. After all, that interview had happened five years ago. Jimmy had almost certainly forgotten all about it. There was no use in making him feel unnecessarily awkward. It was up to Ann. If she wanted to disinter the ancient grievance let her. It was no business of his.

'I thought you weren't coming over!' said Ann.

'I changed my mind.'

Mr Pett, who had been gazing attentively at them, uttered an exclamation.

'I've got it! I've been trying all this while to think where it was I saw you before. It was on the *Atlantic*!'

Ann caught Jimmy's eye. She was relieved to see that he was not disturbed by this sudden development.

'Did you come over on the *Atlantic*, Mr Crocker?' she said. 'Surely not? We crossed on her ourselves. We should have met.'

'Don't call me Mr Crocker,' said Jimmy. 'Call me Jimmy. Your mother's brother's wife's sister's second husband is my father. Blood is thicker than water. No, I came over on the *Caronia*. We docked this morning.'

'Well, there was a fellow just like you on the *Atlantic*,' persisted Mr Pett.

Mrs Pett said nothing. She was watching Jimmy with a keen and suspicious eye.

'I suppose I'm a common type,' said Jimmy.

'You remember the man I mean,' said Mr Pett, innocently unconscious of the unfriendly thoughts he was encouraging in two of his hearers. 'He sat two tables away from us at meals. You remember him, Nesta?'

'As I was too unwell to come to meals, I do not.'

'Why, I thought I saw you once talking to him on deck, Ann.'

'Really?' said Ann. 'I don't remember anyone who looked at all like Jimmy.'

'Well,' said Mr Pett, puzzled, 'it's very strange. I guess I'm wrong.' He looked at his watch. 'Well, I'll have to be getting back to the office.'

'I'll come with you part of the way, Uncle Pete,' said Jimmy. 'I have to go and arrange for my things to be expressed here.'

'Why not phone to the hotel?' said Mr Pett. It seemed to Jimmy and Ann that he was doing this sort of thing on purpose. 'Which hotel did you leave them at?'

'No, I shall have to go there. I have some packing to do.'

'You will be back to lunch?' said Ann.

'Thanks; I shan't be gone more than half an hour.'

For a moment after they had gone Ann relaxed, happy and relieved. Everything had gone splendidly. Then a shock ran through her whole system as Mrs Pett spoke. She spoke excitedly, in a lowered voice, leaning over to Ann.

'Ann, did you notice anything? Did you suspect anything?'

Ann mastered her emotion with an effort.

'Whatever do you mean, Aunt Nesta?'

'About that young man who calls himself Jimmy Crocker.'

Ann clutched the side of the chair.

'Who calls himself Jimmy Crocker? I don't understand.'

Ann tried to laugh. It seemed to her an age before she produced any sound at all, and when it came it was quite unlike a laugh.

'What put that idea into your head? Surely, if he says he is Jimmy Crocker, it's rather absurd to doubt him, isn't it? How could anybody except Jimmy Crocker know that you were anxious to get Jimmy Crocker over here? You didn't tell anyone, did you?'

This reasoning shook Mrs Pett a little, but she did not intend to abandon a perfectly good suspicion merely because it began to seem unreasonable.

'They have their spies everywhere,' she said doggedly.

'Who have?'

'The Secret Service people from other countries. Lord Wisbeach was telling me about it yesterday. He said that I ought to suspect everybody. He said that an attempt might be made on Willie's invention at any moment now.'

'He was joking.'

'He was not. I have never seen anyone so serious. He said that I ought to regard every fresh person who came into the house as a possible criminal.'

'Well, that guy's fresh enough,' muttered Ogden from the settee.

Mrs Pett started.

'Ogden! I had forgotten that you were there.' She uttered a cry of horror, as the fact of his presence started a new train of thoughts. 'Why, this man may have come to kidnap you! I never thought of that.'

Ann felt it time to intervene. Mrs Pett was hovering much too near the truth for comfort.

'You mustn't imagine things, Aunt Nesta. I believe it comes from writing the sort of stories you do. Surely it is impossible for this man to be an impostor. How would he dare take such a risk? He must know that you could detect him at any moment by cabling over to Mrs Crocker to ask if her stepson was really in America.'

It was a bold stroke, for it suggested a plan of action which, if followed, would mean ruin for her schemes, but Ann could not refrain from chancing it. She wanted to know whether her aunt had any intention of asking Mrs Crocker for information, or whether the feud was too bitter for her pride to allow her to communicate with her sister in any way. She breathed again as Mrs Pett stiffened grimly in her chair.

'I should not dream of cabling to Eugenia.'

'I quite understand that,' said Ann. 'But an impostor would not know that you felt like that, would he?'

'I see what you mean.'

Ann relaxed again. The relief was, however, only momentary.

'I cannot understand, though,' said Mrs Pett, 'why your uncle should have been so positive that he saw this young man on the *Atlantic*.'

'Just a chance resemblance, I suppose. Why, Uncle Peter said he saw the man who he imagined was like Jimmy Crocker talking to me. If there had been any real resemblance, shouldn't I have seen it before Uncle Peter?'

Assistance came from an unexpected quarter.

'I know the chap Uncle Peter meant,' said Ogden. 'He wasn't like this guy at all.'

Ann was too grateful for the help to feel astonished at it. Her mind, dwelling for a mere instant on the matter, decided that Ogden must have seen her on deck with somebody else than Jimmy. She had certainly not lacked during the voyage for those who sought her society.

Mrs Pett seemed to be impressed.

'I may be letting my imagination run away with me,' she said.

'Of course you are, Aunt Nesta,' said Ann thankfully. 'You don't realize what a vivid imagination you have got. When I was typing that last story of yours I was simply astounded at the ideas you had thought of. I remember saying so to Uncle Peter. You can't expect to have a wonderful imagination like yours and not imagine things, can you?'

Mrs Pett smiled demurely. She looked hopefully at her niece, waiting for more, but Ann had said her say.

'You are perfectly right, my dear child,' she said, when she was quite sure the eulogy was not to be resumed. 'No doubt I have been foolish to suspect this young man. But Lord Wisbeach's words naturally acted more strongly on a mind like mine than they would have done in the case of another woman.'

'Of course,' said Ann.

She was feeling quite happy now. It had been tense while it had lasted, but everything was all right now.

'And fortunately,' said Mrs Pett, 'there is a way by which we can find out for certain if the young man is really James Crocker.'

Ann became rigid again.

'A way? What way?'

'Why, don't you remember, my dear, that Skinner has known James Crocker for years?'

'Skinner?'

The name sounded familiar, but in the stress of the moment Ann could not identify it.

'My new butler. He came to me straight from Eugenia. It was he who let us in when we called at her house. Nobody could know better than he whether this person is really James Crocker or not.'

Ann felt as if she had struggled to the limit of her endurance. She was not prepared to cope with this unexpected blow. She had not the strength to rally under it. Dully she perceived that her schemes must be dismissed as a failure before they had had a chance of success. Her accomplice must not return to the house to be exposed. She saw that clearly enough. If he came back he would walk straight into a trap. She rose quickly. She must warn him. She must intercept him before he arrived, and he might arrive at any moment now.

'Of course,' she said, steadying herself with an effort, 'I never thought of that. That makes it all simple – I hope lunch won't be late. I'm hungry.'

She sauntered to the door, but directly she had closed it behind her ran to her room, snatched up a hat, and rushed downstairs and out into Riverside Drive. Just as she reached the street Jimmy turned the corner. She ran toward him, holding up her hands.

CHAPTER 14

Jimmy halted in his tracks. The apparition had startled him. He had been thinking of Ann, but he had not expected her to bound out at him, waving her arms.

'What's the matter?' he inquired.

Ann pulled him toward a side street.

'You mustn't go to the house. Everything has gone wrong.'

'Everything gone wrong? I thought I had made a hit. I have with your uncle, anyway. We parted on the friendliest terms. We have arranged to go to the ball game together to-morrow. He is going to tell them at the office that Carnegie wants to see him.'

'It isn't Uncle Peter. It's Aunt Nesta.'

'Ah, there you touch my conscience. I was a little tactless, I'm afraid, with Ogden. It happened before you came into the room. I suppose that is the trouble?'

'It has nothing to do with that,' said Ann impatiently. 'It's much worse. Aunt Nesta is suspicious. She has guessed that you aren't really Jimmy Crocker.'

'Great Scott! How?'

'I tried to calm her down, but she still suspects. So now she decided to wait and see if Skinner, the butler, knows you. If he doesn't, she will know that she was right.'

Jimmy was frankly puzzled.

'I don't quite follow the reasoning. Surely it's a peculiar kind of test. Why should she think a man cannot be honest and true unless her butler knows him? There must be hundreds of worthy citizens whom he does not know.'

'Skinner arrived from England a few days ago. Until then he was employed by Mrs Crocker. Now do you understand?'

Jimmy stopped. She had spoken slowly and distinctly, and there could be no possibility that he had misunderstood her, yet he scarcely believed that he had heard her aright. How could a man named Skinner have been his stepmother's butler? Bayliss had been with the family ever since they had arrived in London.

'Are you sure?'

'Of course, of course I'm sure. Aunt Nesta told me herself. There can't possibly be a mistake, because it was Skinner who let her in when she called on Mrs Crocker. Uncle Peter told me about it. He had a talk with the man in the hall and found that he was a baseball enthusiast—'

A wild, impossible idea flashed upon Jimmy. It was so absurd that he felt ashamed of entertaining it even for a moment. But strange things were happening these times, and it might be—

'What sort of looking man is Skinner?'

'Oh, stout, clean-shaven. I like him. He's much more human than I thought butlers ever were. Why?'

'Oh, nothing.'

'Of course you can't go back to the house. You see that? He would say that you aren't Jimmy Crocker and then you would be arrested.'

'I don't see that. If I am sufficiently like Crocker for his friends to mistake me for him in restaurants, why shouldn't this butler mistake me too?'

'But—'

'And, consider. In any case, there's no harm done. If he fails to recognize me when he opens the door to us, we shall know that the game is up, and I shall have plenty of time to disappear. If the likeness deceives him all will be well. I propose that we go to the house, ring the bell, and when he appears, I will say, "Ah, Skinner! Honest fellow!" or words to that effect. He will either stare blankly at me or fawn on me like a faithful watchdog. We will base our further actions on which way the butler jumps.'

The sound of the bell died away. Footsteps were heard. Ann reached for Jimmy's arm and clutched it.

'Now!' she whispered.

The door opened. Next moment Jimmy's suspicion was confirmed. Gaping at them from the open doorway, wonderfully respectable and butler-like in swallow-tails, stood his father. How he came to be there and why he was there Jimmy did not know. But there he was.

Jimmy had little faith in his father's talents as a man of discretion. The elder Crocker was one of those simple, straight-forward people who, when surprised, do not conceal their surprise, and who, not understanding any situation in which they find themselves, demand explanation on the spot. Swift and immediate action was indicated on his part before his amazed parent, finding him on the steps of the one house in New York where he was least likely to be, should utter words that would undo everything. He could see the name Jimmy trembling on Mr Crocker's lips.

He waved his hand cheerily.

'Ah, Skinner, there you are!' he said breezily. 'Miss Chester was telling me that you had left my stepmother. I suppose you sailed on the boat before mine. I came over on the *Caronia*. I suppose you didn't expect to see me again so soon, eh?'

A spasm seemed to pass over Mr Crocker's face, leaving it calm and serene. He had been thrown his cue, and like the old actor he was he took it easily and without confusion. He smiled a respectful smile.

'No, indeed, sir.'

He stepped aside to allow them to enter. Jimmy caught Ann's eye as she passed him. It shone with relief and admiration, and it exhilarated Jimmy like wine. As she moved toward the stairs he gave expression to his satisfaction by slapping his father on the back with a report that rang out like a pistol shot.

'What was that?' said Ann, turning.

'Something out on the drive, I think,' said Jimmy. 'A car back-firing, I fancy, Skinner.'

'Very probably, sir.'

He followed Ann to the stairs. As he started to mount them a faint whisper reached his ears.

"At-a-boy!'

It was Mr Crocker's way of bestowing a father's blessing.

Ann walked into the drawing-room, her head high, triumph in the glance which she cast upon her unconscious aunt.

'Quite an interesting little scene downstairs, Aunt Nesta,' she said. 'The meeting of the faithful old retainer and the young master. Skinner was almost overcome with surprise and joy when he saw Jimmy!'

Mrs Pett could not check an incautious exclamation.

'Did Skinner recognize—' she began, then stopped herself abruptly.

Ann laughed.

'Did he recognize Jimmy? Of course! He was hardly likely to have forgotten him, surely? It isn't much more than a week since he was waiting on him in London.'

'It was a very impressive meeting,' said Jimmy. 'Rather like the reunion of Ulysses and the hound Argos, of which this bright-eyed child here' – he patted Ogden on the head, a proceeding violently resented by that youth – 'has no doubt read in the course of his researches into the classics. I was Ulysses, Skinner enacted the rôle of the exuberant dog.'

Mrs Pett was not sure whether she was relieved or disappointed at this evidence that her suspicions had been without foundation. On the whole, relief may be said to have preponderated.

'I have no doubt he was pleased to see you again. He must have been very much astonished.'

'He was!'

'You will be meeting another old friend in a minute or two,' said Mrs Pett.

Jimmy had been sinking into a chair. This remark stopped him in mid-descent.

'Another!'

Mrs Pett glanced at the clock.

'Lord Wisbeach is coming to lunch.'

'Lord Wisbeach!' cried Ann. 'He doesn't know Jimmy.'

'Eugenia informed me in London that he was one of your best friends, James.'

Ann looked helplessly at Jimmy. She was conscious again of that feeling of not being able to cope with Fate's blows, of not having the strength to go on climbing over the barriers which Fate placed in her path.

Jimmy, for his part, was cursing the ill fortune that had brought Lord Wisbeach across his path. He saw clearly that it only needed recognition by one or two more intimates of Jimmy Crocker to make Ann suspect his real identity. The fact that she had seen him with Bayliss in Paddington Station and had fallen into the error of supposing Bayliss to be his father had kept her from suspecting until now, but this could not last for ever. He remembered Lord Wisbeach well, as a garrulous, irrepressible chatterer who would probably talk about old times to such an extent as to cause Ann to realize the truth in the first five minutes.

The door opened.

'Lord Wisbeach,' announced Mr Crocker.

'I'm afraid I'm late, Mrs Pett,' said his lordship.

'No, you're quite punctual. Lord Wisbeach, here is an old friend of yours, James Crocker.'

There was an almost imperceptible pause. Then Jimmy stepped forward and held out his hand.

'Hello, Wizzy, old man!'

'H-hello, Jimmy!'

Their eyes met. In his lordship's there was an expression of unmistakable relief, mingled with astonishment. His face, which had turned a sickly white, flushed as the blood poured back into it. He had the appearance of a man who has had a bad shock and is just getting over it. Jimmy, eyeing him curiously, was not surprised at his emotion. What the man's game might be he could not say, but of one thing he was sure, which was that this was not Lord Wisbeach but – on the contrary – someone he had never seen before in his life.

'Luncheon is served, madam,' said Mr Crocker sonorously from the doorway.

CHAPTER 15

It was not often that Ann found occasion to rejoice at the presence in her uncle's house of the six geniuses whom Mrs Pett had installed therein. As a rule, she disliked them individually and collectively. But to-day their company was extraordinarily welcome to her. They might have their faults, but at least their presence tended to keep the conversation general and prevent it becoming a duologue between Lord Wisbeach and Jimmy on the subject of old times. She was still feeling weak from the reaction consequent upon the slackening of the tension of her emotions on seeing Lord Wisbeach greet Jimmy as an old acquaintance.

She had never hoped that that barrier would be surmounted. She had pictured Lord Wisbeach drawing back with a puzzled frown on his face and an astonished 'But this is not Jimmy Crocker.' The strain had left her relieved, but in no mood for conversation, and she replied absently to the remarks of Howard Bemis, the poet, who sat on her left. She looked round the table. Willie Partridge was talking to Mrs Pett about the difference between picric acid and trinitrotoluene, than which a pleasanter topic for the luncheon table could hardly be selected, and the voice of Clarence Renshaw rose above all other competing noises, as he spoke of the functions of the trochaic spondee.

There was nothing outwardly to distinguish this meal from any other which she had shared of late in that house.

The only thing that prevented her relief being unmixed was the fact that she could see Lord Wisbeach casting furtive glances at Jimmy, who was eating with the quiet concentration of one who, after days of boarding-house fare, finds himself in the presence of the masterpieces of a chef. In the past few days Jimmy had consumed too much hash to worry now about anything like a furtive glance. He had perceived Lord Wisbeach's roving eye, and had no doubt that at the conclusion of the meal he would find occasion for a little chat. Meanwhile, however, his duty was toward his tissues and their restoration. He helped himself liberally from a dish which his father offered him.

He became aware that Mrs Pett was addressing him.

'I beg your pardon?'

'Quite like old times,' said Mrs Pett genially. Her suspicions had vanished completely since Lord Wisbeach's recognition of the visitor, and remorse that she should have suspected him made her unwontedly amiable. 'Being with Skinner again,' she explained. 'It must remind you of London.'

Jimmy caught his father's expressionless eye.

'Skinner's,' he said handsomely, 'is a character one cannot help but respect. His nature expands before one like some beautiful flower.'

The dish rocked in Mr Crocker's hand, but his face remained impassive.

'There is no vice in Skinner,' proceeded Jimmy. 'His heart is the heart of a little child.'

Mrs Pett looked at this paragon of the virtues in rather a startled way. She had an uncomfortable feeling that she was being laughed at. She began to dislike Jimmy again.

'For many years Skinner has been a father to me,' said Jimmy. 'Who ran to help me when I fell, And would some pretty story tell, Or kiss the place to make it well? Skinner!'

For all her suspense, Ann could not help warming toward an accomplice who carried off an unnerving situation with such a flourish. She had always regarded herself with a fair degree of complacency as possessed of no mean stock of courage and resource, but she could not have spoken then without betraying her anxiety. She thought highly of Jimmy, but all the same she could not help wishing that he would not make himself quite so conspicuous. Perhaps – the thought chilled her – perhaps he was creating quite a new Jimmy Crocker, a character which would cause Skinner and Lord Wisbeach to doubt the evidence of their eyes and begin to suspect the truth. She wished she could warn him to simmer down, but the table was a large one and he and she were at opposite ends of it.

Jimmy, meanwhile, was thoroughly enjoying himself. He felt that he was being the little ray of sunshine about the home and making a good impression. He was completely happy. He liked the food, he liked seeing his father buttle, and he liked these amazing freaks who were, it appeared, fellow-inmates with him of this highly desirable residence. He wished that old Mr Pett could have been present. He had conceived a great affection for Mr Pett, and registered a mental resolve to lose no time in weaning him from his distressing habit of allowing the office to interfere with his pleasures. He was planning a little trip to the Polo Grounds, in which Mr Pett, his father, and a number of pop bottles were to be his companions, when his reverie was interrupted by a sudden cessation of the buzz of talk. He looked up from his plate, to find the entire company regarding Willie Partridge open-mouthed. Willie, with gleaming eyes, was gazing at a small test tube which he had produced from his pocket and placed beside his plate.

'I have enough in this test tube,' said Willie airily, 'to blow half New York to bits.'

The silence was broken by a crash in the background. Mr Crocker had dropped a chafing-dish.

'If I were to drop this little tube like that,' said Willie, using the occurrence as a topical illustration, 'we shouldn't be here.'

'Don't drop it,' advised Jimmy. 'What is it?'

'Partridgite!'

Mrs Pett had risen from the table with blanched face.

'Willie, how can you bring that stuff here? What are you thinking of?'

Willie smiled a patronizing smile.

'There is not the slightest danger, Aunt Nesta. It cannot explode without concussion. I have been carrying it about with me all the morning.'

He bestowed on the test tube the look a fond parent might give his favourite child. Mrs Pett was not reassured.

'Go and put it in your uncle's safe at once. Put it away.'

'I haven't the combination.'

'Call your uncle up at once at the office and ask him.'

'Very well, if you wish it, Aunt Nesta. But there is no danger.'

'Don't take that thing with you,' screamed Mrs Pett, as he rose. 'You might drop it. Come back for it.'

'Very well.'

Conversation flagged after Willie's departure. The presence of the test tube seemed to act on the spirits of the company after the fashion of the corpse at the Egyptian banquet. Howard Bemis, who was sitting next to it, edged away imperceptibly till he nearly crowded Ann off her chair. Presently Willie returned. He picked up the test tube, put it in his pocket with a certain jauntiness, and left the room again.

'Now if you hear a sudden bang and find yourself disappearing through the roof,' said Jimmy, 'that will be it.'

Willie returned and took his place at the table again, but the spirit had gone out of the gathering. The voice of Clarence Renshaw was hushed, and Howard Bemis spoke no more of the influence of Edgar Lee Masters on modern literature. Mrs Pett left the room, followed by Ann. The geniuses drifted away one by one. Jimmy, having lighted a cigarette and finished his coffee, perceived that he was alone with his old friend, Lord Wisbeach, and that his old friend Lord Wisbeach was about to become confidential.

The fair-haired young man opened the proceedings by going to the door and looking out. This done he returned to his seat and gazed fixedly at Jimmy.

'What's your game?' he asked.

Jimmy returned his gaze blandly.

'My game?' he said. 'What do you mean?'

'Can the coy stuff,' urged his lordship brusquely. 'Talk sense and talk it quick. We may be interrupted at any moment. What's your name? What are you here for?'

Jimmy raised his eyebrows.

'I am a prodigal nephew returned to the fold.'

'Oh, quit your kidding. Are you one of Potter's lot?'

'Who is Potter?'

'You know who Potter is.'

'On the contrary, my life has never been brightened by so much as a sight of Potter.'

'Is that true?'

'Absolutely.'

'Are you working on your own, then?'

'I am not working at all at present. There is some talk of my learning to be an Asparagus Adjuster by mail later on.'

'You make me sick,' said Lord Wisbeach. 'Where's the sense of trying to pull this line of talk? Why not put your cards on the table? We've both got in here on the same lay, and there's no use fighting and balling the thing up.'

'Do you wish me to understand,' said Jimmy, 'that you are not my old friend, Lord Wisbeach?'

'No. And you're not my old friend, Jimmy Crocker.'

'What makes you think that?'

'If you had been, would you have pretended to recognize me upstairs just now? I tell you, pal, I was all in for a second, till you gave me the high sign.'

Jimmy laughed.

'It would have been awkward for you if I really had been Jimmy Crocker, wouldn't it?'

'And it would have been awkward for you if I had really been Lord Wisbeach.'

'Who are you, by the way?'

'The boys call me Gentleman Jack.'

'Why?' asked Jimmy, surprised.

Lord Wisbeach ignored the question.

'I'm working with Burke's lot just now. Say, let's be sensible about this. I'll be straight with you, straight as a string.'

'Did you say string or spring?'

'And I'll expect you to be straight with me.'

'Are we to breathe confidences into each other's ears?'

Lord Wisbeach went to the door again and submitted the passage to a second examination.

'You seem nervous,' said Jimmy.

'I don't like that butler, he's up to something.'

'Do you think he's one of Potter's lot?'

'Shouldn't wonder. He isn't on the level anyway, or why did he pretend to recognize you as Jimmy Crocker?'

'Recognition of me as Jimmy Crocker seems to be the acid test of honesty.'

'He was in a tight place, same as I was,' said Lord Wisbeach. 'He couldn't know that you weren't really Jimmy Crocker till you put him wise – same as you did me – by pretending to know him.' He looked at Jimmy with grudging admiration. 'You'd got your nerve with you, pal, coming in here like this. You were taking big chances. You couldn't have known you wouldn't run up against someone who really knew Jimmy Crocker. What would you have done if this butler guy had really been on the level?'

'The risks of the profession!'

'When I think of the work I had to put in,' said Lord Wisbeach, 'it makes me tired to think of someone else just walking in here as you did.'

'What made you choose Lord Wisbeach as your alias?'

'I knew I could get away with it. I came over on the boat with him, and I knew he was travelling round the world and wasn't going to stay more than a day in New York. Even then I had to go some to get into this place. Burke told me to get hold of old Chester and get a letter of introduction from him. And here you come along and just stroll in and tell them you have come to stay!' He brooded for a moment on the injustice of things. 'Well, what are you going to do about it, pal?'

'About what?'

'About us both being here? Are you going to be sensible and work in with me and divvy up later on, or are you going to risk spoiling everything by trying to hog the whole thing? I'll be square with you. It isn't as if there was any use in trying to bluff each other. We're both here for the same thing. You want to get hold of that powder stuff, that Partridgite, and so do I.'

'You believe in Partridgite then?'

'Oh, can it!' said Lord Wisbeach disgustedly. 'What's the use? Of course I believe in it. Burke's had his eye on the thing for a year. You've heard of Dwight Partridge, haven't you? Well, this guy's his son. Everyone knows that Dwight Partridge was working on an explosive when he died, and here his son comes along with a test tube full of stuff which he says could blow this city to bits. What's the answer? The boy's been working on the old man's dope. From what I've seen of him, I guess there wasn't much more to be done on it or he wouldn't have done it. He's pretty well dead from the neck up, as far as I can see. But that doesn't alter the fact that he's got the stuff and that you and I have got to get together and make a deal. If we don't I'm not saying you mightn't gum my game, just as I might gum yours, but where's the sense in that? It only means taking extra chances. Whereas, if we sit in together there's enough in it for both of us. You know as well as I do that there's a dozen markets that'll bid against each other for stuff like that Partridgite. If you're worrying about Burke giving you a square deal, forget it. I'll fix Burke. He'll treat you nice, all right.'

Jimmy ground the butt of his cigarette against his plate.

'I'm no orator, as Brutus is; but, as you know me all, a plain blunt man. And, speaking in the capacity of a plain blunt man, I rise to reply – Nothing doing.'

'What? You won't come in?'

Jimmy shook his head.

'I'm sorry to disappoint you, Wizzy, if I may still call you that, but your offer fails to attract. I will not get together or sit in or anything else. On the contrary I am about to go to Mrs Pett and inform her that there is a snake in her Eden.'

'You're not going to squeal on me?'

'At the top of my voice.'

Lord Wisbeach laughed unpleasantly.

'Yes, you will!' he said. 'How are you going to explain why you recognized me as an old pal before lunch if I'm a crook after lunch? You can't give me away without giving yourself away. If I'm not Lord Wisbeach then you're not Jimmy Crocker.'

Jimmy sighed. 'I get you. Life is very complex, isn't it?'

Lord Wisbeach rose.

'You'd better think it over, son,' he said. 'You aren't going to get anywhere by acting like a fool. You can't stop me going after this stuff, and if you won't come in and go fifty-fifty, you'll find yourself left. I'll beat you to it.'

He left the room, and Jimmy, lighting a fresh cigarette, addressed himself to the contemplation of this new complication in his affairs. It was quite true what Gentleman Jack or Joe or whatever the 'boys' called him had said. To denounce him meant denouncing himself. Jimmy smoked thoughtfully. Not for the first time he wished that his record during the past few years had been of a snowier character. He began to appreciate what must have been the feelings of Dr Jekyll under the handicap of his disreputable second self, Mr Hyde.

CHAPTER 16

Mrs Pett, on leaving the luncheon table, had returned to the drawing-room to sit beside the sick settee of her stricken child. She was troubled about Ogden. The poor lamb was not at all himself to-day. A bowl of clear soup, the midday meal prescribed by Doctor Briginshaw, lay untasted at his side.

She crossed the room softly and placed a cool hand on her son's aching blow.

'Oh, gee!' said Ogden wearily.

'Are you feeling a little better, Oggie darling?'

'No,' said Ogden firmly, 'I'm feeling a lot worse.'

'You haven't drunk your nice soup.'

'Feed it to the cat.'

'Could you eat a nice bowl of bread and milk, precious?'

'Have a heart!' replied the sufferer.

Mrs Pett returned to her seat sorrowfully. It struck her as an odd coincidence that the poor child was nearly always like this on the morning after she had been entertaining guests. She put it down to the reaction from the excitement working on a highly strung temperament. To his present collapse the brutal behaviour of Jerry Mitchell had, of course, contributed. Every drop of her maternal blood boiled with rage and horror whenever she permitted herself to contemplate the excesses of the late Jerry. She had always mistrusted the man. She had never liked his face, not merely on æsthetic grounds, but because she had seemed to detect in it a lurking savagery. How right events had proved this instinctive feeling. Mrs Pett was not vulgar enough to describe the feeling, even to herself, as a hunch, but a hunch it had been, and, like everyone whose hunches have proved correct, she was conscious in the midst of her grief of a certain complacency. It seemed to her that hers must be an intelligence and insight above the ordinary.

The peace of the early afternoon settled upon the drawing-room. Mrs Pett had taken up a book. Ogden, on the settee, breathed stertorously. Faint snores proceeded from the basket in the corner where Aïda, the Pomeranian, lay curled in refreshing sleep. Through the open window floated sounds of warmth and summer. Yielding to the drowsy calm Mrs Pett was just nodding into a pleasant nap, when the door opened and Lord Wisbeach came in.

Lord Wisbeach had been doing some rapid thinking. Rapid thought is one of the essentials in the composition of men who are known as Gentlemen Jack to the boys, and whose livelihood is won only by a series of arduous struggles against the forces of society and the machinations of Potter and his gang. Condensed into capsule form, his lordship's meditations during the minutes after he had left Jimmy in the dining-room amounted to the realization that the best mode of defence is attack. It is your man who knows how to play the bold game on occasions who wins. A duller schemer than Lord Wisbeach might have been content to be inactive after such a conversation as had just taken place between himself and Jimmy. His lordship, giving the matter the concentrated attention of the trained mind, had hit on a better plan, and he had come to the drawing-room now to put it into effect.

His entrance shattered the peaceful atmosphere. Aïda, who had been gurgling apoplectically, sprang snarling from the basket and made for the intruder open-mouthed. Her shrill barking rang through the room.

Lord Wisbeach hated little dogs. He hated and feared them. Many men of action have these idiosyncrasies. He got behind a chair and said, 'There, there!' Aïda, whose outburst was mere sound and fury and who had no intention whatever of coming to blows, continued the demonstration from a safe distance, till Mrs Pett, swooping down, picked her up and held her in her lap, where she consented to remain, growling subdued defiance. Lord Wisbeach came out from behind his chair and sat down warily.

'Can I have a word with you, Mrs Pett?'

'Certainly, Lord Wisbeach.'

His lordship looked meaningly at Ogden.

'In private, you know.'

He then looked meaningly at Mrs Pett.

'Ogden, darling,' said Mrs Pett, 'I think you had better go to your room and undress and go to bed. A little nice sleep might do you all the good in the world.'

With surprising docility the boy rose.

'All right,' he said.

'Poor Oggie is not at all well to-day,' said Mrs Pett, when he was gone. 'He is very subject to these attacks. What do you want to tell me, Lord Wisbeach?'

His lordship drew his chair a little closer.

'Mrs Pett, you remember what I told you yesterday?'

'Of course.'

'Might I ask what you know of this man who has come here calling himself Jimmy Crocker?'

Mrs Pett started. She remembered that she had used almost that very expression to Ann. Her suspicions, which had been lulled by the prompt recognition of the visitor by Skinner and Lord Wisbeach, returned. It is one of the effects of a successful hunch that it breeds other hunches. She had been right about Jerry Mitchell, was she to be proved right about the self-styled Jimmy Crocker?

'You have never seen your nephew, I believe?'

'Never. But—'

'That man,' said Lord Wisbeach impressively, 'is not your nephew.'

Mrs Pett thrilled all down her spine. She had been right.

'But you—'

'But I pretended to recognize him? Just so. For a purpose. I wanted to make him think that I suspected nothing.'

'Then you think—'

'Remember what I said to you yesterday.'

'But Skinner, the butler, recognized him?'

'Exactly. It goes to prove that what I said about Skinner was correct. They are working together. The thing is self-evident. Look at it from your point of view. How simple it is. This man pretends to an intimate acquaintance with Skinner. You take that as evidence of Skinner's honesty. Skinner recognizes this man. You take that as proof that this man is really your nephew. The fact that Skinner recognized as Jimmy Crocker a man who is not Jimmy Crocker condemns him.'

'But why did you—'

'I told you that I pretended to accept this man as the real Jimmy Crocker for a purpose. At present there is nothing that you can do. Mere impersonation is not a crime. If I had exposed him when we met you would have gained nothing beyond driving him from the house. Whereas, if we wait, if we pretend to suspect nothing, we shall undoubtedly catch him red-handed in an attempt on your nephew's invention.'

'You are sure that that is why he has come?'

'What other reason could he have?'

'I thought he might be trying to kidnap Ogden.'

Lord Wisbeach frowned thoughtfully. He had not taken this consideration into account.

'It is possible,' he said. 'There have been several attempts made, have there not, to kidnap your son?'

'At one time,' said Mrs Pett proudly, 'there was not a child in America who had to be more closely guarded. Why, the kidnappers had a special nickname for Oggie. They called him the Little Nugget.'

'Of course, then, it is quite possible that that may be the man's object. In any case, our course must be the same. We must watch every move he makes.' He paused. 'I could help – pardon my suggesting it – I could help a great deal more if you were to invite me to live in the house. You were kind enough to ask me to visit you in the country, but it will be two weeks before you go to the country, and in those two weeks—'

'You must come here at once, Lord Wisbeach. To-night. To-day.'

'I think that would be the best plan.'

'I cannot tell you how grateful I am for all you are doing.'

'You have been so kind to me, Mrs Pett,' said Lord Wisbeach with feeling, 'that it is surely only right that I should try to make some return. Let us leave it at this then. I will come here to-night and will make it my business to watch these two men. I will go and pack my things and have them sent here.'

'It is wonderful of you, Lord Wisbeach.'

'Not at all,' replied his lordship. 'It will be a pleasure.'

He held out his hand, drawing it back rapidly as the dog Aïda made a snap at it. Substituting a long-range leave-taking for the more intimate farewell, he left the room.

When he had gone Mrs Pett remained for some minutes, thinking. She was aflame with excitement. She had a sensational mind, and it had absorbed Lord Wisbeach's revelations eagerly. Her admiration for his lordship was intense, and she trusted him utterly. The only doubt that occurred to her was whether, with the best intentions in the world, he would be able unassisted to foil a pair of schemers so distant from each other geographically as the man who called himself Jimmy Crocker and the man who had called himself Skinner. That was a point on which they had not touched, the fact that one impostor was above stairs, the other below. It seemed to Mrs Pett impossible that Lord Wisbeach, for all his zeal, could watch Skinner without neglecting Jimmy, or foil Jimmy without taking his attention off Skinner. It was manifestly a situation that called for allies. She felt that she must have further assistance.

To Mrs Pett, doubtless owing to her hobby of writing sensational fiction, there was a magic in the word detective that was shared by no other word in the language. She loved detectives – their keen eyes, their quiet smiles, their derby hats. When they came on the stage she leaned forward in her orchestra chair, when they entered her own stories she always wrote with a greater zest. It is not too much to say that she had an almost spiritual attachment for detectives, and the idea of neglecting to employ one in real life, now that circumstances had combined to render his advent so necessary, struck her as both rash and inartistic. In the old days, when Ogden had been kidnapped, the only thing which had brought her balm had been the daily interviews with the detectives. She ached to telephone for one now.

The only consideration that kept her back was a regard for Lord Wisbeach's feelings. He had been so kind and so shrewd that to suggest reinforcing him with outside assistance must infallibly wound him deeply. And yet the situation demanded the services of a trained specialist. Lord Wisbeach had borne himself during their recent conversation in such a manner as to leave no doubt that he considered himself adequate to deal with the matter single-handed; but admirable though he was, he was not a professional exponent of the art of espionage. He needed to be helped in spite of himself.

A happy solution struck Mrs Pett. There was no need to tell him. She could combine the installation of a detective with the nicest respect for her ally's feelings by the simple process of engaging one without telling Lord Wisbeach anything about it.

The telephone stood at her elbow, concealed – at the express request of the interior decorator who had designed the room – in the interior of what looked to the casual eye like a stuffed owl. On a table near at hand, handsomely bound in morocco to resemble a complete works of Shakespeare, was the telephone book. Mrs Pett hesitated no longer. She had forgotten the address of the detective agency which she had employed on the occasion of the kidnapping of Ogden, but she remembered the name, and also the name of the delightfully sympathetic manager or proprietor or whatever he was who had listened to her troubles then.

She unhooked the receiver, and gave a number.

'I want to speak to Mr Sturgis,' she said.

'This is Mr Sturgis,' said a voice.

'Oh, Mr Sturgis,' said Mrs Pett, 'I wonder if you could possibly run up here – yes, now. This is Mrs Peter Pett speaking. You remember we met some years ago, when I was Mrs Ford. Yes, the mother of Ogden Ford. I want to consult ... You will come up at once? Thank you so much. Goodbye.'

Mrs Pett hung up the receiver.

CHAPTER 17

Downstairs, in the dining-room, Jimmy was smoking cigarettes and reviewing in his mind the peculiarities of the situation, when Ann came in.

'Oh, there you are,' said Ann. 'I thought you must have gone upstairs.'

'I have been having a delightful and entertaining conversation with my old chum, Lord Wisbeach.'

'Good gracious! What about?'

'Oh, this and that.'

'Not about old times?'

'No, we did not touch upon old times.'

'Does he still believe that you are Jimmy Crocker? I'm so nervous,' said Ann, 'that I can hardly speak.'

'I shouldn't be nervous,' said Jimmy encouragingly. 'I don't see how things could be going better.'

'That's what makes me nervous. Our luck is too good to last. We are taking such risks. It would have been bad enough without Skinner and Lord Wisbeach. At any moment you may make some fatal slip. Thank goodness, Aunt Nesta's suspicions have been squashed for the time being, now that Skinner and Lord Wisbeach have accepted you as genuine. But then you have only seen them for a few minutes. When they have been with you a little longer they may get suspicious themselves. I can't imagine how you managed to keep it up with Lord Wisbeach. I should have thought he would be certain to say something about the time when you were supposed to be friends in London. We simply mustn't strain our luck. I want you to go straight to Aunt Nesta now and ask her to let Jerry come back.'

'You still refuse to let me take Jerry's place?'

'Of course I do. You'll find Aunt Nesta upstairs.'

'Very well. But suppose I can't persuade her to forgive Jerry?'

'I think she is certain to do anything you ask. You saw how friendly she was to you at lunch. I don't see how anything can have happened since lunch to change her.'

'Very well. I'll go to her now.'

'And when you have seen her, go to the library and wait for me. It's the second room along the passage outside here. I have promised to drive Lord Wisbeach down to his hotel in my car. I met him outside just now and he tells me Aunt Nesta has invited him to stay here, so he wants to go and get his things ready. I shan't be twenty minutes! I shall come straight back!'

Jimmy found himself vaguely disquieted by this piece of information.

'Lord Wisbeach is coming to stay here?'

'Yes. Why?'

'Oh, nothing. Well, I'll go and see Mrs Pett.'

No traces of the disturbance which had temporarily ruffled the peace of the drawing-room were to be observed when Jimmy reached it. The receiver of the telephone was back on its hook, Mrs Pett back in her chair, the dog Aïda back in her basket. Mrs Pett, her mind at ease now that she had taken the step of summoning Mr Sturgis, was reading a book, one of her own, and was absorbed in it. The dog Aïda slumbered noisily.

The sight of Jimmy, however, roused Mrs Pett from her literary calm. To her eye, after what Lord Wisbeach had revealed, there was something sinister in the very way in which he walked into the room. He made her flesh creep. In *A Society Thug* – one dollar and thirty-five cents net, all rights of translation reserved, including the Scandinavian – she portrayed just such a man – smooth, specious and formidable. Instinctively, as she watched Jimmy, her mind went back to the perfectly rotten behaviour of her own Marsden Tuke – it was only in the last chapter but one that they managed to foil his outrageous machinations – and it seemed to her that here was Tuke in the flesh. She had pictured him, she remembered, as a man of agreeable exterior, the better calculated to deceive and undo the virtuous; and the fact that Jimmy was a presentable-looking young man only made him appear viler in her eyes. In a word, she could hardly have been in a less suitable frame of mind to receive graciously any kind of request from him. She would have suspected ulterior motives if he had asked her the time.

Jimmy did not know this. He thought that she eyed him a trifle frostily, but he did not attribute this to any suspicion of him. He tried to ingratiate himself by smiling pleasantly. He could not have made a worse move. Marsden Tuke's pleasant smile had been his deadliest weapon. Under its influence deluded people had trusted him alone with their jewellery, and what not.

'Aunt Nesta,' said Jimmy, 'I wonder if I might ask you a personal favour?'

Mrs Pett shuddered at the glibness with which he brought out the familiar name. This was super-Tuke. Marsden himself, scoundrel as he was, could not have called her Aunt Nesta as smoothly as that.

'Yes?' she said at last. She found it difficult to speak.

'I happened to meet an old friend of mine this morning. He was very sorry for himself. It appears that – for excellent reasons, of course – you had dismissed him. I mean Jerry Mitchell.'

Mrs Pett was now absolutely appalled. The conspiracy seemed to grow more complicated every moment. Already its ramifications embraced this man before her, a trusted butler, and her husband's late physical instructor. Who could say where it would end? She had never liked Jerry Mitchell, but she had never suspected him of being a conspirator. Yet, if this man who called himself Jimmy Crocker was an old friend of his, how could he be anything else?

'Mitchell,' Jimmy went on, unconscious of the emotions that his every word was arousing in his hearer's bosom, 'told me about what happened yesterday. He is very depressed. He said he could not think how he happened to behave in such an abominable way. He entreated me to put in a word for him with you. He begged me to tell you how he regretted the brutal assault, and asked me to mention the fact that his record had hitherto been blameless.' Jimmy paused. He was getting no encouragement and seemed to be making no impression whatever. Mrs Pett was sitting bolt upright in her chair in a stiffly defensive sort of way. She had the appearance of being absolutely untouched by his eloquence. 'In fact,' he concluded lamely, 'he is very sorry.'

There was silence for a moment.

'How do you come to know Mitchell?' asked Mrs Pett.

'We knew each other when I was over here working on the *Chronicle*. I saw him fight once or twice. He is an excellent fellow and used to have a right swing that was a pippin – I should say extremely excellent. Brought it right up from the floor, you know.'

'I strongly object to prize fighters,' said Mrs Pett, 'and I was opposed to Mitchell coming into the house from the first.'

'You wouldn't let him come back, I suppose?' queried Jimmy tentatively.

'I would not. I would not dream of such a thing.'

'He's full of remorse, you know.'

'If he has a spark of humanity I have no doubt of it.'

Jimmy paused. This thing was not coming out so well as it might have done. He feared that, for once in her life, Ann was about to be denied something on which she had set her heart. The reflection that this would be extremely good for her competed for precedence in his mind with the reflection that she would probably blame him for the failure, which would be unpleasant.

'He is very fond of Ogden really.'

'H'm,' said Mrs Pett.

'I think the heat must have made him irritable. In his normal state he would not strike a lamb. I've known him to do it.'

'Do what?'

'Not strike lambs.'

'Isch,' said Mrs Pett – the first time Jimmy had ever heard that remarkable monosyllable proceed from human lips. He took it – rightly – to be intended to convey disapproval, scepticism and annoyance. He was convinced that this mission was going to be one of his failures.

'Then I may tell him,' he said, 'that it's all right?'

'That what is all right?'

'That he may come back here?'

'Certainly not.'

Mrs Pett was not a timid woman, but she could not restrain a shudder as she watched the plot unfold before her eyes. Her gratitude towards Lord Wisbeach, at this point in the proceedings, became almost hero worship. If it had not been for him and his revelations concerning this man before her, she would certainly have yielded to the request that Jerry Mitchell be allowed to return to the house. Much as she disliked Jerry, she had been feeling so triumphant at the thought of Jimmy Crocker coming to her in spite of his stepmother's wishes and so pleased at having unexpectedly got her own way, that she could have denied him nothing that he might have cared to ask. But now it was as if, herself unseen, she were looking on at a gang of conspirators hatching some plot. She was in the strong strategic position of the person who is apparently deceived, but who in reality knows all.

For a moment she considered the question of admitting Jerry to the house. Evidently his presence was necessary to the consummation of the plot, whatever it might be; and it occurred to her that it might be as well, on the principle of giving the schemers enough rope to hang themselves with, to let him come back and play his part. Then she reflected that, with the self-styled Jimmy Crocker as well as the fraudulent Skinner in the house, Lord Wisbeach and the detective would have their hands quite full enough. It would be foolish to complicate matters. She glanced at the clock on the mantelpiece. Mr Sturgis would be arriving soon, if he had really started at once from his office, as he had promised. She drew comfort from the imminence of his coming. It would be pleasant to put herself in the hands of an expert.

Jimmy had paused midway to the door, and was standing there as if reluctant to accept her answer to his plea.

'It would never occur again. What happened yesterday I mean. You need not be afraid of that.'

'I am not afraid of that,' responded Mrs Pett tartly.

'If you had seen him when I did—'

'When did you? You landed from the boat this morning, you went to Mr Pett's office, and then came straight up here with him. I am interested to know when you did see Mitchell?'

She regretted this thrust a little, for she felt it might put the man on his guard by showing that she suspected something, but she could not resist it, and it pleased her to see that her companion was momentarily confused.

'I met him when I was going for my luggage,' said Jimmy.

It was just the way Marsden Tuke would have got out of it. Tuke was always wriggling out of corners like that. Mrs Pett's horror of Jimmy grew.

'I told him, of course,' said Jimmy, 'that you had very kindly invited me to stay with you, and he told me all about his trouble and implored me to plead for him. If you had seen him when I did, all gloom and repentance, you would have been sorry for him. Your woman's heart—'

Whatever Jimmy was about to say regarding Mrs Pett's woman's heart was interrupted by the opening of the door and the deep respectful voice of Mr Crocker.

'Mr Sturgis.'

The detective entered briskly, as if time were money with him – as, indeed, it was, for the International Detective Agency, of which he was the proprietor, did a thriving business. He was a gaunt, hungry-looking man of about fifty, with sunken eyes and thin lips. It was his habit to dress in the height of fashion, for one of his favourite axioms was that a man might be a detective and still look a gentleman, and his appearance was that of the individual usually described as a popular clubman. That is to say, he looked like a floorwalker taking a Sunday stroll. His prosperous exterior deceived Jimmy satisfactorily, and the latter left the room little thinking that the visitor was anything but an ordinary caller.

The detective glanced keenly at him as he passed. He made a practice of glancing keenly at nearly everything. It cost nothing and impressed clients.

'I am so glad you have come, Mr Sturgis,' said Mrs Pett. 'Won't you sit down?'

Mr Sturgis sat down, pulled up the knees of his trousers – that half inch which keeps them from bagging and so preserves the gentlemanliness of the appearance – and glanced keenly at Mrs Pett.

'Who was that young man who just went out?'

'It is about him that I wish to consult you, Mr Sturgis.'

Mr Sturgis leaned back and placed the tips of his fingers together.

'Tell me how he comes to be here.'

'He pretends that he is my nephew, James Crocker.'

'Your nephew? Have you never seen your nephew?'

'Never. I ought to tell you that a few years ago my sister married for the second time. I disapproved of the marriage and refused to see her husband or his son – he was a widower. A few weeks ago, for private reasons, I went over to England, where they are living, and asked my sister to let the boy come here to work in my husband's office. She refused, and my husband and I returned to New York. This morning I was astonished to get a telephone call from Mr Pett at his office, saying that James Crocker had unexpectedly arrived after all and was then at the office. They came up here, and the young man seemed quite genuine. Indeed, he had an offensive jocularity that would be quite in keeping with the character of the real James Crocker, from what I have heard of him.'

Mr Sturgis nodded.

'Know what you mean. Saw that thing in the paper,' he said briefly. 'Yes?'

'Now it is very curious, but almost from the start I was uneasy. When I say that the young man seemed genuine I mean that he completely deceived my husband and my niece, who lives with us. But I had reasons, which I need not go into now, for being on my guard, and I was suspicious. What aroused my suspicion was the fact that my husband thought that he remembered this young man as a fellow-traveller of ours on the *Atlantic*, on our return voyage, while he claimed to have landed that morning on the *Caronia*.'

'You are certain of that, Mrs Pett? He stated positively that he had landed this morning?'

'Yes. Quite positively. Unfortunately I myself had no chance of judging the truth of what he said, as I am such a bad sailor that I was seldom out of my stateroom from beginning to end of the voyage. However, as I say, I was suspicious. I did not see how I could confirm my suspicions, until I remembered that my new butler, Skinner, had come straight from my sister's house.'

'That is the man who just admitted me?'

'Exactly. He entered my employment only a few days ago, having come direct from London. I decided to wait until Skinner should meet this young man. Of course when this impostor first came into the house he was with my husband, who opened the door with his key, so that he did not meet Skinner then.'

'I understand,' said Mr Sturgis, glancing keenly at the dog Aïda, who had risen and was sniffing at his ankles. 'You thought that if Skinner recognized this young man, it would be proof of his identity?'

'Exactly.'

'Did he recognize him?'

'Yes, but wait. I have not finished. He recognized him and for the moment I was satisfied, but I had had my suspicions of Skinner too. I ought to tell you that I had been warned against him by a great friend of mine, Lord Wisbeach, an English peer whom we have known intimately for a very long time. He is one of the Shropshire Wisbeaches, you know.'

'No doubt,' said Mr Sturgis.

'Lord Wisbeach used to be intimate with the real Jimmy Crocker. He came to lunch to-day and met this impostor. Lord Wisbeach pretended to recognize him, in order to put him off his guard, but after lunch he came to me here and told me that in reality he had never seen the man before in his life and that, whoever else he might be, he was certainly not James Crocker, my nephew.'

She broke off and looked at Mr Sturgis expectantly. The detective smiled a quiet smile.

'And even that is not all. There is another thing. Mr Pett used to employ as a physical instructor a man named Jerry Mitchell. Yesterday I dismissed him for reasons it is not necessary to go into. Today – just as you arrived, in fact – the man who calls himself Jimmy Crocker was begging me to allow Mitchell to return to the house and resume his work here. Does that not strike you as suspicious, Mr Sturgis?'

The detective closed his eyes and smiled his quiet smile again. He opened his eyes and fixed them on Mrs Pett.

'As pretty a case as I have come across in years,' he said. 'Mrs Pett, let me tell you something. It is one of my peculiarities that I never forget a face. You say that this young man pretends to have landed this morning from the steamer? Well I saw him myself more than a week ago in a Broadway café.'

'You did?'

'Talking to – Jerry Mitchell. I know Mitchell well by sight.'

Mrs Pett uttered an exclamation.

'And this butler of yours – Skinner. Shall I tell you something about him? You perhaps know that when the big detective agencies, Anderson's and the others, are approached in the matter of tracing a man who is wanted for anything, they sometimes ask the smaller agencies like my own to work in with them. It saves time and widens the field of operations. We are very glad to do Anderson's a service, and Anderson's are big enough to be able to afford to let us do it. Now, a few days ago, a friend of mine in Anderson's came to me with a sheaf of photographs that had been sent to them from London. Whether from some private client in London or from Scotland Yard I do not know. Nor do I know why the original of the photographs was wanted. But Anderson's had been asked to trace him and make a report. My peculiar gift for remembering faces has enabled me to oblige the Anderson people once or twice before in this way. I studied the photographs very carefully and kept two of them for reference. I have one with me now.' He felt in his pocket. 'Do you recognize it?'

Mrs Pett stared at the photograph. It was the presentment of a stout, good-humoured man of middle age, whose solemn gaze dwelt on the middle distance, in the fixed way that a man achieves only in photographs.

'Skinner!'

'Exactly,' said Mr Sturgis, taking the photograph from her and putting it back in his pocket. 'I recognized him directly he opened the door to me.'

'But – but I am almost certain that Skinner is the man who let me in when I called on my sister in London.'

'Almost,' repeated the detective. 'Did you observe him very closely?'

'No, I suppose I did not.'

'The type is a very common one. It would be very easy, indeed, for a clever crook to make himself up as your sister's butler, closely enough to deceive anyone who had only seen the original once and for a short time then. What their game is I could not say at present, but, taking everything into consideration, there can be no doubt whatever that the man who calls himself your nephew and the man who calls himself your sister's butler are working together, and that Jerry Mitchell is working in with them. As I say, I cannot tell you what they are after at present, but there is no doubt that your unexpected dismissal of Mitchell must have upset their plans. That would account for the eagerness to get back into the house again.'

'Lord Wisbeach thought that they were trying to steal my nephew's explosive. Perhaps you have read in the papers that my nephew, Willie Partridge, has completed an explosive that is more powerful than any at present known. His father – you have heard of him, of course – was Dwight Partridge.'

Mr Sturgis nodded.

'His father was working on it at the time of his death, and Willie has gone on with his experiments where his father left off. To-day at lunch he showed us a test tube full of the explosive. He put it in my husband's safe in the library. Lord Wisbeach is convinced that these scoundrels are trying to steal this sample, but I cannot help feeling that it is another of those attempts to kidnap my son Ogden. What do you think?'

'It is impossible to say at this stage of the proceedings. All we can tell is that there is some plot going on. You refused, of course, to allow Mitchell to come back to the house?'

'Yes. You think that was wise?'

'Undoubtedly. If his absence did not handicap them they would not be so anxious to have him on the spot.'

'What shall we do?'

'You wish me to undertake the case?'

'Of course.'

Mr Sturgis frowned thoughtfully.

'It would be useless for me to come here myself. By bad luck the man who pretends to be your nephew has seen me. If I were to come to stay here he would suspect something. He would be on his guard.' He pondered with closed eyes. 'Miss Trimble,' he explained.

'I beg your pardon.'

'You want Miss Trimble. She is the smartest worker in my office. This is precisely the type of case she could handle to perfection.'

'A woman?' said Mrs Pett doubtfully.

'A woman in a thousand,' said Mr Sturgis; 'a woman in a million.'

'But physically would a woman be—'

'Miss Trimble knows more about ju-jitsu than the Japanese professor who taught her. At one time she was a strong woman in small-time vaudeville. She is an expert revolver shot. I am not worrying about Miss Trimble's capacity to do the work. I am only wondering in what capacity it would be best for her to enter the house. Have you a vacancy for a parlour-maid?'

'I could make one.'

'Do so at once! Miss Trimble is at her best as a parlour-maid. She handled the Marling divorce case in that capacity. Have you a telephone in the room?'

Mrs Pett opened the stuffed owl. The detective got in touch with his office.

'Mr Sturgis speaking. Tell Miss Trimble to come to the phone...Miss Trimble? I am speaking from Mrs Pett's on Riverside Drive. You know the house? I want you to come up at once. Take a taxi! Go to the back door and ask to see Mrs Pett! Say you have come about getting a place here as a maid! Understand? Right. Say, listen, Miss Trimble! Hello? Yes, don't hang up for a moment! Do you remember those photographs I showed you yesterday? Yes, the photographs from Anderson's. I've found the man. He's the butler here. Take a look at him when you get to the house! Now go and get a taxi! Mrs Pett will explain everything when you arrive.' He hung up the receiver. 'I think I had better go now, Mrs Pett. It would not do for me to be here while these fellows are on guard. I can safely leave the matter to Miss Trimble. I wish you good afternoon.'

After he had gone, Mrs Pett vainly endeavoured to interest herself again in her book, but, in competition with the sensations of life, fiction – even though she had written it herself – had lost its power and grip. It seemed to her that Miss Trimble must be walking to the house instead of journeying thither in a taxicab. But a glance at the clock assured her that only five minutes had elapsed since the detective's departure. She went to the window and looked out. She was hopelessly restless.

At last a taxicab stopped at the corner and a young woman got out and walked towards the house. If this were Miss Trimble she certainly looked capable. She was a stumpy, square-shouldered person, and even at that distance it was possible to perceive that she had a face of no common shrewdness and determination. The next moment she had turned down the side street in the direction of the back premises of Mrs Pett's house; and a few minutes later Mr Crocker presented himself.

'A young person wishes to see you, madam, a young person of the name of Trimble.' A pang passed through Mrs Pett as she listened to his measured tones. It was tragic that so perfect a butler should be a scoundrel. 'She says that you desired her to call in connection with a situation.'

'Show her up here, Skinner! She is the new parlour-maid. I will send her down to you when I have finished speaking to her.'

'Very good, madam.'

There seemed to Mrs Pett to be a faint touch of defiance in Miss Trimble's manner as she entered the room. The fact was that Miss Trimble held strong views on the equal distribution of property, and rich people's houses always affected her adversely. Mr Crocker retired, closing the door gently behind him.

A meaning sniff proceeded from Mrs Pett's visitor, as she looked at the achievements of the interior decorator, who had lavished his art unsparingly in this particular room. At this close range she more than fulfilled the promise of that distant view that Mrs Pett had had of her from the window. Her face was not only shrewd and determined, it was menacing. She had thick eyebrows, from beneath which small glittering eyes looked out like dangerous beasts in undergrowth. And the impressive effect of these was accentuated by the fact, that while the left eye looked straight out at its object the right eye had a sort of roving commission and now was, while its colleague fixed Mrs Pett with a gimlet stare, examining the ceiling.

As to the rest of the appearance of this remarkable woman, her nose was stubby and aggressive and her mouth had the coldly forbidding look of the closed door of a subway express when you have just missed the train. It bade you keep your distance on pain of injury. Mrs Pett, though herself a strong woman, was conscious of a curious weakness, as she looked at a female of the species so much deadlier than any male whom she had ever encountered. She came near feeling a half pity for the unhappy wretches on whom this dynamic maiden was to be unleashed. She hardly knew how to open the conversation.

Miss Trimble, however, was equal to the occasion. She always preferred to open conversation herself. Her lips parted, and words flew out as if shot from a machine gun. As far as Mrs Pett could observe, Miss Trimble considered it unnecessary to part her teeth, preferring to speak with them clenched. This gave an additional touch of menace to her speech.

'Dafternoon,' said Miss Trimble, and Mrs Pett backed convulsively into the padded recesses of her chair, feeling as if somebody had thrown a brick at her.

'Good afternoon,' she said faintly.

'Gladda meecher, siz Pett. Mr Sturge semme up. Said y'ad job f'r me. Came here squick scould.'

'I beg your pardon?'

'Squick scould. Got slow taxi.'

'Oh, yes.'

Miss Trimble's right eye flashed about the room like a searchlight, but she kept the other hypnotically on her companion's face.

'Whass trouble?' The right eye rested for a moment on a magnificent Corot over the mantelpiece, and she sniffed again.

'Not s'prised y'have trouble. All rich people 've trouble. Noth' t'do with their time 'c'pt get 'nto trouble.'

She frowned disapprovingly at a Canaletto.

'You – ah – appear to dislike the rich,' said Mrs Pett, as nearly in her grand manner as she could contrive.

Miss Trimble bowled over the grand manner as if it had been a small fowl and she an automobile. She rolled over it and squashed it flat.

'Hate 'em! Sogelist!'

'I beg your pardon?' said Mrs Pett humbly. This woman was beginning to oppress her to an almost unbelievable extent.

'Sogelist! No use f'r idle rich! Ev' read B'nard Shaw? Huh? Or Upton Sinclair? Uh? Read'm. Make y'think a bit. Well, y'haven't told me whasser trouble.'

Mrs Pett was, by this time, heartily regretting the impulse that had caused her to telephone to Mr Sturgis. In a career that had had more than its share of detectives, both real and fictitious, she had never been confronted with a detective like this. The galling thing was that she was helpless. After all, one engaged a detective for his or her shrewdness and efficiency, not for suavity and polish. A detective who hurls speech at you through clenched teeth and yet detects is better value for the money than one who – though an ideal companion for the drawing-room – is incompetent; and Mrs Pett, like most other people, subconsciously held the view that the ruder a person is the more efficient he must be. It is but rarely that anyone is found who is not dazzled by the glamour of incivility.

Mrs Pett crushed down her resentment at her visitor's tone, and tried to concentrate her mind on the fact that this was a business matter and that what she wanted was results rather than fair words. She found it easier to do this when looking at the other's face. It was a capable face. Not beautiful, perhaps, but full of promise of action. Miss Trimble having ceased temporarily to speak, her mouth was in repose, and when her mouth was in repose it looked more efficient than anything else of its size in existence.

'I want you,' said Mrs Pett, 'to come here and watch some men—'

'Men! Thought so! Wh' there's trouble always men't bottom'f it!'

'You do not like men?'

'Hate 'em! Suff-gist!' She looked penetratingly at Mrs Pett. Her left eye seemed to pounce out from under its tangled brow. 'You s'porter of th' cause?'

Mrs Pett was an anti-suffragist, but, though she held strong opinions, nothing would have induced her to air them at that moment. Her whole being quailed at the prospect of arguing with this woman. She returned hurriedly to the main theme.

'A young man arrived here this morning, pretending to be my nephew, James Crocker. He is an impostor. I want you to watch him very carefully.'

'Whassiz game?'

'I do not know. Personally I think he is here to kidnap my son Ogden.'

'I'll fix 'm,' said the fair Trimble confidently. 'Say, that butler 'f yours. He's a crook!'

Mrs Pett opened her eyes. This woman was manifestly competent at her work.

'Have you found that out already?'

'D'rectly saw him.' Miss Trimble opened her purse. 'Go' one 'f his phot'graphs here. Brought it from office. He's th'man that's wanted'll right.'

'Mr Sturgis and I both think he is working with the other man, the one who pretends to be my nephew.'

'Sure. I'll fix 'm.'

Miss Trimble returned the photograph to her purse and snapped the catch with vicious emphasis.

'There is another possibility,' said Mrs Pett. 'My nephew, Mr William Partridge, has invented a wonderful explosive, and it is quite likely that these men are here to try and steal it.'

'Sure. Men'll do anything. If y' put all the men in the world in the cooler, wouldn't be 'ny more crime.'

She glowered at the dog Aïda, which had risen from the basket and was removing the last remains of sleep from her system by a series of calisthenics of her own invention, as if suspecting her of masculinity. Mrs Pett could not help wondering what tragedy in the dim past had caused this hatred of males on the part of her visitor. Miss Trimble had not the appearance of one who would lightly be deceived by man; still less the appearance of one whom man, unless short-sighted and extraordinarily susceptible, would go out of his way to deceive. She was still turning this mystery over in her mind, when her visitor spoke.

'Well, gimme th' rest of the dope,' said Miss Trimble.

'I beg your pardon?'

'More facts. Spill 'm!'

'Oh, I understand,' said Mrs Pett hastily, and embarked on a brief narrative of the suspicious circumstances which had caused her to desire skilled assistance.

'Lor' W'sbeach?' said Miss Trimble, breaking the story. 'Who's he?'

'A very great friend of ours.'

'You vouch f'r him pers'n'lly? He's all right, huh? Not a crook, huh?'

'Of course he is not!' said Mrs Pett indignantly. 'He's a great friend of mine.'

'S'll right. Well, I guess thass 'bout all, huh? I'll be going downstairs an' starting in.'

'You can come here immediately?'

'Sure. Got parlour-maid rig round at m' boarding house round corner. Come back with it 'n ten minutes. Same dress I used when I w's working on th' Marling d'vorce case. D'jer know th' Marlings? Idle rich! Bound t' get 'nto trouble. I fixed 'm. Well, g'-by. Mus' be going. No time t' waste.'

Mrs Pett leaned back faintly in her chair. She felt overcome.

Downstairs, on her way out, Miss Trimble had paused in the hall to inspect a fine statue that stood at the foot of the stairs. It was a noble work of art, but it seemed to displease her. She snorted.

'Idle rich!' she muttered scornfully. 'B-r-rh!'

The portly form of Mr Crocker loomed up from the direction of the back stairs. She fixed her left eye on him piercingly. Mr Crocker met it and quailed. He had that consciousness of guilt that philosophers tell us is the worst drawback to crime. Why this woman's gaze should disturb him so thoroughly, he could not have said. She was a perfect stranger to him. She could know nothing about him. Yet he quailed.

'Say,' said Miss Trimble. 'I'm c'ming here's parlour-maid.'

'Oh, ah?' said Mr Crocker feebly.

'G-r-r-rh!' observed Miss Trimble and departed.

CHAPTER 18

The library, whither Jimmy had made his way after leaving Mrs Pett, was a large room on the ground floor, looking out on the street that ran parallel to the south side of the house. It had French windows opening on to a strip of lawn that ended in a high stone wall with a small gate in it, the general effect of these things being to create a resemblance to a country house rather than to one in the centre of the city. Mr Pett's town residence was full of these surprises.

In one corner of the room a massive safe had been let into the wall, striking a note of incongruity, for the remainder of the wall space was completely covered with volumes of all sorts and sizes, which filled the shelves and overflowed into a small gallery, reached by a short flight of stairs and running along the north side of the room over the door.

Jimmy cast a glance at the safe, behind the steel doors of which he presumed the test tube of Partridgite that Willie had carried from the luncheon table lay hid; then transferred his attention to the shelves. A cursory inspection of these revealed nothing that gave promise of whiling away entertainingly the moments that must elapse before the return of Ann. Jimmy's tastes in literature lay in the direction of the lighter kind of modern fiction, and Mr Pett did not appear to possess a single volume that had been written later than the eighteenth century – and mostly poetry at that. He turned to the writing desk near the window, on which he had caught sight of a standing shelf, full of books of a more modern aspect. He picked one up at random and opened it.

He threw it down disgustedly. It was poetry. This man Pett appeared to have a perfect obsession for poetry. One would never have suspected it, to look at him. Jimmy had just resigned himself, after another glance at the shelf, to a bookless vigil, when his eye was caught by a name – on the cover of the last in the row – so unexpected that he had to look again to verify the discovery.

He had been perfectly right. There it was – in gold letters.

THE LONELY HEART

BY

ANN CHESTER

He extracted the volume from the shelf in a sort of stupor. Even now he was inclined to give his goddess of the red hair the benefit of the doubt and to assume that someone else of the same name had written it. For it was a defect in Jimmy's character – one of his many defects – that he loathed and scorned minor poetry and considered minor poets, especially when feminine, an unnecessary affliction. He declined to believe that Ann, his Ann, a girl full of the finest traits of character, the girl who had been capable of encouraging a comparative stranger to break the law by impersonating her cousin, Jimmy Crocker, could also be capable of writing *The Lonely Heart* and other poems. He skimmed through the first one he came across and shuddered. It was pure slush. It was the sort of stuff they filled up pages with in the magazines when the detective story did not run long enough. It was the sort of stuff that long-haired blighters read alone to other long-haired blighters in English suburban drawing-rooms. It was the sort of stuff that – to be brief – gave him the Willies. No, it could not be Ann who had written it.

The next moment the horrid truth was thrust upon him. There was an inscription on the title-page:

> *To my dearest Uncle Peter,*
> *with love from the author,*
> ANN CHESTER.

The room seemed to reel before Jimmy's eyes. He felt as if a friend had wounded him in his tenderest feelings. He felt as if some loved one had smitten him over the back of the head with a sandbag. For one moment, in which time stood still, his devotion to Ann wobbled. It was as if he had found her out in some terrible crime that revealed unsuspected flaws in her hitherto ideal character.

Then his eye fell upon the date on the title-page, and a strong spasm of relief shook him. The clouds rolled away, and he loved her still. This frightful volume had been published five years ago.

A wave of pity swept over Jimmy. He did not blame her now. She had been a mere child five years ago, scarcely old enough to distinguish right from wrong. You couldn't blame her for writing sentimental verse at that age. Why, at a similar stage in his own career he had wanted to be a vaudeville singer. Everything must be excused to youth. It was with a tender glow of affectionate forgiveness that he turned the pages.

As he did so a curious thing happened to him. He began to have that feeling, which everyone has experienced at some time or other, that he had done this very thing before. He was almost convinced that this was not the first time he had seen that poem on page twenty-seven entitled 'A Lament'. Why, some of the lines seemed extraordinarily familiar. The people who understood these things explained this phenomenon, he believed, by some stuff about the cells of the brain working simultaneously or something. Something about cells anyway. He supposed that that must be it.

But that was not it. The feeling that he had read all this before grew instead of vanishing, as is generally the way on these occasions. He had read this stuff before. He was certain of it. But when? And where? And above all, why? Surely he had not done it from choice.

It was the total impossibility of his having done it from choice that led his memory in the right direction. There had only been a year or so in his life when he had been obliged to read things that he would not have read of his own free will, and that had been when he worked on the *Chronicle*. Could it have been that they had given him this book of poems to review? Or—

And then memory, in its usual eccentric way, having taken all this time to make the first part of the journey, finished the rest of it with one lightning swoop, and he knew. And with the illumination came dismay, worse than dismay – horror.

'Gosh!' said Jimmy.

He knew now why he had thought on the occasion of their first meeting in London that he had seen hair like Ann's before. The mists rolled away and he saw everything clear and stark. He knew what had happened at that meeting five years before, to which she had so mysteriously alluded. He knew what she had meant that evening on the boat, when she had charged one Jimmy Crocker with having cured her of sentiment. A cold sweat sprang into being about his temples. He could remember that interview now, as clearly as if it had happened five minutes ago instead of five years.

He could recall the article for the *Sunday Chronicle* that he had written from the interview, and the ghoulish gusto with which he had written it. He had had a boy's undisciplined sense of humour in those days, the sense of humour that riots like a young colt, careless of what it bruises and crushes. He shuddered at the recollection of the things he had hammered out so gleefully on his typewriter down at the *Chronicle* office. He found himself recoiling in disgust from the man he had been, the man who could have done a wanton thing like that without compunction or ruth. He had read extracts from the article to an appreciative colleague— A great sympathy for Ann welled up in him. No wonder she hated the memory of Jimmy Crocker.

It is probable that remorse would have tortured him even further had he not chanced to turn absently to page forty-six and read a poem entitled 'Love's Funeral'. It was not a long poem, and he had finished it inside of two minutes; but by that time a change had come upon his mood of self-loathing. He no longer felt like a particularly mean murderer. 'Love's Funeral' was like a tonic. It braced and invigorated him. It was so unspeakably absurd, so poor in every respect. All things, he now perceived, had worked together for good.

Ann had admitted on the boat that it was his satire that had crushed out of her the fondness for this sort of thing. If that was so then the part he had played in her life had been that of a rescuer. He thought of her as she was now and as she must have been then, to have written stuff like this, and he rejoiced at what he had done. In a manner of speaking the Ann of to-day, the glorious creature who went about the place kidnapping Ogdens, was his handiwork. It was he who had destroyed the minor poetry virus in her. The refrain of an old song came to him.

> You made me what I am to-day!
> I hope you're satisfied!

He was more than satisfied. He was proud of himself. He rejoiced, however, after the first flush of enthusiasm, somewhat moderately. There was no disguising the penalty of his deed of kindness. To Ann, Jimmy Crocker was no rescuer, but a sort of blend of ogre and vampire. She must never learn his real identity – or not until he had succeeded by assiduous toil, as he hoped he would, in neutralizing that prejudice of the distant past.

A footstep outside broke in on his thoughts. He thrust the book quickly back into its place. Ann came in and shut the door behind her.

'Well?' she said eagerly.

Jimmy did not reply for a moment. He was looking at her and thinking how perfect in every way she was now, as she stood there purged of sentimentality, all aglow with curiosity to know how her nefarious plans had succeeded. It was his Ann who stood there, not the author of *The Lonely Heart*.

'Did you ask her?'

'Yes, but—'

Ann's face fell.

'Oh! She won't let him come back?'

'She absolutely refused. I did my best.'

'I know you did.'

There was a silence.

'Well, this settles it,' said Jimmy. 'Now you will have to let me help you.'

Ann looked troubled.

'But it's such a risk. Something terrible might happen to you. Isn't impersonation a criminal offence?'

'What does it matter? They tell me prisons are excellent places nowadays. Concerts, picnics – all that sort of thing. I shan't mind going there. I have a nice singing voice. I think I will try to make the glee club.'

'I suppose we are breaking the law,' said Ann seriously. 'I told Jerry that nothing could happen to us, except the loss of his place to him and my being sent to my grandmother to me, but I'm bound to say I said that just to encourage him. Don't you think we ought to know what the penalty is, in case we are caught?'

'It would enable us to make our plans. If it's a life sentence I shouldn't worry about selecting my future career.'

'You see,' explained Ann, 'I suppose they would hardly send me to prison, as I'm a relation – though I would far rather go there than to Grandmother's. She lives all alone, miles away in the country and is strong on discipline; but they might do all sorts of things to you, in spite of my pleadings. I really think you had better give up the idea. I'm afraid my enthusiasm carried me away. I didn't think of all this before.'

'Never! This thing goes through or fails over my dead body. What are you looking for?'

Ann was deep in a bulky volume that stood on a lectern by the window.

'Catalogue,' she said briefly, turning the pages. 'Uncle Peter has heaps of law books. I'll look up kidnapping. Here we are: "Law encyclopædia – shelf X." Oh, that's upstairs. I shan't be a minute.'

She ran to the little staircase and disappeared. Her voice came from the gallery.

'Here we are! I've got it!'

'Shoot,' said Jimmy.

'There's such a lot of it,' called the voice from above, 'pages and pages. I'm just skimming. Wait a moment!'

A rustling followed fron the gallery, then a sneeze.

'This is the dustiest place I was ever in,' said the voice. 'It's inches deep everywhere. It's full of cigarette ends too. I must tell Uncle. Oh, here it is. Kidnapping penalties—'

'Hush!' called Jimmy. 'There's someone coming.'

The door opened.

'Hello,' said Ogden, strolling in. 'I was looking for you. Didn't think you would be here.'

'Come right in, my little man, and make yourself at home,' said Jimmy.

Ogden eyed him with disfavour.

'You're pretty fresh, aren't you?'

'This is praise from Sir Hubert Stanley.'

'Eh? Who's he?'

'Oh, a gentleman who knew what was what.'

Ogden closed the door.

'Well, I know what's what too. I know what you are for one thing.' He chuckled. 'I've got your number all right.'

'In what respect?'

Another chuckle proceeded from the bulbous boy.

'You think you're smooth, don't you? But I'm on to you, Jimmy Crocker! A lot of Jimmy Crocker you are. You're a crook. Get me? And I know what you're after, at that. You're going to try to kidnap me.'

From the corner of his eye Jimmy was aware of Ann's startled face, looking over the gallery rail and withdrawn hastily. No sound came from the heights, but he knew that she was listening intently.

'What makes you think that?'

Ogden lowered himself into the depth of his favourite easy-chair and, putting his feet restfully on the writing table, met Jimmy's gaze with a glassy but knowing eye.

'Got a cigarette?' he said.

'I have not,' said Jimmy. 'I'm sorry.'

'So am I.'

'Returning with your permission to our original subject,' said Jimmy, 'what makes you think that I have come here to kidnap you?'

Ogden yawned.

'I was in the drawing-room after lunch, and that guy Lord Wisbeach came in and said he wanted to talk to Mother privately. Mother sent me out of the room, so, of course, I listened at the door.'

'Do you know where little boys go who listen to private conversations?' said Jimmy severely.

'To the witness stand generally, I guess. Well, I listened, and I heard this Lord Wisbeach tell Mother that he had only pretended to recognize you as Jimmy Crocker and that really he had never seen you before in his life. He said you were a crook and that they had got to watch you. Well, I knew then why you had come here. It was pretty smooth, getting in the way you did. I've got to hand it to you.'

Jimmy did not reply. His mind was occupied with the contemplation of this dashing counterstroke on the part of Gentleman Jack. He could hardly refrain from admiring the simple strategy with which the latter had circumvented him. There was an artistry about the move that compelled respect.

'Well, now, see here,' said Ogden, 'you and I have got to get together on this proposition. I've been kidnapped twice before, and the only guys that made anything out of it were the kidnappers. It's pretty soft for them. They couldn't have got a cent without me, and they never dreamed of giving me a rake-off. I'm getting good and tired of being kidnapped for other people's benefit, and I've made up my mind that the next guy that wants me has got to come across. See? My proposition is fifty-fifty. If you like it I'm game to let you go ahead. If you don't like it then the deal's off, and you'll find that you've a darned poor chance of getting me. When I was kidnapped before I was just a kid, but I can look after myself now. Well, what do you say?'

Jimmy found it hard at first to say anything. He had never properly understood the possibilities of Ogden's character before. The longer he contemplated him, the more admirable Ann's scheme appeared. It seemed to him that only a resolute keeper of a home for dogs would be adequately equipped for dealing with this remarkable youth.

'This is a commercial age,' he said.

'You bet it is!' said Ogden. 'My middle name is business. Say, are you working this on your own, or are you in with Buck Maginnis and his crowd?'

'I don't think I know Mr Maginnis.'

'He's the guy who kidnapped me the first time. He's a roughneck. Smooth Sam Fisher got away with me the second time. Maybe you're in with Sam?'

'No.'

'No, I guess not. I heard that he had married and retired from business. I rather wish you were one of Buck's lot. I like Buck.

When he kidnapped me I lived with him and he gave me a swell time. When I left him a woman came and interviewed me about it for one of the Sunday papers. Sob stuff. Called the piece "Even Kidnappers Have Tender Hearts Beneath a Rough Exterior". I've got it upstairs in my press-clipping album. It was pretty bad slush. Buck Maginnis hasn't got any tender heart beneath his rough exterior, but he's a good sort and I liked him. We used to shoot craps, and he taught me to chew. I'd be tickled to death to have Buck get me again. But, if you're working on your own, all right. It's all the same to me, provided you meet me on the terms.'

'You certainly are a fascinating child.'

'Less of it, less of it. I've troubles enough to bear without having you getting fresh. Well, what about it? Talk figures. If I let you take me away, do we divvy up or don't we? That's all you've got to say.'

'That's easily settled. I'll certainly give you half of whatever I get.'

Ogden looked wistfully at the writing desk.

'I wish I could have that in writing. But I guess it wouldn't stand in law. I suppose I shall have to trust you.'

'Honour among thieves.'

'Less of the thieves. This is just a straight business proposition. I've got something valuable to sell, and I'm darned if I'm going to keep giving it away. I've been too easy. I ought to have thought of this before. All right, then, that's settled. Now it's up to you! You can think out the rest of it yourself!'

He heaved himself out of the chair and left the room. Ann, coming down from the gallery, found Jimmy meditating. He looked up at the sound of her step.

'Well, that seems to make it pretty easy for us, doesn't it?' he said. 'It solves the problem of ways and means.'

'But this is awful. This alters everything. It isn't safe for you to stay here. You must go away at once. They've found you out. You may be arrested at any moment.'

'That's a side issue. The main point is to put this thing through. Then we can think about what is going to happen to me.'

'But can't you see the risk you're running?'

'I don't mind. I want to help you.'

'I won't let you.'

'You must.'

'But do be sensible. What would you think of me if I allowed you to face this danger—'

'I wouldn't think any differently of you. My opinion of you is a fixed thing. Nothing can alter it. I tried to tell you on the boat, but you wouldn't let me. I think you're the most perfect, wonderful girl in all the world. I've loved you since the first moment I saw you. I knew who you were when we met for half a minute that day in London. We were utter strangers, but I knew you. You were the girl I had been looking for all my life. Good heavens, you talk of risks! Can't you understand that just being with you and speaking to you and knowing that we share this thing is enough to wipe out any thought of risk? I'd do anything for you; and you expect me to back out of this thing because there is a certain amount of danger!'

Ann had retreated to the door and was looking at him with wide eyes. With other young men – and there had been many – who had said much the same sort of thing to her since her *débutante* days, she had been cool and composed – a little sorry, perhaps, but in no doubt as to her own feelings and her ability to resist their pleadings. But now her heart was racing and the conviction had begun to steal over her that the cool and composed Ann Chester was in imminent danger of making a fool of herself. Quite suddenly, without any sort of warning, she realized that there was some quality in Jimmy that called aloud to some corresponding quality in herself – a nebulous something that made her know that he and she were mates. She knew herself hard to please where men were concerned. She could not have described what it was in her that all the men she had met – the men with whom she had golfed and ridden and yachted – had failed to satisfy; but, ever since she had acquired the power of self-analysis, she had known that it was something that was a solid and indestructible part of her composition. She could not have put into words what quality she demanded in man, but she had always known that she would recognize it when she found it – and she recognized it now in Jimmy. It was a recklessness, an irresponsibility, a cheerful dare-deviltry, the complement to her own gay lawlessness.

'Ann!' said Jimmy.

'It's too late!'

She had not meant to say that. She had meant to say that it was impossible, out of the question. But her heart was running away with her, goaded on by the irony of it all. A veil seemed to have fallen from before her eyes, and she knew now why she had been drawn to Jimmy from the very first. They were mates, and she had thrown away her happiness.

'I've promised to marry Lord Wisbeach!'

Jimmy stopped dead, as if the blow had been a physical one.

'You've promised to marry Lord Wisbeach!'

'Yes.'

'But – but when?'

'Just now – only a few minutes ago, when I was driving him to his hotel. He had asked me to marry him before I left for England, and I had promised to give him his answer when I got back. But when I got back somehow I couldn't make up my mind. The days slipped by. Something seemed to be holding me back. He pressed me to say that I would marry him, and it seemed absurd to go on refusing to be definite, so I said I would.'

'You can't love him? Surely you do not—'

Ann met his gaze frankly.

'Something seems to have happened to me in the last few minutes,' she said, 'and I can't think clearly. A little while ago it didn't seem to matter much. I liked him. He was good-looking and good-tempered. I felt that we should get along quite well and be as happy as most people are. That seemed as near perfection as one could expect to get nowadays, so – well, that's how it was.'

'But you can't marry him! It's out of the question!'

'I've promised.'

'You must break your promise!'

'I can't do that.'

'You must!'

'I can't. One must play the game.'

Jimmy groped for words.

'But in this case – you mustn't – it's awful – in this special case—' He broke off. He saw the trap he was in. He could not denounce that crook without exposing himself. And from that he still shrank. Ann's prejudice against Jimmy Crocker might have its root in a trivial and absurd grievance, but it had been growing through the years, and who could say how strong it was now?

Ann came a step toward him, then paused doubtfully. Then, as if making up her mind, she drew near and touched his sleeve.

'I'm sorry,' she said.

There was a silence.

'I'm sorry!'

She moved away. The door closed softly behind her. Jimmy scarcely knew that she had gone. He sat down in that deep chair that was Mr Pett's favourite and stared sightlessly at the ceiling. And then – how many minutes or hours later he did not know – the sharp click of the door handle roused him. He sprang from the chair. Was it Ann come back?

It was not Ann. Round the edge of the door came inquiringly the fair head of Lord Wisbeach.

'Oh!' said his lordship, sighting Jimmy.

The head withdrew itself.

'Come here!' shouted Jimmy.

The head appeared again.

'Talking to me?'

'Yes, I was talking to you.'

Lord Wisbeach followed his superstructure into the room. He was outwardly all that was bland and unperturbed, but there was a wary look in the eye that cocked itself at Jimmy, and he did not move far from the door. His fingers rested easily on the handle behind him. He did not think it probable that Jimmy could have heard of his visit to Mrs Pett, but there had been something menacing in the latter's voice, and Lord Wisbeach believed in safety first.

'They told me Miss Chester was here,' he said, by way of relaxing any possible strain there might be in the situation.

'And what the devil do you want with Miss Chester, you slimy, crawling, second-story worker, you oily yegg?' inquired Jimmy.

The sunniest optimist could not have deluded himself into the belief that the words were spoken in a friendly and genial spirit. Lord Wisbeach's fingers tightened on the door handle, and he grew a little flushed about the cheek bones.

'What's all this about?' he said.

'You infernal crook!'

Lord Wisbeach looked anxious.

'Don't shout like that! Are you crazy? Do you want people to hear?'

Jimmy drew a deep breath.

'I shall have to get farther away from you,' he said more quietly. 'There's no knowing what may happen, if I don't. I don't want to kill you. At least I do, but I had better not.'

He retired slowly, until brought to a halt by the writing desk. To this he anchored himself with a firm grip. He was extremely anxious to do nothing rash, and the spectacle of Gentleman Jack invited rashness. He leaned against the desk, clutching its solidity with both hands. Lord Wisbeach held steadfastly to the door handle. And in this tense fashion the interview proceeded.

'Miss Chester,' said Jimmy, forcing himself to speak calmly, 'has just been telling me that she has promised to marry you.'

'Quite true,' said Lord Wisbeach. 'It will be announced to-morrow.' A remark trembled on his lips, to the effect that he relied on Jimmy for a fish slice, but prudence kept it unspoken. He was unable at present to understand Jimmy's emotion. Why Jimmy should object to his being engaged to Ann he could not imagine. But it was plain that for some reason he had taken the thing to heart and, dearly as he loved a bit of quiet fun, Lord Wisbeach decided that the other was at least six inches too tall and fifty pounds too heavy to be bantered in his present mood by one of his own physique. 'Why not?'

'It won't be announced to-morrow,' said Jimmy. 'Because by to-morrow you will be as far away from here as you can get, if you have any sense.'

'What do you mean?'

'Just this – if you haven't left this house by breakfast time to-morrow I shall expose you.'

Lord Wisbeach was not feeling particularly happy, but he laughed at this.

'You!'

'That's what I said.'

'Who do you think you are, to go about exposing people?'

'I happen to be Mrs Pett's nephew, Jimmy Crocker.'

Lord Wisbeach laughed again.

'Is that the line you are going to take?'

'It is.'

'You are going to Mrs Pett to tell her that you are Jimmy Crocker and that I am a crook, and that you only pretended to recognize me for reasons of your own?'

'Just that.'

'Forget it!' Lord Wisbeach had forgotten to be alarmed in his amusement. He smiled broadly. 'I'm not saying it's not good stuff to pull, but it is old stuff now. I'm sorry for you, but I thought of it before you did. I went to Mrs Pett directly after lunch and sprang that line of talk myself. Do you think she'll believe you after that? I tell you I'm ace high with that dame. You can't queer me with her.'

'I think I can – for the simple reason that I really am Jimmy Crocker.'

'Yes, you are!'

'Exactly. Yes, I am.'

Lord Wisbeach smiled tolerantly.

'It was worth trying the bluff, I guess, but it won't work. I know you'd be glad to get me out of this house, but you've got to make a better play than that to do it.'

'Don't deceive yourself with the idea that I'm bluffing. Look here!' He suddenly removed his coat, and threw it to Lord Wisbeach. 'Read the tailor's label inside the pocket! See the name, also the address – "J. Crocker, Drexdale House, Grosvenor Square, London"!'

Lord Wisbeach picked up the garment and looked as directed. His face turned a little sallower, but he still fought against his growing conviction.

'That's no proof.'

'Perhaps not. But, when you consider the reputation of the tailor whose name is on the label, it's hardly likely that he would be standing in with an impostor, is it? If you want real proof I have no doubt that there are half a dozen men working on the *Chronicle* who can identify me. Or are you convinced already?'

Lord Wisbeach capitulated.

'I don't know what fool game you think you're playing, but I can't see why you couldn't have told me this when we were talking after lunch.'

'Never mind, I had my reasons. They don't matter. What matters is that you are going to get out of here to-morrow. Do you understand that?'

'I get you.'

'Then that's about all, I think. Don't let me keep you!'

'Say, listen!' Gentleman Jack's voice was plaintive. 'I think you might give a fellow a chance to get out good. Give me time to have a guy in Montreal send me a telegram, telling me to go up there right away. Otherwise you might just as well put the cops on me at once. The old lady knows I've got business in Canada. You don't need to be rough on a fellow.'

Jimmy pondered this point.

'All right, I don't object to that.'

'Thanks.'

'Don't start anything, though!'

'I don't know what you mean.'

Jimmy pointed to the safe.

'Come, come, friend of my youth. We have no secrets from each other. I know you're after what's in there, and you know that I know. I don't want to harp on it, but you'll be spending to-night in the house, and I think you had better make up your mind to spend it in your room, getting a nice sleep to prepare you for your journey. Do you follow me, old friend?'

'I get you.'

'That will be all then, I think. Wind a smile round your neck and recede.'

The door slammed. Lord Wisbeach had restrained his feelings successfully during the interview, but he could not deny himself that slight expression of them. Jimmy crossed the room and took his coat from the chair where the other had dropped it. As he did so a voice spoke:

'Say!'

Jimmy spun round. The room was apparently empty. The thing was beginning to assume an uncanny aspect when the voice spoke again.

'You think you're darned funny, don't you!'

It came from above. Jimmy had forgotten the gallery. He directed his gaze thither and perceived the heavy face of Ogden, hanging over the rail like a gargoyle.

'What are you doing there?' he demanded.

'Listening.'

'How did you get there?'

'There's a door back here that you get to from the stairs. I often come here for a quiet cigarette. Say, you think yourself some josher, don't you, telling me you were a kidnapper! You strung me like an onion. So you're really Jimmy Crocker after all? Where was the sense in pulling all that stuff about taking me away and divvying up the ransom? Aw, you make me tired!'

The head was withdrawn, and Jimmy heard heavy steps followed by the banging of a door. Peace reigned in the library.

Jimmy sat down in the chair that was Mr Pett's favourite, which Ogden was accustomed to occupy to that gentleman's displeasure. The swiftness of recent events had left him a little dizzy, and he desired to think matters over and find out exactly what had happened.

The only point that appeared absolutely clear to him, in a welter of confusing occurrences, was the fact that he had lost the chance of kidnapping Ogden. Everything had arranged itself so beautifully simply and conveniently, as regarded that venture, until a moment ago; but now that the boy had discovered his identity it was impossible for him to attempt it. He was loath to accept this fact. Surely, even now, there was a way— Quite suddenly an admirable plan occurred to him. It involved the co-operation of his father. And at that thought he realized, with a start, that life had been moving so rapidly for him, since his return to the house, that he had not paid any attention at all to what was really as amazing a mystery as any. He had been too busy to wonder why his father was there.

Jimmy debated the best method of getting in touch with him. It was out of the question to descend to the pantry, or wherever it was that his father lived in this new incarnation of his. Then the happy thought struck him that results might be obtained by the simple process of ringing the bell. It might produce some other unit of the domestic staff. However, it was worth trying. He rang the bell.

A few moments later the door opened. Jimmy looked up. It was not his father. It was a dangerous-looking female of uncertain age, dressed as a parlour-maid, who eyed him with – what seemed to his conscience-stricken soul – dislike and suspicion. She had a tight-lipped mouth and beady eyes beneath heavy brows. Jimmy had seldom seen a woman who attracted him less at first sight.

'Jer ring, s'?'

Jimmy blinked and almost ducked. The words had come at him like a projectile.

'Oh, ah, yes.'

'J' want anything, s'?'

With an effort, Jimmy induced his mind to resume its interrupted equilibrium.

'Oh, ah, yes. Would you mind sending Skinner, the butler, to me?'

'Y's'r.'

The apparition vanished. Jimmy drew out his handkerchief and dabbed at his forehead. He felt weak and guilty. He felt as if he had just been accused of nameless crimes and had been unable to deny the charge. Such was the magic of Miss Trimble's eye – the left one, which looked directly at its object. Conjecture pauses, baffled at the thought of the effect that her gaze might have created in the breasts of the sex she despised, had it been double instead of single-barrelled. But half of it had wasted itself on a spot some few feet to his right.

Presently the door opened again and Mr Crocker appeared, looking like a benevolent priest.

CHAPTER 19

'Well, Skinner, my man,' said Jimmy, 'how goes it?' Mr Crocker looked about him cautiously. Then his priestly manner fell from him like a robe, and he bounded forward.

'Jimmy!' he exclaimed, seizing his son's hand and shaking it violently. 'Say, it's great seeing you again, Jim!'

Jimmy drew himself up haughtily.

'Skinner, my good menial, you forget yourself strangely! You will be getting fired if you mitt the handsome guest in this chummy fashion!' He slapped his father on the back. 'Dad, this is great! How on earth do you come to be here? What's the idea? Why the buttling? When did you come over? Tell me all!'

Mr Crocker hoisted himself nimbly on to the writing desk and sat there, beaming, with dangling legs.

'It was your letter that did it, Jimmy. Say, Jim, there wasn't any need for you to do a thing like that just for me.'

'Well, I thought you would have a better chance of being a peer without me round. By the way, Dad, how did my stepmother take the Lord Percy episode?'

A shadow fell upon Mr Crocker's happy face.

'I don't like to do much thinking about your stepmother,' he said. 'She was pretty sore about Percy. And she was pretty sore about your lighting out for America. But, gee, what she must be feeling like now that I've come over, I daren't let myself think!'

'You haven't explained that yet. Why did you come over?'

'Well, I'd been feeling homesick – I always do over there in the baseball season – and then talking with Pett made it worse—'

'Talking with Pett? Did you see him, then, when he was in London?'

'See him? I let him in!'

'How?'

'Into the house, I mean. I had just gone to the front door to see what sort of a day it was – I wanted to know if there had been enough rain in the night to stop my having to watch that cricket game – and just as I got there the bell rang. I opened the door.'

'A revoltingly plebeian thing to do! I'm ashamed of you, Dad! They won't stand for that sort of thing in the House of Lords!'

'Well, before I knew what was happening they had taken me for the butler. I didn't want your stepmother to know I'd been opening doors – you remember how touchy she was always about it – so I just let it go at that and jollied them along. But I just couldn't help asking the old man how the pennant race was making out, and that tickled him so much that he offered me a job here as butler if I ever wanted to make a change. And then your note came saying that you were going to New York, and – well, I couldn't help myself. You couldn't have kept me in London with ropes. I sneaked out next day and bought a passage on the *Carmantic* – she sailed the Wednesday after you left – and came straight here. They gave me this job right away.' Mr Crocker paused, and a holy light of enthusiasm made his homely features almost beautiful. 'Say, Jim, I've seen a ball game every darned day since I landed! Say, two days running Larry Doyle made home runs! But, gosh, that guy Klem is one swell robber!

See here!' Mr Crocker sprang down from the desk and snatched up a handful of books, which he proceeded to distribute about the floor. 'There were two men on bases in the sixth and What's-his-Name came to bat. He lined one out to centre field – where this book is – and—'

'Pull yourself together, Skinner! You can't monkey about with the employer's library like that.' Jimmy restored the books to their places. 'Simmer down and tell me more. Postpone the gossip from the diamond. What plans have you made? Have you considered the future at all? You aren't going to hold down this buttling job for ever, are you? When do you go back to London?'

The light died out of Mr Crocker's face.

'I guess I shall have to go back some time. But how can I yet, with the Giants leading the league like this?'

'But did you just light out without saying anything?'

'I left a note for your stepmother telling her I had gone to America for a vacation. Jimmy, I hate to think what she's going to do to me when she gets me back!'

'Assert yourself, Dad! Tell her that woman's place is the home and man's the ball park! Be firm!'

Mr Crocker shook his head dubiously.

'It's all very well to talk that way when you're three thousand miles from home, but you know as well as I do, Jim, that your stepmother, though she's a delightful woman, isn't the sort you can assert yourself with. Look at this sister of hers here! I guess you haven't been in the house long enough to have noticed, but she's very like Eugenia in some ways. She's the boss all right, and old Pett does just what he's told to. I guess it's the same with me, Jim. There's a certain type of man that's just born to have it put over on him by a certain type of woman. I'm that sort of man and your stepmother's that sort of woman. No, I guess I'm going to get mine all right, and the only thing to do is to keep it from stopping me having a good time now.'

There was truth in what he said, and Jimmy recognized it. He changed the subject.

'Well, never mind that. There's no sense in worrying oneself about the future. Tell me, Dad, where did you get all the "dinner-is-served, madam" stuff? How did you ever learn to be a butler?'

'Bayliss taught me back in London. And, of course, I've played butlers when I was on the stage.'

Jimmy did not speak for a moment.

'Did you ever play a kidnapper, Dad?' he asked at length.

'Sure, I was Chicago Ed in a crook play called "This Way Out". Why, surely you saw me in that? I got some good notices.'

Jimmy nodded.

'Of course. I knew I'd seen you play that sort of part some time. You came on during the dark scene and—'

'Switched on the lights and—'

'Covered the bunch with your gun while they were still blinking! You were great in that part, Dad.'

'It was a good part,' said Mr Crocker modestly. 'It had fat. I'd like to have got a chance to play a kidnapper again. There's a lot of pep to kidnappers.'

'You shall play one again,' said Jimmy. 'I am putting on a little sketch with a kidnapper as the star part.'

'Eh? A sketch? You, Jim? Where?'

'Here – in this house! It is entitled "Kidnapping Ogden", and it opens to-night.'

Mr Crocker looked at his only son in concern. Jimmy appeared to him to be rambling.

'Amateur theatricals?' he hazarded.

'In the sense that there is no pay for performing, yes. Dad, you know that kid Ogden upstairs? Well, it's quite simple. I want you to kidnap him for me.'

Mr Crocker sat down heavily. He shook his head.

'I don't follow all this.'

'Of course not. I haven't begun to explain. Dad, in your rambles through this joint you've noticed a girl with glorious red-gold hair, I imagine?'

'Ann Chester?'

'Ann Chester. I'm going to marry her.'

'Jimmy!'

'But she doesn't know it yet. Now follow me carefully, Dad! Five years ago Ann Chester wrote a book of poems. It's on that desk there. You were using it a moment back as second base or something. Now I was working at that time on the *Chronicle*. I wrote a skit on those poems for the Sunday paper. Do you begin to follow the plot?'

'She's got it in for you? She's sore?'

'Exactly. Get that firmly fixed in your mind, because it's the source from which all the rest of the story springs.'

Mr Crocker interrupted.

'But I don't understand. You say she's sore at you. Well, how is it that you came in together looking as if you were good friends when I let you in this morning?'

'I was waiting for you to ask that. The explanation is that she doesn't know that I am Jimmy Crocker.'

'But you came here saying that you were Jimmy Crocker.'

'Quite right. And that is where the plot thickens. I made Ann's acquaintance first in London and then on the boat. I had found out that Jimmy Crocker was the man she hated most in the world, so I took another name. I called myself Bayliss.'

'Bayliss!'

'I had to think of something quick, because the clerk at the shipping office was waiting to fill in my ticket. I had just been talking to Bayliss on the phone, and his was the only name that came into my mind. You know how it is when you try to think of a name suddenly. Now mark the sequel! Old Bayliss came to see me off at Paddington. Ann was there and saw me. She said "Good evening, Mr Bayliss" or something, and naturally old Bayliss replied "What ho!" or words to that effect. The only way to handle the situation was to introduce him as my father. I did so. Ann, therefore, thinks that I am a young man named Bayliss, who has come over to America to make his fortune. We now come to the third reel. I met Ann by chance at the Knicker-bocker and took her to lunch. While we were lunching, that confirmed congenital idiot, Reggie Bartling, who for some reason has come over to America, came up and called me by my name. I knew that if Ann discovered who I really was she would have nothing more to do with me, so I gave Reggie the haughty stare and told him that he had made a mistake. He ambled away – and possibly committed suicide in his anguish at having made such a bloomer – leaving Ann discussing with me the extraordinary coincidence of my being Jimmy Crocker's double. Do you follow the story of my life so far?'

Mr Crocker, who had been listening with wrinkled brow and other signs of rapt attention, nodded.

'I understand all that. But how did you come to get into this house?'

'That is reel four. I am getting to that. It seems that Ann, who is the sweetest girl on earth and always on the lookout to do someone a kindness, had decided, in the interest of the boy's future, to remove young Ogden Ford from his present sphere where he is being spoiled and ruined, and send him down to a man on Long Island who would keep him for a while and instil the first principles of decency into him. Her accomplice in this admirable scheme was Jerry Mitchell.'

'Jerry Mitchell!'

'Who, as you know, got fired yesterday. Jerry was to have done the rough work of the job. But, being fired, he was no longer available. I, therefore, offered to take his place. So here I am.'

'You're going to kidnap that boy?'

'No, you are.'

'Me!'

'Precisely. You are going to play a benefit performance of your world-famed success, Chicago Ed. Let me explain further. Owing to circumstances which I need not go into, Ogden has found out that I am really Jimmy Crocker, so he refuses to have anything more to do with me. I had deceived him into believing that I was a professional kidnapper, and he came to me and offered to let me kidnap him if I would go fifty-fifty with him in the ransom!'

'Gosh!'

'Yes, he's an intelligent child, full of that sort of bright ideas. Well, now he has found that I am not all his fancy painted me, he wouldn't come away with me; and I want you to under-study me while the going is good. In the fifth reel, which will be released to-night, after the household has retired to rest, you will be featured. It's got to be to-night, because it has just occurred to me that Ogden, knowing that Lord Wisbeach is a crook, may go to him with the same proposal that he has made to me.'

'Lord Wisbeach a crook!'

'Of the worst description. He is here to steal that explosive stuff of Willie Partridge's. But, as I have blocked that play, he may turn his attention to Ogden.'

'But, Jimmy, if that fellow is a crook— How do you know he is?'

'He told me so himself.'

'Well, then, why don't you expose him?'

'Because in order to do so, Skinner, my man, I should have to explain that I was really Jimmy Crocker, and the time is not yet ripe for that. To my thinking, the time will not be ripe till you have got safely away with Ogden Ford. I can then go to Ann and say: "I may have played you a rotten trick in the past, but I have done you a good turn now, so let's forget the past!" So you see that everything now depends on you, Dad. I'm not asking you to do anything difficult. I'll go round to the boarding house now and tell Jerry Mitchell about what we have arranged, and have him waiting outside here in a car. Then all you will have to do is to go to Ogden, play a short scene as Chicago Ed, escort him to the car, and then go back to bed and have a good sleep. Once Ogden thinks you are a professional kidnapper, you won't have any difficulty at all. Get it into your head that he wants to be kidnapped. Surely you can tackle this light and attractive job? Why, it will be a treat for you to do a bit of character acting once more!'

Jimmy had struck the right note. His father's eyes began to gleam with excitement. The scent of the footlights seemed to dilate his nostrils.

'I was always good at that roughneck stuff,' he murmured meditatively. 'I used to eat it!'

'Exactly,' said Jimmy. 'Look at it in the right way, and I am doing you a kindness in giving you this chance!'

Mr Crocker rubbed his neck with his forefinger.

'You'd want me to make up for the part?' he asked wistfully.

'Of course!'

'You'd want me to do it to-night?'

'At about two in the morning, I thought.'

'I'll do it, Jim!'

Jimmy grasped his hand.

'I knew I could rely on you, Dad.'

Mr Crocker was following a train of thought.

'Dark wig . . . blue chin . . . heavy eyebrows . . . I guess I can't do better than my old Chicago Ed make-up. Say, Jimmy, how am I to get to the kid?'

'That'll be all right. You can stay in my room till the time comes to go to him. Use it as a dressing-room.'

'How am I to get him out of the house?'

'Through this room. I'll tell Jerry to wait out on the side street with the car from two o'clock on.'

Mr Crocker considered these arrangements.

'That seems to be about all,' he said.

'I don't think there's anything else.'

'I'll slip down town and buy the props.'

'I'll go and tell Jerry.'

A thought struck Mr Crocker.

'You'd better tell Jerry to make up too. He doesn't want the kid recognizing him and squealing on him later.'

Jimmy was lost in admiration of his father's resource.

'You think of everything, Dad! That wouldn't have occurred to me. You certainly do take to crime in the most wonderful way. It seems to come naturally to you!'

Mr Crocker smirked modestly.

CHAPTER 20

A plot is only as strong as its weakest link. The best-laid schemes of mice and men gang oft a-gley, if one of the mice is a mental defective, or if one of the men is a Jerry Mitchell.

Celestine, Mrs Pett's maid – she who was really Maggie O'Toole and whom Jerry loved with a strength that deprived him of even the small amount of intelligence bestowed upon him by Nature – came into the housekeeper's room at about ten o'clock that night. The domestic staff had gone in a body to the moving pictures, and the only occupant of the room was the new parlour-maid, who was sitting in a hard chair, reading Schopenhauer.

Celestine's face was flushed, her dark hair was ruffled, and her eyes were shining. She breathed a little quickly, and her left hand was out of sight behind her back. She eyed the new parlour-maid doubtfully for a moment. The latter was a woman of a somewhat unencouraging exterior, not the kind that invites confidences. But Celestine had confidences to bestow, and the exodus to the movies had left her in a position where she could not pick and choose. She was faced with the alternative of locking her secret in her palpitating bosom or of revealing it to this one auditor. The choice was one that no impulsive damsel in like circumstances would have hesitated to make.

'Say!' said Celestine.

A face rose reluctantly from behind Schopenhauer. A gleaming eye met Celestine's. A second eye – no less gleaming – glared at the ceiling.

'Say, I just been talking to my feller outside,' said Celestine with a coy simper. 'Say, he's a grand man!'

A snort of uncompromising disapproval proceeded from the thin-lipped mouth beneath the gleaming eyes. But Celestine was too full of her news to be discouraged.

'I'm strong for Jer!' she said.

'Huh?' said the student of Schopenhauer.

'Jerry Mitchell, you know. You ain't never met him, have you? Say, he's a grand man!'

For the first time she had the other's undivided attention. The new parlour-maid placed her book upon the table.

'Uh?' she said.

Celestine could hold back her dramatic surprise no longer. Her concealed left hand flashed into view. On the third finger glittered a ring. She gazed at it with awed affection.

'Ain't it a beaut?'

She contemplated its sparkling perfection for a moment in rapturous silence.

'Say, you could have knocked me down with a feather!' she resumed. 'He telephones me a while ago and says to be outside the back-door at ten to-night, because he'd something he wanted to tell me. Of course he couldn't come in and tell me here, because he'd been fired and everything. So I goes out, and there he is. "Hello, kid!" he says to me. "Fresh!" I says to him. "Say, I got something to be fresh about!" he says to me. And then he reaches into his jeans and hauls out the sparkler. "What's that?" I says to him. "It's an engagement ring," he says to me.

"For you, if you'll wear it!" I came over so weak I could have fell! And the next thing I know he's got it on my finger and—'

Celestine broke off modestly.

'Say, ain't it a beaut, honest!' She gave herself over to contemplation once more. 'He says to me how he's on Easy Street now, or will be pretty soon. I says to him, "Have you got a job, then?" He says to me, "Naw, I ain't got a job, but I'm going to pull off a stunt to-night that's going to mean enough to me to start that health farm I've told you about." Say, he's always had a line of talk about starting a health farm down on Long Island, he knowing all about training and health and everything through having been one of them fighters. I asks him what the stunt is, but he won't tell me yet. He says he'll tell me after we're married, but he says it's sure fire and he's going to buy the licence to-morrow.'

She paused for comment and congratulations, eyeing her companion expectantly.

'Huh!' said the new parlour-maid briefly and resumed her Schopenhauer. Decidedly hers was not a winning personality.

'Ain't it a beaut?' demanded Celestine, damped.

The new parlour-maid uttered a curious sound at the back of her throat.

'He's a beaut!' she said cryptically. She added another remark in a lower tone, too low for Celestine's ears. It could hardly have been that, but it sounded to Celestine like: 'I'll fix 'im!'

Riverside Drive slept. The moon shone on darkened windows and deserted sidewalks. It was past one o'clock in the morning. The wicked Forties were still ablaze with light and noisy with fox trots; but in the virtuous Hundreds, where Mr Pett's house stood, respectable slumber reigned. Only the occasional drone of a passing automobile broke the silence or the love-sick cry of some feline Romeo, patrolling a wall top.

Jimmy was awake. He was sitting on the edge of his bed, watching his father put the finishing touches to his make-up, which was of a shaggy and intimidating nature. The elder Crocker had conceived the outward aspect of Chicago Ed, King of the Kidnappers, on broad and impressive lines, and one glance would have been enough to tell the sagacious observer that there was no white-souled comrade for a nocturnal saunter down lonely lanes and out-of-the-way alleys.

Mr Crocker seemed to feel this himself.

'The only trouble is, Jim,' he said, peering at himself in the glass, 'shan't I scare the boy to death directly he sees me? Oughtn't I to give him some sort of warning?'

'How? Do you suggest sending him a formal note?'

Mr Crocker surveyed his repellent features doubtfully.

'It's a good deal to spring on a kid at one in the morning,' he said. 'Suppose he has a fit!'

'He's far more likely to give you one. Don't you worry about Ogden, Dad! I shouldn't think there was a child alive more equal to handling such a situation.'

There was an empty glass standing on a tray on the dressing-table. Mr Crocker eyed this sadly.

'I wish you hadn't thrown that stuff away, Jim. I could have done with it. I'm feeling nervous.'

'Nonsense, Dad! You're all right! I had to throw it away. I'm on the waggon now, but how long I should have stayed on with that smiling up at me, I don't know. I've made up my mind never to lower myself to the level of the beasts that perish with the demon rum again, because my future wife has strong views on the subject; but there's no sense in taking chances. Temptation is all very well, but you don't need it on your dressing-table. It was a kindly thought of yours to place it there, Dad, but—'

'Eh? I didn't put it there.'

'I thought that sort of thing came in your department. Isn't it the butler's job to supply drinks to the nobility and gentry? Well, it doesn't matter. It is now distributed over the neighbouring soil, thus removing a powerful temptation from your path. You're better without it.' He looked at his watch. 'Well, it ought to be all right now.' He went to the window. 'There's an automobile down there. I suppose it's Jerry. I told him to be outside at one sharp, and it's nearly half-past. I think you might be starting, Dad. Oh, by the way, you had better tell Ogden that you represent a gentleman of the name of Buck Maginnis. It was Buck who got away with him last time, and a firm friendship seems to have sprung up between them. There's nothing like coming with a good introduction.'

Mr Crocker took a final survey of himself in the mirror.

'Gee! I'd hate to meet myself on a lonely road!'

He opened the door and stood for a moment listening. From somewhere down the passage came the murmur of a muffled snore.

'Third door on the left,' said Jimmy. 'Three – count 'em – three. Don't go getting mixed!'

Mr Crocker slid into the outer darkness like a stout ghost, and Jimmy closed the door gently behind him.

Having launched his indulgent parent safely on a career of crime, Jimmy switched off the light and returned to the window. Leaning out he gave himself up for a moment to sentimental musings. The night was very still. Through the trees that flanked the house the dimmed headlights of what was presumably Jerry Mitchell's hired car shone faintly like enlarged fireflies. A boat of some description was tooting reflectively far down the river. Such was the seductive influence of the time and the scene that Jimmy might have remained there indefinitely weaving dreams, had he not been under the necessity of making his way down to the library. It was his task to close the French windows after his father and Ogden had passed through, and he proposed to remain hid in the gallery there until the time came for him to do this. It was imperative that he avoid being seen by Ogden.

Locking his door behind him he went downstairs. There were no signs of life in the house. Everything was still. He found the staircase leading to the gallery without having to switch on the lights.

It was dusty in the gallery, and a smell of old leather enveloped him. He hoped his father would not be long. He lowered himself cautiously to the floor and, resting his head against a convenient shelf, began to wonder how the interview between Chicago Ed and his prey was progressing.

Mr Crocker, meanwhile, masked to the eyes, had crept in fearful silence to the door that Jimmy had indicated. A good deal of the gay enthusiasm with which he had embarked on this enterprise had ebbed away from him. Now that he had become accustomed to the novelty of finding himself once more playing a character part, his innate respectability began to assert itself. It was one thing to play Chicago Ed at a Broadway theatre, but quite another to give a benefit performance like this. As he tiptoed along the passage, the one thing that presented itself most clearly to him was the appalling outcome of this act of his, should anything go wrong. He would have turned back but for the thought that Jimmy was depending on him, and that success would mean Jimmy's happiness. Stimulated by this reflection, he opened Ogden's door inch by inch and went in. He stole softly across the room.

He had almost reached the bed and had just begun to wonder how on earth, now that he was here, he could open the proceedings tactfully and without alarming the boy, when he was saved the trouble of pondering further on this problem. A light flashed out of the darkness with the suddenness of a bursting bomb, and a voice from the same general direction said: 'Hands up!'

When Mr Crocker had finished blinking and had adjusted his eyes to the glare, he perceived Ogden sitting up in bed with a revolver in his hand. The revolver was resting on his knee, and its muzzle pointed directly at Mr Crocker's ample stomach.

Exhaustive as had been the thought that Jimmy's father had given to the possible developments of his enterprise, this was a contingency of which he had not dreamed. He was entirely at a loss.

'Don't do that!' he said huskily. 'It might go off!'

'I shouldn't worry!' replied Ogden coldly. 'I'm at the right end of it. What are you doing here?' He looked fondly at the lethal weapon. 'I got this with cigarette coupons to shoot rabbits when we went to the country. Here's where I get a chance at something part human.'

'Do you want to murder me?'

'Why not?'

Mr Crocker's make-up was trickling down his face in sticky streams. The mask, however, prevented Ogden from seeing this peculiar phenomenon. He was glaring interestedly at his visitor. An idea struck him.

'Say, did you come to kidnap me?'

Mr Crocker felt that sense of relief that he had sometimes experienced on the stage when memory had failed him during a scene and a fellow-actor had thrown him the line. It would be exaggerating to say that he was himself again. He could never be completely at his ease with that pistol pointing at him; but he felt considerably better. He lowered his voice an octave or so and spoke in a husky growl:

'Aw, cheese it, kid! Nix on the rough stuff!'

'Keep those hands up!' advised Ogden.

'Sure! Sure!' growled Mr Crocker. 'Can the gun play, bo! Say, you've soitanly grown some since de last time we got youse!'

Ogden's manner became magically friendly.

'Are you one of Buck Maginnis' lot?' he inquired almost politely.

'Dat's right!' Mr Crocker blessed the inspiration that had prompted Jimmy's parting words. 'I'm wit' Buck.'

'Why didn't Buck come himself?'

'He's woiking on anudder job!'

To Mr Crocker's profound relief, Ogden lowered the pistol.

'I'm strong for Buck,' he said conversationally. 'We're old pals. Did you see the piece in the paper about him kidnapping me last time? I've got it in my press-clipping album.'

'Sure,' said Mr Crocker.

'Say, listen! If you take me now Buck's got to come across. I like Buck, but I'm not going to let myself be kidnapped for his benefit. It's fifty-fifty or nothing doing. See?'

'I get you, kid.'

'Well, if that's understood, all right. Give me a minute to get some clothes on, and I'll be with you.'

'Don't make a noise,' said Mr Crocker.

'Who's making a noise? Say, how did you get in here?'

'T'roo de libery windows.'

'I always knew some yegg would stroll in that way. It beats me why they didn't have bars fixed on them.'

'Dere's a buzz waggon outside, waitin'.'

'You do it in style, don't you!' observed Ogden, pulling on his shirt. 'Who's working this with you? Anyone I know?'

'Naw. A new guy.'

'Oh? Say, I don't remember you, if it comes to that.'

'You don't?' said Mr Crocker, a little discomposed.

'Well, maybe I wouldn't, with that mask on you. Which of them are you?'

'Chicago Ed's my monaker.'

'I don't remember any Chicago Ed.'

'Well, you will after dis!' said Mr Crocker, happily inspired.

Ogden was eyeing him with sudden suspicion.

'Take that mask off and let's have a look at you.'

'Nothing doin'.'

'How am I to know you're on the level?'

Mr Crocker played a daring card.

'All right,' he said, making a move toward the door. 'It's up to youse. If you t'ink I'm not on de level I'll beat it.'

'Here, stop a minute,' said Ogden hastily, unwilling that a promising business deal should be abandoned in this summary manner. 'I'm not saying anything against you. There's no need to fly off the handle like that.'

'I'll tell Buck I couldn't get you,' said Mr Crocker, moving another step.

'Here, stop! What's the matter with you?'

'Are youse comin' wit' me?'

'Sure, if you get the conditions. Buck's got to slip me half of whatever he gets out of this.'

'Dat's right. Buck'll slip youse half of anyt'ing he gets.'

'All right then. Wait till I've got this shoe on and let's start. Now I'm ready.'

'Beat it quietly!'

'What did you think I was going to do? Sing?'

'Step dis way!' said Mr Crocker jocosely.

They left the room cautiously. Mr Crocker for a moment had a sense of something missing. He had reached the stairs before he realized what it was. Then it dawned upon him that what was lacking was the applause. The scene had deserved a round.

Jimmy, vigilant in the gallery, heard the library door open softly and, peering over the rail, perceived two dim forms in the darkness. One was large, the other small. They crossed the room together.

Whispered words reached him.

'I thought you said you came in this way.'

'Sure.'

'Then why's the shutter closed?'

'I fixed it after I was in.'

There was a faint scraping sound, followed by a click. The darkness of the room was relieved by moonlight. The figures passed through. Jimmy ran down from the gallery and closed the windows softly. He had just fastened the shutter, when from the passage outside there came the unmistakable sound of a footstep.

CHAPTER 22

Jimmy's first emotion on hearing the footstep was the crude instinct of self-preservation. All that he was able to think of at the moment was the fact that he was in a questionable position and one that would require a good deal of explaining away if he were found, and his only sensation was a strong desire to avoid discovery. He made a silent scrambling leap for the gallery stairs and reached their shelter just as the door opened. He stood there, rigid, waiting to be challenged, but apparently he had moved in time, for no voice spoke. The door closed so gently as to be almost inaudible, and then there was silence again. The room remained in darkness, and it was this perhaps that first suggested to Jimmy the comforting thought that the intruder was equally desirous of avoiding the scrutiny of his fellows. Jimmy had taken it for granted, in his first panic, that he himself was the only person in that room whose motives for being there would not have borne inspection. But now, safely hidden in the gallery, out of sight from the floor below, he had the leisure to consider the newcomer's movements and to draw conclusions from them.

An honest man's first act would surely have been to switch on the lights. And an honest man would hardly have crept so stealthily. It became apparent to Jimmy, as he leaned over the rail and tried to pierce the darkness, that there was sinister work afoot; and he had hardly reached this conclusion when his mind took a further leap and he guessed the identity of the soft-footed person below. It could be none but his old friend, Lord Wisbeach, known to the boys as Gentleman Jack. It surprised him that he had not thought of this before. Then it surprised him that, after the talk they had had only a few hours earlier in that very room, Gentleman Jack should have dared to risk this raid.

At this moment the blackness was relieved as if by the striking of a match. The man below had brought an electric torch into play, and now Jimmy could see clearly. He had been right in his surmise. It was Lord Wisbeach. He was kneeling in front of the safe. What he was doing to the safe Jimmy could not see, for the man's body was in the way; but the electric torch shone on his face, lighting up grim, serious features, quite unlike the amiable and slightly vacant mask that his lordship was wont to present to the world. As Jimmy looked, something happened in the pool of light beyond his vision. Gentleman Jack gave a muttered exclamation of satisfaction and then Jimmy saw that the door of the safe had swung open. The air was full of a penetrating smell of scorched metal. Jimmy was not an expert in these matters, but he had read from time to time of modern burglars and their methods, and he gathered that an oxy-acetylene blowpipe, with its flame that cuts steel as a knife cuts cheese, had been at work.

Lord Wisbeach flashed the torch into the open safe, plunged his hand in, and drew it out again, holding something. Handling this in a cautious and gingerly manner, he placed it carefully in his breast pocket. Then he straightened himself. He switched off the torch, and moved to the window, leaving the rest of his implements by the open safe. He unfastened the shutter, then raised the catch of the window. At this point it seemed to Jimmy that the time had come to interfere.

'Tut, tut!' he said in a tone of mild reproof.

The effect of the rebuke on Lord Wisbeach was remarkable. He jumped convulsively away from the window, then, revolving on his own axis, flashed the torch into every corner of the room.

'Who's that?' he gasped.

'Conscience!' said Jimmy.

Lord Wisbeach had overlooked the gallery in his researches. He now turned his torch upward. The light flooded the gallery on the opposite side of the room from where Jimmy stood. There was a pistol in Gentleman Jack's hand now. It followed the torch uncertainly.

Jimmy, lying flat on the gallery floor, spoke again.

'Throw that gun away and the torch too,' he said. 'I've got you covered!'

The torch flashed above his head, but the raised edge of the gallery rail protected him.

'I'll give you five seconds. If you haven't dropped that gun by then I shall shoot!'

As he began to count, Jimmy heartily regretted that he had allowed his appreciation of the dramatic to lead him into this situation. It would have been so simple to have roused the house in a prosaic way and avoided this delicate position. Suppose his bluff did not succeed! Suppose the other still clung to his pistol at the end of the five seconds! He wished that he had made it ten instead. Gentleman Jack was an enterprising person, as his previous act had showed. He might very well decide to take a chance. He might even refuse to believe that Jimmy was armed. He had only Jimmy's word for it. Perhaps he might be as deficient in simple faith as he had been proved to be in Norman blood! Jimmy lingered lovingly over his count.

'Four!' he said reluctantly.

There was a breathless moment. Then, to Jimmy's unspeakable relief, gun and torch dropped simultaneously to the floor. In an instant Jimmy was himself again.

'Go and stand with your face to that wall!' he said crisply. 'Hold your hands up!'

'Why?'

'I'm going to see how many more guns you've got.'

'I haven't another.'

'I'd like to make sure of that for myself. Get moving!'

Gentleman Jack reluctantly obeyed. When he had reached the wall Jimmy came down. He switched on the lights. He felt in the other's pockets and almost at once encountered something hard and metallic.

He shook his head reproachfully.

'You are very loose and inaccurate in your statements,' he said. 'Why all these weapons? I didn't raise my boy to be a soldier! Now you can turn round and put your hands down.'

Gentleman Jack's appeared to be a philosophical nature. The chagrin consequent upon his failure seemed to have left him. He sat on the arm of a chair and regarded Jimmy without apparent hostility. He even smiled a faint smile.

'I thought I had fixed you,' he said. 'You must have been smarter than I took you for. I never supposed you would get on to that drink and pass it up.'

Understanding of an incident that had perplexed him came to Jimmy.

'Was it you who put that highball in my room? Was it doped?'

'Didn't you know?'

'Well,' said Jimmy, 'I never knew before that virtue got its reward so darned quick in this world. I rejected that highball not because I suspected it but out of pure goodness, because I had made up my mind that I was through with all that sort of thing.'

His companion laughed. If Jimmy had had a more intimate acquaintance with the resourceful individual whom the boys called Gentleman Jack he would have been disquieted by that laugh. It was an axiom among those who knew him well that, when Gentleman Jack chuckled in that reflective way, he generally had something unpleasant up his sleeve.

'It's your lucky night,' said Gentleman Jack.

'It looks like it.'

'Well, it isn't over yet.'

'Very nearly. You had better go and put that test tube back in what is left of the safe now. Did you think I had forgotten it?'

'What test tube?'

'Come, come, old friend! The one filled with Partridge's explosive, that you have in your breast pocket!'

Gentleman Jack laughed again, then he moved toward the safe.

'Place it gently on the top shelf,' said Jimmy.

The next moment every nerve in his body was leaping and quivering. A great shout split the air. Gentleman Jack, apparently insane, was giving tongue at the top of his voice.

'Help! Help! Help!'

The conversation having been conducted up to this point in undertones, the effect of this unexpected uproar was like an explosion. The cries seemed to echo round the room and shake the very walls. For a moment Jimmy stood paralysed, staring feebly; then there was a sudden deafening increase in the din.

Something living seemed to writhe and jump in his hand. He dropped it incontinently and found himself gazing in a stupefied way at a round, smoking hole in the carpet. Such had been the effect of Gentleman Jack's unforeseen outburst, that he had quite forgotten that he held the revolver, and he had been unfortunate enough at this juncture to pull the trigger.

There was a sudden rush and swirl of action. Something hit Jimmy under the chin. He staggered back, and when he had recovered himself found himself looking into the muzzle of the revolver that had nearly blown a hole in his foot a moment back. The sardonic face of Gentleman Jack smiled grimly over the barrel.

'I told you the night wasn't over yet!' he said.

The blow under the chin had temporarily dulled Jimmy's mentality. He stood, swallowing and endeavouring to pull himself together and to get rid of a feeling that his head was about to come off. He backed to the desk and steadied himself against it.

As he did so, a voice from behind him spoke.

'Whassall this?'

He turned his head. A curious procession was filing in through the open French window. First came Mr Crocker, still wearing his hideous mask; then a heavily bearded individual with round spectacles, who looked like an automobile coming through a haystack; then Ogden Ford; and finally a sturdy, determined-looking woman, with glittering but poorly co-ordinated eyes, who held a large revolver in her unshaking right hand and looked the very embodiment of the modern female who will stand no nonsense. It was part of the nightmare-like atmosphere that seemed to brood inexorably over this particular night that this person looked to Jimmy exactly like the parlour-maid who had come in answer to his bell and who had sent his father to him. Yet how could it be she? Jimmy knew little of the habits of parlour-maids, but surely they did not wander about with revolvers, in the small hours?

While he endeavoured feverishly to find reason in this chaos, the door opened and a motley crowd, roused from sleep by the cries, poured in. Jimmy, turning his head back again to attend to this invasion, perceived Mrs Pett, Ann, two or three of the geniuses, and Willie Partridge, in various stages of negligée and babbling questions.

The woman with the pistol, assuming instant and unquestioned domination of the assembly, snapped out an order.

'Shutatdoor!'

Somebody shut the door.

'Now whassall this?' she said, turning to Gentleman Jack.

CHAPTER 23

Gentleman Jack had lowered his revolver and was standing waiting to explain all, with the insufferable look of the man who is just going to say that he has only done his duty and requires no thanks.

'Who are you?' he said.

'Nev' min' who I am!' said Miss Trimble curtly. 'Siz Pett knows who I am.'

'I hope you won't be offended, Lord Wisbeach,' said Mrs Pett from the group by the door. 'I engaged a detective to help you. I really thought you could not manage everything by yourself. I hope you do not mind.'

'Not at all, Mrs Pett; very wise.'

'I am so glad to hear you say so.'

'An excellent move.'

Miss Trimble broke in on these amiable exchanges.

'Whassall this? Howjer mean – help me?'

'Lord Wisbeach most kindly offered to do all he could to protect my nephew's explosive,' said Mrs Pett.

Gentleman Jack smiled modestly.

'I hope I have been of some slight assistance! I think I came down in the nick of time. Look' – he pointed to the safe – 'he had just got it open! Luckily I had my pistol with me. I covered him and called for help. In another moment he would have got away.'

Miss Trimble crossed to the safe and inspected it with a frown, as if she disliked it. She gave a grunt and returned to her place by the window.

'Made good job 'f it!' was her comment.

Ann came forward. Her face was glowing and her eyes shone.

'Do you mean to say that you found Jimmy breaking into the safe? I never heard anything so absurd!'

Mrs Pett intervened.

'This is not James Crocker, Ann! This man is an impostor, who came into the house in order to steal Willie's invention.' She looked fondly at Gentleman Jack. 'Lord Wisbeach told me so. He only pretended to recognize this young man this afternoon.'

A low gurgle proceeded from the open mouth of little Ogden – the proceedings bewildered him. The scene he had overheard in the library between the two men had made it clear to him that Jimmy was genuine and Lord Wisbeach a fraud, and he could not understand why Jimmy did not produce his proofs as before. He was not aware that Jimmy's head was only just beginning to clear from the effects of the blow on the chin. Ogden braced himself for resolute lying, in the event of Jimmy calling him as a witness. He did not intend to have his little business proposition dragged into the open.

Ann was looking at Jimmy with horror-struck eyes. For the first time it came to her how little she knew of him and how very likely it was – in the face of the evidence it was almost certain – that he should have come to the house with the intention of stealing Willie's explosive. She fought against it, but a voice seemed to remind her that it was she who had suggested the idea of posing as Jimmy Crocker. She could not help remembering how smoothly and willingly he had embarked on the mad scheme. But had it been so mad? Had it not been a mere cloak for this other venture? If Lord Wisbeach had found him in this room, with the safe blown open, what other explanation could there be?

And then, simultaneously with her conviction that he was a criminal, came the certainty that he was the man she loved. It had only needed the spectacle of him in trouble to make her sure. She came to his side, with the vague idea of doing something to help him, of giving him her support. Once there, she found that there was nothing to do and nothing to say. She put her hand on his and stood waiting helplessly for she knew not what.

It was the touch of her fingers that woke Jimmy from his stupor. He came to himself almost with a jerk. He had been mistily aware of what had been said, but speech had been beyond him. Now, quite suddenly, he was a whole man once more. He threw himself into the debate with energy.

'Good heavens!' he cried. 'You're all wrong. I found him blowing open the safe.'

Gentleman Jack smiled superciliously.

'A likely story, what! I mean to say, it's a bit thin!'

'Ridiculous!' said Mrs Pett. She turned to Miss Trimble with a gesture. 'Arrest that man!'

'Wait a mom'nt,' replied that clear-headed maiden, picking her teeth thoughtfully with the muzzle of her revolver. 'Wait mom'nt. Gotta look 'nto this. Hear both these guys' stories.'

'Really,' said Gentleman Jack suavely, 'it seems somewhat absurd—'

'Nev' mind how 'bsurd 't sounds,' returned the fair Trimble rebukingly. 'You close y'r face 'n' lissen t'me. Thass all you've got ta do.'

'I know you didn't do it!' cried Ann, tightening her hold on Jimmy's arm.

'Less 'f it, please, less 'f it!' Miss Trimble removed the pistol from her mouth and pointed it at Jimmy. 'What've you to say? Talk quick!'

'I happened to be down there—'

'Why?' asked Miss Trimble, as if she had touched off a bomb.

Jimmy stopped short. He perceived difficulties in the way of explanation.

'I happened to be down there,' he resumed stoutly, 'and that man came into the room with an electric torch and a blowpipe and began working on the safe—'

The polished tones of Gentleman Jack cut in on his story.

'Really now, is it worth while?' He turned to Miss Trimble. 'I came down here, having heard a noise. I did not happen to be here for some unexplained purpose. I was lying awake and something attracted my attention. As Mrs Pett knows, I was suspicious of this worthy and expected him to make an attempt on the explosive at any moment – so I took my pistol and crept downstairs. When I got here the safe was open and this man making for the window.'

Miss Trimble scratched her chin caressingly with the revolver and remained for a moment in thought. Then she turned to Jimmy like a striking rattlesnake.

'Y' gotta pull someth'g better th'n that,' she said. 'I got y'r number. Y're caught with th' goods.'

'No!' cried Ann.

'Yes!' said Mrs Pett; 'the thing is obvious.'

'I think the best thing I can do,' said Gentleman Jack smoothly, 'is to go and telephone for the police.'

'You think of everything, Lord Wisbeach,' said Mrs Pett.

'Not at all,' said his lordship.

Jimmy watched him moving to the door. At the back of his mind there was a dull feeling that he could solve the whole trouble if only he could remember one fact which had escaped him. The effects of the blow he had received still handicapped him. He struggled to remember, but without result. Gentleman Jack reached the door and opened it and as he did so a shrill yapping, hitherto inaudible because of the intervening oak and the raised voices within, made itself heard from the passage outside. Gentleman Jack closed the door with a hasty bang.

'I say, that dog's out there!' he said plaintively.

The scratching of Aïda's busy feet on the wood bore out his words. He looked about him, baffled.

'That dog's out there!' he repeated gloomily.

Something seemed to give way in Jimmy's brain. The simple fact that had eluded him till now sprang into his mind.

'Don't let that man get out!' he cried. 'I've only just remembered. You say you found me breaking into the safe! You say you heard a noise and came down to investigate! Well, then, what's that test tube of the explosive doing in your breast pocket?' He swung round to Miss Trimble. 'You needn't take my word or his word. There's a much simpler way of finding out who's the real crook. Search us both!' He began to turn out his pockets rapidly. 'Look here – and here – and here! Now ask him to do the same!'

He was pleased to observe a spasm pass across Gentleman Jack's hitherto composed countenance. Miss Trimble was eyeing the latter with sudden suspicion.

'Thasso!' she said. 'Say, Bill, I've f'gott'n y'r name – 'sup to you to show us! Less've a look 't what y' got inside there.'

Gentleman Jack drew himself up haughtily.

'I really could not agree to—'

Mrs Pett interrupted indignantly.

'I never heard of such a thing! Lord Wisbeach is an old friend—'

'Less 'f it!' ordered Miss Trimble, whose left eye was now like the left eye of a basilisk. 'Y' gotta show us, Bill, so b' quick 'bout 't!'

A tired smile played over Gentleman Jack's face. He was the bored aristocrat, mutely protesting against something that 'wasn't done'. He dipped his slender fingers into his pocket. Then, drawing out the test tube and holding it up, he spoke with a drawling calm for which even Jimmy could not help admiring him.

'All right! If I'm done, I'm done!'

The sensation caused by this action and his words was the kind usually described as profound. Mrs Pett uttered a strangled shriek. Willie Partridge yelped like a dog. Sharp exclamations came simultaneously from each of the geniuses.

Gentleman Jack waited for the clamour to subside, then he resumed his gentle drawl.

'But I'm not done,' he exclaimed. 'I'm going out now through that window. And if anybody tries to stop me it will be his or her' – he bowed politely to Miss Trimble – 'last act in the world. If anyone makes a move to stop me I shall drop this test tube and blow the whole place to pieces!'

If his first speech had made a marked impression on his audience his second paralysed them. A silence followed as of the tomb. Only the yapping of the dog Aïda refused to be stilled.

'Y' stay where y' are!' said Miss Trimble, as the speaker moved toward the window. She held the revolver poised, but for the first time that night – possibly for the first time in her life – she spoke irresolutely. Superbly competent woman though she was, here was a situation that baffled her.

Gentleman Jack crossed the room slowly, the test tube held aloft between forefinger and thumb. He was level with Miss Trimble, who had lowered her revolver and had drawn to one side, plainly at a loss to know how to handle this unprecedented crisis when the door flew open. For an instant the face of Howard Bemis, the poet, was visible.

'Mrs Pett, I have telephoned—'

Then another voice interrupted him.

'Yipe! Yipe! Yipe!'

Through the opening the dog Aïda, rejoicing in the removing of the obstacle, raced like a fur muff mysteriously endowed with legs and a tongue. She tore across the room to where Gentleman Jack's ankles waited invitingly. Ever since their first meeting she had wanted a fair chance at those ankles, but someone had always prevented her.

'Damn!' shouted Gentleman Jack.

The word was drowned in one vast cataclysm of noise. From every throat in the room there proceeded a shout, a shriek, or some other variety of cry, as the test tube, slipping from beneath the victim's fingers, described a parabola through the air.

Ann flung herself into Jimmy's arms, and he held her tight. He shut his eyes. Even as he waited for the end the thought flashed through his mind that if he must die this was the manner of death that he would prefer.

The test tube crashed on the writing desk and burst into a million pieces ... Jimmy opened his eyes. Things seemed to be much about the same as before. He was still alive. The room in which he stood was solid and intact. Nobody was in fragments. There was only one respect in which the scene differed from what it had been a moment before. Then it had contained Gentleman Jack. Now it did not.

A great sigh seemed to sweep through the room. There was a long silence. Then, from the direction of the street, came the roar of a starting automobile. And at that sound the bearded man with the spectacles who had formed part of Miss Trimble's procession uttered a wailing cry.

'Gee! He's beat it in my bubble – and it was a hired one!'

The words seemed to relieve the tension in the air. One by one the company became masters of themselves once more. Miss Trimble, that masterly woman, was the first to recover. She raised herself from the floor – for with a confused idea that she would be safer there, she had flung herself down – and, having dusted her skirt with a few decisive dabs of her strong left hand, addressed herself once more to business.

'I let 'm bluff me with a fake bomb!' she commented bitterly. She brooded on this for a moment. 'Say, shut th' door 'gain, someone, and turn this mutt out. I can't think with th't yapping going on.'

Mrs Pett, pale and scared, gathered Aïda into her arms. At the same time Ann removed herself from Jimmy's. She did not look at him. She was feeling oddly shy. Shyness had never been a failing of hers, but she would have given much now to have been elsewhere.

Miss Trimble again took charge of the situation. The sound of the automobile had died away. Gentleman Jack had passed out of their lives. This fact embittered Miss Trimble. She spoke with asperity.

'Well, he's gone!' she said acidly. 'Now we can get down t' cases again. Say!' She addressed Mrs Pett, who started nervously. The experience of passing through the shadow of the valley of death and of finding herself in one piece instead of several thousand had robbed her of all her wonted masterfulness. 'Say, list'n t' me! There's been a double game on here t'-night. That guy that's jus' gone was th' first part of th' entertainment. Now we c'n start th' sec'nd part. You see these ducks?' She indicated with a wave of the revolver Mr Crocker and his bearded comrade. 'They've been trying t' kidnap y'r son!'

Mrs Pett uttered a piercing cry.

'Oggie!'

'Oh, can it!' muttered that youth uncomfortably. He foresaw awkward moments ahead, and he wished to concentrate his faculties entirely on the part he was to play in them. He looked sideways at Chicago Ed. In a few minutes, he supposed, Ed would be attempting to minimize his own crimes, by pretending that he, Ogden, had invited him to come and kidnap him. Stout denial must be his weapon.

'I had m' suspicions,' resumed Miss Trimble, 'that someth'ng was goin' t' be pulled off t'-night, 'nd I was waiting outside f'r it to break loose. This guy here,' she indicated the bearded plotter, who blinked deprecatingly through his spectacles, 'h's been waiting on the c'rner of th' street for the last hour with 'n automobile. I've b'n watching him right along. I was on to h's game! Well, just now out came the kid with this plug-ugly here.' She turned to Mr Crocker. 'Say, you, take off th't mask. Let's have a l'k at you!'

Mr Crocker reluctantly drew the cambric from his face.

'Gosh!' exclaimed Miss Trimble in strong distaste. 'Say, 've you got some kind of a plague, or wh't is it? Y' look like a coloured comic supplement!' She confronted the shrinking Mr Crocker and ran a bony finger over his cheek. 'Make-up!' she said, eyeing the stains disgustedly. 'Grease paint! Gosh!'

'Skinner!' cried Mrs Pett.

Miss Trimble scanned her victim more closely.

'So 'tis, if y' do a bit 'f excavating' – she turned on the bearded one – "nd I guess all this shrubbery is fake, 'f you come down to it!' She wrenched at the unhappy Jerry's beard. It came off in her hands, leaving a square chin behind it. 'If this ain't a wig y'll have a headache t'morrow,' observed Miss Trimble, weaving her fingers into his luxuriant head covering and pulling. 'Wish y' luck! Ah, 'twas a wig! Gimme those spect'cles.' She surveyed the results of her handiwork grimly. 'Say, Clarence,' she remarked, 'y'r a wise guy. Y' look handsomer with 'em on. Does anyone know this duck?'

'It is Mitchell,' said Mrs Pett, 'my husband's physical instructor.'

Miss Trimble turned and, walking to Jimmy, tapped him meaningly on the chest with her revolver.

'Say, this is gett'n' int'resting! This is where y' 'xplain, y'ng man, how 'twas you happened to be down in this room when th't crook who's just gone was monkeyin' with the safe. L'ks t' me as if you were in with these two.'

A feeling of being on the verge of one of those crises that dot the smooth path of our lives came to Jimmy. To conceal his identity from Ann any longer seemed impossible. He was about to speak, when Ann broke in.

'Aunt Nesta,' she said, 'I can't let this go on any longer. Jerry Mitchell isn't to blame. I told him to kidnap Ogden!'

There was an awkward silence. Mrs Pett laughed nervously.

'I think you had better go to bed, my dear child. You have had a severe shock. You are not yourself!'

'But it's true! I did tell him, didn't I, Jerry?'

'Say!' Miss Trimble silenced Jerry with a gesture. 'You beat 't back t' y'r little bed, honey, like y'r aunt says. Y' say y' told this guy t' steal th' kid. Well, what about this here Skinner? Y' didn't tell him, did y'?'

'I – I—' Ann began confusedly. She was utterly unable to account for Skinner, and it made her task of explaining difficult.

Jimmy came to the rescue. He did not like to think how Ann would receive the news, but for her own sake he must speak now. It would have required a harder-hearted man than himself to resist the mute pleading of his father's grease-painted face. Mr Crocker was a game sport. He would not have said a word without the sign from Jimmy, even to save himself from a night in prison, but he hoped that Jimmy would speak.

'It's perfectly simple,' said Jimmy, with an attempt at airiness that broke down miserably under Miss Trimble's eye. 'Perfectly simple! I really am Jimmy Crocker, you know.' He avoided Ann's gaze. 'I can't think what you are making all this fuss about.'

'Th'n why did y' sit in at a plot to kidnap this boy?'

'That, of course – ha, ha – might seem at first sight to require a little explanation—'

'Y' admit it, then?'

'Yes. As a matter of fact I did have the idea of kidnapping Ogden. Wanted to send him to a dogs' hospital, if you understand what I mean.' He tried to smile a conciliatory smile, but, encountering Miss Trimble's left eye, abandoned the project. He removed a bead of perspiration from his forehead with his handkerchief. It struck him as a very curious thing that the simplest explanations were so often quite difficult to make.

'Before I go any further, I ought to explain one thing. Skinner there is my father.'

Mrs Pett gasped.

'Skinner was my sister's butler, in London.'

'In a way of speaking,' said Jimmy, 'that is correct. It's rather a long story. It was this way, you see—'

Miss Trimble uttered an ejaculation of supreme contempt.

'I n'ver saw such a lot of babbl'ng crooks in m' life! 'T beats me what y' hope to get pulling this stuff. Say' – she indicated Mr Crocker – 'this guy's wanted f'r something over in England. We've got h's photographs 'n th' office. If y' ask me he lit out with the spoons 'r something. Say' – she fixed one of the geniuses with her compelling eye – ''bout time y' made y'rself useful. Go 'n' call up th' Astorbilt on the phone. There's a dame there that's been making the inquiries f'r this duck. She told Anderson's – and Anderson's handed it on to us – to call her up any hour 'f the day 'r night when they found him. You go get her on the wire and t'll her t' come right up here 'n a taxi and identify h'm!'

The genius paused at the door.

'Whom shall I ask for?'

'Mrs Crocker,' snapped Miss Trimble. 'Siz Bingley Crocker. Tell her we've found th' guy she's been looking for!'

The genius backed out. There was a howl of anguish from the doorway.

'I beg your pardon!' said the genius.

'Can't you look where you're going!'

'I am exceedingly sorry—'

'Brrh!'

Mr Pett entered the room, hopping. He was holding one slippered foot in his hand and appeared to be submitting it to some form of massage. It was plain that the usually mild and gentle little man was in a bad temper. He glowered round him at the company assembled.

'What the devil's the matter here?' he demanded. 'I stood it as long as I could, but a man can't get a wink of sleep with this noise going on!'

'Yipe! Yipe! Yipe!' barked Aïda from the shelter of Mrs Pett's arms.

Mr Pett started violently.

'Kill that dog! Throw her out! Do something to her!'

Mrs Pett was staring blankly at her husband. She had never seen him like this before. It was as if a rabbit had turned and growled at her. Coming on top of the crowded sensations of the night it had the effect of making her feel curiously weak. In all her married life she had never known what fear was. She had coped dauntlessly with the late Mr Ford, a man of a spirited temperament, and as for the mild Mr Pett she had trampled on him. But now she felt afraid. This new Peter intimidated her.

CHAPTER 24

To this remarkable metamorphosis in Mr Peter Pett several causes had contributed. In the first place, the sudden dismissal of Jerry Mitchell had obliged him to go two days without the physical exercises to which his system had become accustomed; and this had produced a heavy, irritable condition of body and mind. He had brooded on the injustice of his lot until he had almost worked himself up to rebellion. And then, as sometimes happened with him when he was out of sorts, a touch of gout came to add to his troubles. Being a patient man by nature, he might have borne up against these trials had he been granted an adequate night's rest. But, just as he had dropped off after tossing restlessly for two hours, things had begun to happen noisily in the library. He awoke to a vague realization of tumult below.

Such was the morose condition of his mind as the result of his misfortune that at first not even the cries for help could interest him sufficiently to induce him to leave his bed. He knew that walking in his present state would be painful, and he declined to submit to any more pain just because some party unknown was apparently being murdered in his library. It was not until the shrill barking of the dog Aïda penetrated his nerve centres and began to tie them into knots that he found himself compelled to descend. Even when he did so, it was in no spirit of kindness. He did not come to rescue anybody or to interfere between any murderer and his victim. He came in a fever of militant wrath to suppress Aïda. On the threshold of the library, however, the genius, by treading on his gouty foot, had diverted his anger and caused it to become more general. He had ceased to concentrate his venom on Aïda. He wanted to assail everybody.

'What's the matter here?' he demanded, red-eyed. 'Isn't somebody going to tell me? Have I got to stop here all night? Who on earth is this?' He glared at Miss Trimble. 'What's she doing with that pistol?' He stamped incautiously with his bad foot and emitted a dry howl of anguish.

'She is a detective, Peter,' said Mrs Pett timidly.

'A detective? Why? Where did she come from?'

Miss Trimble took it upon herself to explain.

"Ster Pett, siz Pett sent f'r me t' watch out so's nobody kidnapped her son.'

'Oggie,' explained Mrs Pett. 'Miss Trimble was guarding darling Oggie.'

'Why?'

'To – to prevent him being kidnapped, Peter.'

Mr Pett glowered at the stout boy. Then his eye was attracted by the forlorn figure of Jerry Mitchell. He started.

'Was this fellow kidnapping the boy?' he asked.

'Sure,' said Miss Trimble. 'Caught h'm with th' goods. He w's waiting outside there with a car. I held h'm and this other guy up w'th a gun and brought 'em back!'

'Jerry,' said Mr Pett, 'it wasn't your fault that you didn't bring it off, and I'm going to treat you right. You'd have done it if nobody had butted in to stop you. You'll get the money to start that health farm of yours all right. I'll see to that. Now you run off to bed! There's nothing to keep you here.'

'Say!' cried Miss Trimble, outraged. 'D'y' mean t' say y' aren't going t' pros'cute? Why, aren't I tell'ng y' I caught h'm kidnapping the boy?'

'I told him to kidnap the boy!' snarled Mr Pett.

'Peter!'

Mr Pett looked like an undersized lion, as he faced his wife. He bristled. The recollection of all that he had suffered from Ogden came to strengthen his determination.

'I've tried for two years to get you to send that boy to a good boarding-school, and you wouldn't do it. I couldn't stand having him loafing round the house any longer, so I told Jerry Mitchell to take him away to a friend of his, who keeps a dogs' hospital on Long Island, and to tell his friend to hold Ogden there till he got some sense into him. Well, you've spoiled that for the moment with your detectives, but it still looks good to me. I'll give you a choice. You can either send that boy to a boarding-school next week, or he goes to Jerry Mitchell's friend. I'm not going to have him in the house any longer, loafing in my chair and smoking my cigarettes. Which is it to be?'

'But, Peter!'

'Well?'

'If I send him to a school he may be kidnapped.'

'Kidnapping can't hurt him. It's what he needs. And, anyway, if he is I'll pay the bill and be glad to do it. Take him off to bed now! To-morrow you can start looking up schools. Great Godfrey!' He hopped to the writing desk and glared disgustedly at the débris on it. 'Who's been making this mess on my desk? It's hard! It's darned hard! The only room in the house that I ask to have for my own, where I can get a little peace, and I find it turned into a bear garden, and coffee or some messy thing spilled all over my writing desk!'

'That isn't coffee, Peter,' said Mrs Pett mildly. This cave man whom she had married, under the impression that he was a gentle domestic pet, had taken all the spirit out of her. 'It's Willie's explosive!'

'Willie's explosive?'

'Lord Wisbeach – I mean the man who pretended to be Lord Wisbeach – dropped it there.'

'Dropped it there? Well, why didn't it explode and blow the place to Hoboken, then?'

Mrs Pett looked helplessly at Willie, who thrust his fingers into his mop of hair and rolled his eyes.

'There was fortunately some slight miscalculation in my formula, Uncle Peter,' he said. 'I shall have to look into it to-morrow. Whether the trinitrotuluol—'

Mr Pett uttered a sharp howl. He beat the air with his clenched fists. He seemed to be having a brain storm.

'Has this – this fish been living on me all this time – have I been supporting this – this buzzard in luxury all these years, while he fooled about with an explosive that won't explode!' He pointed an accusing finger at the inventor. 'Look into it to-morrow, will you! Yes, you can look into it to-morrow after six o'clock! Until then you'll be working – for the first time in your life – working in my office, where you ought to have been all along.' He surveyed the crowded room belligerently. 'Now perhaps you will all go back to bed and let people get a little sleep! Go home!' he said to the detective.

Miss Trimble stood her ground. She watched Mrs Pett pass away with Ogden, and Willie Partridge head a stampede of geniuses, but she declined to move.

'Y' gotta cut th' rough stuff, 'ster Pett,' she said calmly. 'I need my sleep, j'st 's much 's everyb'dy else, but I gotta stay here. There's a lady c'ming right up in a taxi fr'm th' Astorbilt, to identify this gook. She's after 'm f'r something.'

'What! Skinner?'

''S what he calls h'mself.'

'What's he done?'

'I d'no. Th' lady'll tell us that.'

There was a violent ringing at the front door bell.

'I guess that's her,' said Miss Trimble. 'Who's going to let h'r in? I can't go.'

'I will,' said Ann.

Mr Pett regarded Mr Crocker with affectionate encouragement.

'I don't know what you've done, Skinner,' he said, 'but I'll stand by you. You're the best fan I ever met, and if I can keep you out of the penitentiary I will.'

'It isn't the penitentiary!' said Mr Crocker unhappily.

A tall, handsome and determined-looking woman came into the room. She stood in the doorway, looking about her. Then her eyes rested on Mr Crocker. For a moment she gazed incredulously at his discoloured face. She drew a little nearer, peering.

'D'y' 'dentify 'm, ma'am?' said Miss Trimble.

'Bingley!'

'Is 't th' guy y' wanted?'

'It's my husband!' said Mrs Crocker.

'Y' can't arrest 'm f'r that!' said Miss Trimble disgustedly.

She thrust her revolver back into the hinterland of her costume.

'Guess I'll be beatin' it,' she said, with a sombre frown. She was plainly in no sunny mood. ''F all th' bunk jobs I was ever on, this is th' bunkest. I'm told off t' watch a gang of crooks, and after I've lost a night's sleep doing it, it turns out it's a nice jolly fam'ly party!' She jerked her thumb toward Jimmy. 'Say, this guy says he's that guy's son. I s'pose it's all right?'

'That is my stepson, James Crocker!'

Ann uttered a little cry, but it was lost in Miss Trimble's stupendous snort. The detective turned to the window.

'I guess I'll beat it,' she observed caustically, 'before it turns out that I'm y'r l'il daughter Genevieve.'

CHAPTER 25

Mrs Crocker turned to her husband. 'Well, Bingley?' she said, a steely tinkle in her voice.

'Well, Eugenia?' said Mr Crocker.

A strange light was shining in Mr Crocker's mild eyes. He had seen a miracle happen that night. He had seen an even more formidable woman than his wife dominated by an even meeker man than himself, and he had been amazed and impressed by the spectacle. It had never even started to occur to him before, but apparently it could be done. A little resolution, a little determination – nothing more was needed. He looked at Mr Pett. And yet Mr Pett had crumpled up Eugenia's sister with about three firm speeches. It could be done.

'What have you to say, Bingley?'

Mr Crocker drew himself up.

'Just this!' he said. 'I'm an American citizen, and the way I've figured it out is that my place is in America. It's no good talking about it, Eugenia. I'm sorry if it upsets your plans, but I – am – not – going – back – to – London!' He eyed his speechless wife unflatteringly. 'I'm going to stick on here and see the pennant race out. And after that I'm going to take in the World's Series.'

Mrs Crocker opened her mouth to speak, closed it, re-opened it. Then she found that she had nothing to say.

'I hope you'll be sensible, Eugenia, and stay on this side, and we can all be happy. I'm sorry to have to take this stand, but you tried me too high. You're a woman, and you don't know what it is to go five years without seeing a ball game; but take it from me it's more than any real fan can stand. It nearly killed me, and I'm not going to risk it again. If Mr Pett will keep me on as his butler I'll stay here in this house. If he won't I'll get another job somewhere. But, whatever happens, I stick to this side!'

Mr Pett uttered a whoop of approval.

'There's always been a place for you in my house, old man!' he cried. 'When I get a butler who—'

'But, Bingley, how can you be a butler?'

'You ought to watch him!' said Mr Pett enthusiastically. 'He's a wonder! He can pull all the starchy stuff, as if he'd lived with the Duke of Whoosis for the last forty years, and then go right off and fling a pop bottle at an umpire! He's all right!'

The eulogy was wasted on Mrs Crocker. She burst into tears. It was a new experience for her husband, and he watched her awkwardly, his resolute demeanour crumbling under this unexpected assault.

'Eugenia!'

Mrs Crocker wiped her eyes.

'I can't stand it!' she sobbed. 'I've worked and worked all these years, and now, just as success has nearly come! . . . Bingley, do come back! It will only be for a little longer.'

Mr Crocker stared.

'A little longer? Why, that Lord Percy Whipple business – I know you must have had excellent reasons for soaking him, Jimmy, but it did put the lid on it – surely, after that Lord Percy affair there's no chance—'

'There is! There is! It has made no difference at all! Lord Percy came to call next day – with a black eye, poor boy – and said that James was a sportsman and that he wanted to know him better! He said he had never felt so drawn toward anyone in his life and he wanted him to show him how he made some blow which he called a right hook. The whole affair has simply endeared James to him, and Lady Corstorphine says that the Duke of Devizes read the account of the fight to the premier that very evening, and they both laughed till they nearly got apoplexy.'

Jimmy was deeply touched. He had not suspected such a sporting spirit in his antagonist.

'Percy's all right!' he said enthusiastically. 'Dad, you ought to go back. It's only fair!'

'But, Jimmy, surely you can understand? There's only a game separating the Giants and the Phillies, with the Braves coming along just behind – and the season only half over!'

Mrs Crocker looked imploringly at him.

'It will only be for a little while, Bingley. Lady Corstorphine, who has means of knowing, says that your name is certain to be in the next honours list. After that you can come back as often as you like. We could spend the summer here and the winter in England, or whatever you pleased.'

Mr Crocker capitulated.

'All right, Eugenia. I'll come!'

'Bingley! We shall have to go back by the next boat, dear. People are beginning to wonder where you are. I've told them that you are taking a rest in the country. But they will suspect something if you don't come back at once.'

Mr Crocker's face wore a drawn look. He had never felt so attached to his wife as now, when she wept these unexpected tears, and begged favours of him with that unfamiliar catch in her voice. On the other hand – a vision rose before him of the Polo Grounds on a warm afternoon – he crushed it down.

'Very well,' he said.

Mr Pett offered a word of consolation.

'Maybe you'll be able to run over for the World's Series?'

Mr Crocker's face cleared.

'That's true.'

'And I'll cable you the scores every day, Dad,' said Jimmy.

Mrs Crocker looked at him, with a touch of disapproval clouding the happiness of her face.

'Are you staying over here, James? There is no reason why you should not come back too. If you make up your mind to change your habits—'

'I have made up my mind to change them, but I'm going to do it in New York. Mr Pett is going to give me a job in his office. I am going to start at the bottom and work my way still farther down.'

Mr Pett yapped with rapture. He was experiencing something of the emotion of the preacher at the camp meeting, who sees the sinners' bench filling up. To have secured Willie Partridge, whom he intended to lead gradually into the realms of high finance by way of envelope addressing, was much; but that Jimmy, with a choice in the matter, should have chosen the office filled him with such content that he only just stopped himself from dancing on his bad foot.

'Don't worry about me, Dad. I shall do wonders. It's quite easy to make a large fortune. I watched Uncle Pete in his office this morning, and all he does is sit at a mahogany table and tell the office boy to tell callers that he has gone away for the day. I think I ought to rise to great heights in that branch of industry. From the little I have seen of it, it seems to have been made for me!'

Jimmy looked at Ann. They were alone. Mr Pett had gone back to bed, Mrs Crocker to her hotel. Mr Crocker was removing his make-up in his room. A silence had followed their departure.

'This is the end of a perfect day!' said Jimmy.

Ann took a step toward the door.

'Don't go!'

Ann stopped.

'Mr Crocker!' she said.

'Jimmy,' he corrected.

'Mr Crocker!' repeated Ann firmly.

'Or Algernon, if you prefer it.'

'May I ask—' Ann regarded him steadily. 'May I ask—'

'Nearly always,' said Jimmy, 'when people begin with that, they are going to say something unpleasant.'

'May I ask why you went to all this trouble to make a fool of me? Why could you not have told me who you were from the start?'

'Have you forgotten all the harsh things you said to me from time to time about Jimmy Crocker? I thought that if you knew who I was you would have nothing more to do with me.'

'You were quite right.'

'Surely, though, you won't let a thing that happened five years ago make so much difference?'

'I shall never forgive you!'

'And yet, a little while ago, when Willie's bomb was about to go off, you flung yourself into my arms.'

Ann's face flamed.

'I lost my balance.'

'Why try to recover it?'

Ann bit her lip.

'You did a cruel, heartless thing. What does it matter how long ago it was? If you were capable of it then—'

'Be reasonable! Don't you admit the possibility of reformation? Take your own case! Five years ago you were a minor poetess. Now you are an amateur kidnapper – a bright, lovable girl, at whose approach people lock up their children and sit on the key. As for me, five years ago I was a heartless brute. Now I am a sober, serious business man, specially called in by your uncle to help jack up his tottering firm. Why not bury the dead past? Besides, I don't want to praise myself, I just want to call your attention to it – think what I have done for you! You admitted yourself that it was my influence that had revolutionized your character. But for me, you would now be doing worse than write poetry. You would be writing *vers libre*. I saved you from that, and you spurn me!'

'I hate you!' said Ann.

Jimmy went to the writing desk and took up a small book.

'Put that down!'

'I just wanted to read you, "Love's Funeral"! It illustrates my point. Think of yourself as you are now and remember that it is I who am responsible for the improvement. Here we are! "Love's Funeral". "My heart is dead—"'

Ann snatched the book from his hands and flung it away. It soared up, clearing the gallery rails, and fell with a thud on the gallery floor. She stood facing him with sparkling eyes. Then she moved away.

'I beg your pardon,' she said stiffly. 'I lost my temper.'

'It's your hair,' said Jimmy soothingly. 'You're bound to be quick-tempered with hair of that glorious red shade. You must marry some nice, determined fellow, blue-eyed, dark-haired, clean-shaven, about five feet eleven, with a future in business. He will keep you in order.'

'Mr Crocker!'

'Gently, of course. Kindly – lovingly – the velvet thingummy rather than the iron what's-its-name, but, nevertheless, firmly.'

Ann was at the door.

'To a girl with your ardent nature someone with whom you can quarrel is an absolute necessity of life. You and I are affinities. Ours will be an ideally happy marriage. You would be miserable if you had to go through life with a human doormat with Welcome written on him. You want someone made of sterner stuff. You want, as it were, a sparring partner, someone with whom you can quarrel happily, with the certain knowledge that he will not curl up in a ball for you to kick but will be there with the return wallop. I may have my faults—' He paused expectantly.

Ann remained silent.

'No, no!' he went on. 'But I am such a man. Brisk give-and-take is the foundation of the happy marriage. Do you remember that beautiful line of Tennyson's, "We fell out, my wife and I"? It always conjures up for me a vision of wonderful domestic happiness. I seem to see us in our old age, you on one side of the radiator, I on the other, warming our old limbs and thinking up snappy stuff to hand each other – sweethearts still! If I were to go out of your life now you would be miserable. You would have nobody to quarrel with. You would be in the position of the female jaguar of the Indian jungle, who, as you doubtless know, expresses her affection for her mate by biting him shrewdly in the fleshy part of the leg. If she should snap sideways one day and find nothing there—'

Of all the things that Ann had been trying to say during this discourse, only one succeeded in finding expression. To her mortification, it was the only weak one in the collection.

'Are you asking me to marry you?'

'I am.'

'I won't!'

'You think so now, because I am not appearing at my best. You see me nervous, diffident, tongue-tied. All this will wear off, however, and you will be surprised and delighted as you begin to understand my true self. Beneath the surface – I speak conservatively – I am a corker!'

The door banged behind Ann. Jimmy found himself alone. He walked thoughtfully to Mr Pett's armchair and sat down. There was a feeling of desolation upon him. He lit a cigarette and began to smoke pensively. What a fool he had been to talk like that! What girl of spirit could possibly stand it? If ever there had been a time for being soothing and serious and pleading it had been these last few minutes – and he talked like that!

Ten minutes passed. Jimmy sprang from the chair. He thought he had heard a footstep. He flung the door open. The passage was empty. He returned miserably to his chair. Of course she had not come back. Why should she?

A voice spoke.

'Jimmy!'

He leaped up again and looked wildly round. Then he looked up. Ann was leaning over the gallery rail. She was smiling.

'Jimmy, I've been thinking it over. There's something I want to ask you. Do you admit that you behaved abominably five years ago?'

'Yes!' shouted Jimmy.

'And that you've been behaving just as badly ever since?'

'Yes!'

'And that you are really a pretty awful sort of person?'

'Yes!'

'Then it's all right. You deserve it!'

'Deserve it?'

'Deserve to marry a girl like me. I was worried about it, but now I see that it's the only punishment bad enough for you!' She raised her arm. 'Here's the dead past, Jimmy! Go and bury it! Good night!'

A small book fell squashily at Jimmy's feet. He regarded it dully for a moment. Then, with a wild yell that penetrated even to Mr Pett's bedroom and woke that sufferer just as he was dropping off to sleep for the third time that night, Jimmy bounded for the gallery stairs. At the farther end of the gallery a musical laugh sounded, and a door closed. Ann had gone.

THE END

P. G. Wodehouse

IN ARROW BOOKS

If you have enjoyed *Piccadilly Jim*, you'll love *The Heart of a Goof*

FROM

The Heart of a Goof

It was a morning when all nature shouted 'Fore!' The breeze, as it blew gently up from the valley, seemed to bring a message of hope and cheer, whispering of chip-shots holed and brassies landing squarely on the meat. The fairway, as yet unscarred by the irons of a hundred dubs, smiled greenly up at the azure sky; and the sun, peeping above the trees, looked like a giant golf-ball perfectly lofted by the mashie of some unseen god and about to drop dead by the pin of the eighteenth. It was the day of the opening of the course after the long winter, and a crowd of considerable dimensions had collected at the first tee. Plus fours gleamed in the sunshine, and the air was charged with happy anticipation.

In all that gay throng there was but one sad face. It belonged to the man who was waggling his driver over the new ball perched on its little hill of sand. This man seemed careworn, hopeless. He gazed down the fairway, shifted his feet, waggled, gazed down the fairway again, shifted the dogs once more, and waggled afresh. He waggled as Hamlet might have waggled, moodily, irresolutely. Then, at last, he swung, and, taking from his caddie the niblick which the intelligent lad had been holding in readiness from the moment when he had walked on to the tee, trudged wearily off to play his second.

The Oldest Member, who had been observing the scene with a benevolent eye from his favourite chair on the terrace, sighed.

'Poor Jenkinson,' he said, 'does not improve.'

'No,' agreed his companion, a young man with open features and a handicap of six. 'And yet I happen to know that he has been taking lessons all the winter at one of those indoor places.'

'Futile, quite futile,' said the Sage with a shake of his snowy head. 'There is no wizard living who could make that man go round in an average of sevens. I keep advising him to give up the game.'

'You!' cried the young man, raising a shocked and startled face from the driver with which he was toying. '*You* told him to give up golf! Why I thought—'

'I understand and approve of your horror,' said the Oldest Member, gently. 'But you must bear in mind that Jenkinson's is not an ordinary case. You know and I know scores of men who have never broken a hundred and twenty in their lives, and yet contrive to be happy, useful members of society. However badly they may play, they are able to forget. But with Jenkinson it is different. He is not one of those who can take it or leave it alone. His only chance of happiness lies in complete abstinence. Jenkinson is a goof.'

'A what?'

'A goof,' repeated the Sage. 'One of those unfortunate beings who have allowed this noblest of sports to get too great a grip upon them, who have permitted it to eat into their souls, like some malignant growth. The goof, you must understand, is not like you and me. He broods. He becomes morbid. His goofery unfits him for the battles of life. Jenkinson, for example, was once a man with a glowing future in the hay, corn, and feed business, but a constant stream of hooks, tops, and slices gradually made him so diffident and mistrustful of himself, that he let opportunity after opportunity slip, with the result that other, sterner, hay, corn, and feed merchants passed him in the race. Every time he had the chance to carry through some big deal in hay, or to execute some flashing *coup* in corn and feed, the fatal diffidence generated by a hundred rotten rounds would undo him. I understand his bankruptcy may be expected at any moment.'

'My golly!' said the young man, deeply impressed. 'I hope I never become a goof. Do you mean to say there is really no cure except giving up the game?'

The Oldest Member was silent for a while.

'It is curious that you should have asked that question,' he said at last, 'for only this morning I was thinking of the one case in my experience where a goof was enabled to overcome his deplorable malady. It was owing to a girl, of course. The longer I live, the more I come to see that most things are. But you will, no doubt, wish to hear the story from the beginning.'

The young man rose with the startled haste of some wild creature, which, wandering through the undergrowth, perceives the trap in his path.

'I should love to,' he mumbled, 'only I shall be losing my place at the tee.'

'The goof in question,' said the Sage, attaching himself with quiet firmness to the youth's coat-button, 'was a man of about your age, by name Ferdinand Dibble. I knew him well. In fact, it was to me—'

'Some other time, eh?'

'It was to me,' proceeded the Sage, placidly, 'that he came for sympathy in the great crisis of his life, and I am not ashamed to say that when he had finished laying bare his soul to me there were tears in my eyes. My heart bled for the boy.'

'I bet it did. But—'

The Oldest Member pushed him gently back into his seat.

'Golf,' he said, 'is the Great Mystery. Like some capricious goddess—'

The young man, who had been exhibiting symptoms of feverishness, appeared to become resigned. He sighed softly.

'Did you ever read "The Ancient Mariner"?' he said.

'Many years ago,' said the Oldest Member. 'Why do you ask?'

'Oh, I don't know,' said the young man. 'It just occurred to me.'

Golf (resumed the Oldest Member) is the Great Mystery. Like some capricious goddess, it bestows its favours with what would appear an almost fat-headed lack of method and discrimination. On every side we see big two-fisted he-men floundering round in three figures, stopping every few minutes to let through little shrimps with knock knees and hollow cheeks, who are tearing off snappy seventy-fours. Giants of finance have to accept a stroke per from their junior clerks. Men capable of governing empires fail to control a small, white ball, which presents no difficulties whatever to others with one ounce more brain than a cuckoo-clock. Mysterious, but there it is. There was no apparent reason why Ferdinand Dibble should not have been a competent golfer. He had strong wrists and a good eye. Nevertheless, the fact remains that he was a dub. And on a certain evening in June I realised that he was also a goof. I found it out quite suddenly as the result of a conversation which we had on this very terrace.

I was sitting here that evening thinking of this and that, when by the corner of the club-house I observed young Dibble in conversation with a girl in white. I could not see who she was, for her back was turned. Presently they parted and Ferdinand came slowly across to where I sat. His air was dejected. He had had the boots licked off him earlier in the afternoon by Jimmy Fothergill, and it was to this that I attributed his gloom. I was to find out in a few moments that I was partly but not entirely correct in this surmise. He took the next chair to mine, and for several minutes sat staring moodily down into the valley.

'I've just been talking to Barbara Medway,' he said, suddenly breaking the silence.

'Indeed?' I said. 'A delightful girl.'

'She's going away for the summer to Marvis Bay.'

'She will take the sunshine with her.'

'You bet she will!' said Ferdinand Dibble, with extraordinary warmth, and there was another long silence.

Presently Ferdinand uttered a hollow groan.

'I love her, dammit!' he muttered brokenly. 'Oh, golly, how I love her!'

I was not surprised at his making me the recipient of his confidences like this. Most of the young folk in the place brought their troubles to me sooner or later.

'And does she return your love?'

'I don't know. I haven't asked her.'

'Why not? I should have thought the point not without its interest for you.'

Ferdinand gnawed the handle of his putter distractedly.

'I haven't the nerve,' he burst out at length. 'I simply can't summon up the cold gall to ask a girl, least of all an angel like her, to marry me. You see, it's like this. Every time I work myself up to the point of having a dash at it, I go out and get trimmed by someone giving me a stroke a hole. Every time I feel I've mustered up enough pep to propose, I take ten on a bogey three. Every time I think I'm in good mid-season form for putting my fate to the test, to win or lose it all, something goes all blooey with my swing, and I slice into the rough at every tee. And then my self-confidence leaves me. I become nervous, tongue-tied, diffident. I wish to goodness I knew the man who invented this infernal game. I'd strangle him. But I suppose he's been dead for ages. Still, I could go and jump on his grave.'

It was at this point that I understood all, and the heart within me sank like lead. The truth was out. Ferdinand Dibble was a goof.

'Come, come, my boy,' I said, though feeling the uselessness of any words. 'Master this weakness.'

'I can't.'

'Try!'

'I have tried.'

He gnawed his putter again.

'She was asking me just now if I couldn't manage to come to Marvis Bay, too,' he said.

'That surely is encouraging? It suggests that she is not entirely indifferent to your society.'

'Yes, but what's the use? Do you know,' a gleam coming into his eyes for a moment, 'I have a feeling that if I could ever beat some really fairly good player − just once − I could bring the thing off.' The gleam faded. 'But what chance is there of that?'

It was a question which I did not care to answer. I merely patted his shoulder sympathetically, and after a little while he left me and walked away. I was still sitting there, thinking over his hard case, when Barbara Medway came out of the clubhouse.

She, too, seemed grave and pre-occupied, as if there was

something on her mind. She took the chair which Ferdinand had vacated, and sighed wearily.

'Have you ever felt,' she asked, 'that you would like to bang a man on the head with something hard and heavy? With knobs on?'

I said I had sometimes experienced such a desire, and asked if she had any particular man in mind. She seemed to hesitate for a moment before replying, then, apparently, made up her mind to confide in me. My advanced years carry with them certain pleasant compensations, one of which is that nice girls often confide in me. I frequently find myself enrolled as a father-confessor on the most intimate matters by beautiful creatures from whom many a younger man would give his eye-teeth to get a friendly word. Besides, I had known Barbara since she was a child. Frequently – though not recently – I had given her her evening bath. These things form a bond.

'Why are men such chumps?' she exclaimed.

'You still have not told me who it is that has caused these harsh words. Do I know him?'

'Of course you do. You've just been talking to him.'

'Ferdinand Dibble? But why should you wish to bang Ferdinand Dibble on the head with something hard and heavy with knobs on?'

'Because he's such a goop.'

'You mean a goof?' I queried, wondering how she could have penetrated the unhappy man's secret.

'No, a goop. A goop is a man who's in love with a girl and won't tell her so. I am as certain as I am of anything that Ferdinand is fond of me.'

'Your instinct is unerring. He has just been confiding in me on that very point.'

'Well, why doesn't he confide in *me*, the poor fish?' cried the high-spirited girl, petulantly flicking a pebble at a passing grasshopper. 'I can't be expected to fling myself into his arms unless he gives some sort of a hint that he's ready to catch me.'

'Would it help if I were to repeat to him the substance of this conversation of ours?'

'If you breathe a word of it, I'll never speak to you again,' she cried. 'I'd rather die an awful death than have any man think I wanted him so badly that I had to send relays of messengers begging him to marry me.'

I saw her point.

'Then I fear,' I said, gravely, 'that there is nothing to be done. One can only wait and hope. It may be that in the years to come Ferdinand Dibble will acquire a nice lissom, wristy swing, with the head kept rigid and the right leg firmly braced and—'

'What are you talking about?'

'I was toying with the hope that some sunny day Ferdinand Dibble would cease to be a goof.'

'You mean a goop?'

'No, a goof. A goof is a man who—' And I went on to explain the peculiar psychological difficulties which lay in the way of any declaration of affection on Ferdinand's part.

'But I never heard of anything so ridiculous in my life,' she ejaculated. 'Do you mean to say that he is waiting till he is good at golf before he asks me to marry him?'

'It is not quite so simple as that,' I said sadly. 'Many bad golfers marry, feeling that a wife's loving solicitude may improve their game. But they are rugged, thick-skinned men, not sensitive and introspective, like Ferdinand. Ferdinand has allowed himself to become morbid. It is one of the chief merits of golf that non-success at the game induces a certain amount of decent humility, which keeps a man from pluming himself too much on any petty triumphs he may achieve in other walks of life; but in all things there is a happy mean, and with Ferdinand this humility has gone too far. It has taken all the spirit out of him. He feels crushed and worthless. He is grateful to caddies when they accept a tip instead of drawing themselves up to their full height and flinging the money in his face.'

'Then do you mean that things have got to go on like this for ever?'

I thought for a moment.

'It is a pity,' I said, 'that you could not have induced Ferdinand to go to Marvis Bay for a month or two.'

'Why?'

'Because it seems to me, thinking the thing over, that it is just possible that Marvis Bay might cure him. At the hotel there he would find collected a mob of golfers – I used the term in its broadest sense, to embrace the paralytics and the men who play left-handed – whom even he would be able to beat. When I was last at Marvis Bay, the hotel links were a sort of Sargasso Sea into which had drifted all the pitiful flotsam and jetsam of golf. I have seen things done on that course at which I shuddered and averted my eyes – and I am not a weak man. If Ferdinand can polish up his game so as to go round in a fairly steady hundred and five, I fancy there is hope. But I understand he is not going to Marvis Bay.'

'Oh yes, he is,' said the girl.

'Indeed! He did not tell me that when we were talking just now.'

'He didn't know it then. He will when I have had a few words with him.'

And she walked with firm steps back into the club-house.

Also available in Arrow

The Heart of a Goof

P.G. Wodehouse

A Golf collection

From his favourite chair on the terrace above the ninth hole,
The Oldest Member tells a series of hilarious golfing stories.
From Evangeline, Bradbury Fisher's fifth wife and a notorious
'golfing giggler', to poor Rollo Podmarsh whose game was so
unquestionably inept that 'he began to lose his appetite and
would moan feebly at the sight of a poached egg', the game of
golf, its players and their friends and enemies are here shown in
all their comic glory.

arrow books

Also available in Arrow

Uncle Fred in the Springtime

P.G. Wodehouse

A Blandings novel

Uncle Fred is one of the hottest earls that ever donned a
coronet. Or as he crisply said, 'There are no limits, literally
none, to what I can achieve in the springtime.'

Even so, his gifts are stretched to the limit when he is urged
by Lord Emsworth to save his prize pig, the Empress of
Blandings, from the enforced slimming cure of the haughty
Duke of Dunstable. Pongo Twistleton knows his debonair but
wild uncle shouldn't really be allowed at large – especially
when disguised as a brain surgeon. He fears the worst. And
his fears are amply justified.

arrow books

Also available in Arrow

The Mating Season

P.G. Wodehouse

A Jeeves and Wooster novel

At Deverill Hall, an idyllic Tudor manor in the picture-perfect village of King's Deverill, impostors are in the air. The prime example is man-about-town Bertie Wooster, doing a good turn to Gussie Fink-Nottle by impersonating him while he enjoys fourteen days away from society after being caught taking an unscheduled dip in the fountains of Trafalgar Square. Bertie is of course one of nature's gentlemen, but the stakes are high: if all is revealed, there's a danger that Gussie's simpering fiancée Madeline may turn her wide eyes on Bertie instead.

It's a brilliant plan – until Gussie himself turns up, imitating Bertram Wooster. After that, only the massive brain of Jeeves (himself in disguise) can set things right.

arrow books

Also available in Arrow

Full Moon

P.G. Wodehouse

A Blandings novel

When the moon is full at Blandings, strange things happen: among them the painting of a portrait of The Empress, twice in succession winner in the Fat Pigs Class at the Shropshire Agricultural Show. What better choice of artist, in Lord Emsworth's opinion, than Landseer. The renowned painter of The Stag at Bay may have been dead for decades, but that doesn't prevent Galahad Threepwood from introducing him to the castle – or rather introducing Bill Lister, Gally's godson, so desperately in love with Prudence that he's determined to enter Blandings in yet another imposture. Add a gaggle of fearsome aunts, uncles and millionaires, mix in Freddie Threepwood, Beach the Butler and the gardener McAllister, and the moon is full indeed.

arrow books

Also available in Arrow

Ukridge

P.G. Wodehouse

Money makes the world go round for Stanley
Featherstonehaugh Ukridge – and when there isn't enough of
it, the world just has to spin a bit faster.

Ever on the lookout for a quick buck, a solid gold fortune, or at
least a plausible little scrounge, the irrepressible Ukridge gives
con men a bad name. Looking like an animated blob of mustard
in his bright yellow raincoat, he invests time, passion and
energy (but seldom actual cash) in a series of increasingly
bizarre money-making schemes. Finance for a dog college? It's
yours. Shares in an accident syndicate? Easily arranged.
Promoting a kind-hearted heavyweight boxer? A snip.

Poor Corky Corcoran, Ukridge's old school chum and
confidant, trails through these pages in the ebullient wake of
Wodehouse's most disreputable but endearing hero and hopes
to escape with his shirt at least.

arrow books

Also available in Arrow

The Inimitable Jeeves

P.G. Wodehouse

A Jeeves and Wooster collection

A classic collection of stories featuring some of the funniest
episodes in the life of Bertie Wooster, gentleman, and Jeeves, his
gentleman's gentleman – in which Bertie's terrifying Aunt Agatha
stalks the pages, seeking whom she may devour, while Bertie's
friend Bingo Little falls in love with seven different girls in
succession (he marries the last, the bestselling romantic novelist
Rosie M. Banks). And Bertie, with Jeeves's help, just evades the
clutches of the terrifying Honoria Glossop . . . At its heart is one
of Wodehouse's most delicious stories, 'The Great Sermon
Handicap'.

Also available in Arrow

Summer Lightning

P.G. Wodehouse

A Blandings novel

The Empress of Blandings, prize-winning pig and all-consuming
passion of Clarence, Ninth Earl of Emsworth, has disappeared.

Blandings Castle is in uproar and there are suspects a-plenty –
from Galahad Threepwood (who is writing memoirs so
scandalous they will rock the aristocracy to its foundations) to
the Efficient Baxter, chilling former secretary to Lord
Emsworth. Even Beach the Butler seems deeply embroiled. And
what of Sir Gregory Parsloe-Parsloe, Clarence's arch-rival, and
his passion for prize-winning pigs?

With the castle full of deceptions and impostors, will Galahad's
memoirs ever see the light of day? And will the Empress be
returned. . . ?

arrow books

Also available in Arrow

Right Ho, Jeeves

P.G. Wodehouse

A Jeeves and Wooster novel

Gussie Fink-Nottle's knowledge of the common newt is unparalleled. Drop him in a pond of newts and his behaviour will be exemplary, but introduce him to a girl and watch him turn pink, yammer, and suddenly stampede for the great open spaces. Even with Madeline Bassett, who feels that the stars are God's daisy chain, his tongue is tied in reef-knots. And his chum Tuppy Glossop isn't getting on much better with Madeline's delectable friend Angela.

With so many broken hearts lying about him, Bertie Wooster can't sit idly by. The happiness of a pal – two pals, in fact – is at stake. But somehow Bertie's best-laid plans land everyone in the soup, and so it's just as well that Jeeves is ever at hand to apply his bulging brains to the problems of young love.

arrow books

Also available in Arrow

Leave it to Psmith

P.G. Wodehouse

A Blandings novel

Lady Constance Keeble, sister of Lord Emsworth of Blandings
Castle, has both an imperious manner and a valuable diamond
necklace. The precarious peace of Blandings is shattered when
her necklace becomes the object of dark plottings, for within the
castle lurk some well-connected jewel thieves – among them the
Honourable Freddie Threepwood, Lord Emsworth's younger
son, who wants the reward money to set up a bookmaking
business. Psmith, the elegant socialist, is also after it for his
newly married chum Mike. And on patrol with the impossible
task of bringing management to Blandings is the Efficient
Baxter, whose strivings for order lead to a memorable encounter
with the castle flowerpots.

Will peace ever return to Blandings Castle. . . ?

arrow books

The P G Wodehouse Society (UK)

The P G Wodehouse Society (UK) was formed in 1997 to promote the enjoyment of the writings of the twentieth century's greatest humorist. The Society publishes a quarterly magazine, *Wooster Sauce*, which includes articles, features, reviews, and current Society news. Occasional special papers are also published. Society events include regular meetings in central London, cricket matches and a formal biennial dinner, along with other activities. The Society actively supports the preservation of the Berkshire pig, a rare breed, in honour of the incomparable Empress of Blandings.

MEMBERSHIP ENQUIRIES

Membership of the Society is open to applicants from all parts of the world. The cost of a year's membership in 2008 is £15. Enquiries and requests for membership forms should be made to the Membership Secretary, The P G Wodehouse Society (UK), 26 Radcliffe Rd, Croydon, Surrey, CRO 5QE, or alternatively from info@pgwodehousesociety.org.uk

The Society's website can be viewed at www.pgwodehousesociety.org.uk

Visit our special P.G. Wodehouse website
www.wodehouse.co.uk

Find out about P.G. Wodehouse's books now
reissued with appealing new covers

Read extracts from all your favourite titles

Read the exclusive extra content and immerse
yourself in Wodehouse's world

Sign up for news of future publications
and upcoming events

arrow books